A Quick Trip to Moab

"A page turning trip into a desert nightmare. Jones brings a sharp focus to the issues confronting public lands in the West, while mindful to not polarize perspectives. You'll be cheering everyone on in this race to survival. . . except the Viking.

I was out hiking a few days ago and heard some gunshots. I was instantly transported to one of the scenes in your book!"

—Morgan Sjogren, author of the
forthcoming book *Path of Light*

A Quick Trip to Moab

Insurrection in the Wilderness

Kevin T. Jones

LOST SOULS PRESS

Colorado

Published in the United States by
Lost Souls Press
Colorado
www.lostsoulspress.com

ISBN: 978-1-7346553-4-6 (paperback)
ISBN: 978-0-578-349954 (ebook)

Cover illustration and design by Shley Kinser and Nick Jones
Cover art by Cody Rex Chamberlain, www.codyrexchamberlain.art
Design and typography by Dan R. Miller

Utah: Antigovernment Protest Grows
The Salt Lake Tribune

Price, UT—What started late last week with six men and women on all-terrain vehicles (ATVs) protesting a recent wilderness designation in Utah has grown to include over 100 sympathizers, according to Carbon County, Utah, Sheriff Cortland Hackney. Dozens of pickup trucks and ATVs have entered the area known as the San Rafael Swell Wilderness, violating the order closing it to all motorized vehicles. The protesters, who call themselves the Recapture Brigade, contend that the closure deprives them of their existing rights to use the area. They claim, among other things, that a closed trail has been a road since the 1800s and is vital to commerce. The protesters have declared the wilderness designation to be "null and void" and have set up a camp in the disputed area. Many of the protesters openly displayed firearms, including handguns, rifles, shotguns and assault-type weapons. Law enforcement personnel have taken a wait-and-see attitude, pending investigations by state and federal officials and discussions with representatives of the protesters. "More protesters are arriving daily," Sheriff Hackney told reporters.

Bring a Gun When You Come Down

"Be careful on the way," Bill said. "The protesters down by Price are causing a lot of trouble. There are hundreds of them. They've pulled all the law enforcement people out. Kind of scary. Be careful, that's all."

"You're exaggerating," I said. "They've been peaceful, so far, haven't they? Their beef is with the Feds, not some guy driving by."

My friend Bill had called from Moab to tell me that the painting I had purchased from local artist Joe Cain was framed and ready to be picked up. It was perfect timing, since my wife, Chris's birthday was in a couple weeks, and the painting was to be her present. I'd been worried it wouldn't be ready in time, and at the same time worried she wouldn't like it, or the price tag. At any rate, I loved the painting and couldn't wait to get it and give it to Chris. I told Bill I'd be down on Saturday to pick it up.

"Be sure to call or text when you head out," he said, "and then again when you're leaving Price. You can spend the night here. We can jam a little or go out to Woody's or something."

I told him how much I appreciated his concern. I agreed to call from home, and again when I was leaving Price, which is about two hours from Moab.

I'd made the four-hour drive from Salt Lake City to Moab dozens of times and spent many months working as a geomorphologist on environmental impact studies in the area around the San Rafael Swell in central Utah, so I know the area the protesters are concerned about, and the roads. Years ago the highway was notoriously dangerous—narrow, winding, and crowded with traffic. Much of the highway is divided now, with two lanes in both directions, so the weekly reports of deadly head-on collisions have pretty much gone away. It isn't the road that concerns us today; it's the protesters along it.

"Bring a gun when you come down," Bill said. "And have it handy. You never know."

"Really? Bring a gun? What would I do with a gun?"

"I'm serious, Stan," he said. "The federal marshals have blocked off the entire area as unsafe. Only the highways are open. They're afraid somebody's going to get hurt. I just don't want it to be you, that's all. Those people scare me."

"You know they're protesting that trail that went past our camp when we worked on the Questco pipeline, don't you," said Bill. "That place Crazy Uncle Billy called The Motel."

"I sure do. But that's no highway, it's not even a road," I said. "OK, if it will make you feel better, I'll bring a gun. See you Saturday."

My border collie mix, Speck, gave me the sad-eyed look she always gets when I load the truck. What the heck, I thought, and threw in her leash, bowl, and some food. "You can play with Knuckles at Bill's," I told her, and I think she knew exactly what I'd said, because she ran to the truck.

We left mid-morning on Saturday. Speck sat attentively in her customary spot on a small folded blanket on the back seat. In the back I had a cooler with some snacks and drinks and in a canvas case, my rifle and pistol, some clips, and ammunition. I'd bought the guns as a favor from my friend Ted shortly before he moved to Canada, where they were not allowed. "They're fun to shoot, and who knows, you might need them someday," he'd said. I'd shot them exactly twice—once when Ted sold them to me, and the other time at a Fourth of July campout in the West Desert. I wasn't really much of a gun lover, but I had them, and well, I guess situations like this were why people have guns, although I couldn't imagine actually using them. And, as Bill had said, "you never know."

HELP US! PLEASE HELP US!

The drive was routine. I stopped in Price, picked up a gyro sandwich at the Greek Stop, gassed up, and gave Bill a call. "Be there around three," I told him. I was a few miles past Woodside when Speck whined to get out, so I pulled off the pavement and looked around. A small dirt road angled away from the highway, and I could see that there were no vehicles or any reason to be concerned. I drove down the graveled road 100 yards or so and stopped to let Speck out without fear of her running into traffic. I had used this place as a pit stop many times, and both Speck and I knew it well. We got out of the truck, I peed on a sagebrush, and Speck raced around, sniffing and checking out all the enticing odors swirling on the breeze and gracing the trees and bushes.

A lovely day, I thought to myself. The breeze ruffled my hair. Chris had been after me lately to get it trimmed. I'll make an appointment when I get back. I guess I need to make one with the dentist, too. It seems I always put things off that make me uncomfortable. Sitting in a chair while somebody does something to me. Maybe that's it.

I took a quick look around, whistled for Speck, and headed back toward the truck. When she didn't immediately come, I turned and looked for her and spotted her a short distance away. She headed toward me, and then I saw her stop, lower her front quarters a slight bit, and alert on something in the junipers. I whistled again. "Come on Speck, let's go." When she didn't move, I took a step toward her, and as I did, she barked and backed toward me. Looking closer, I saw a head lean out from behind the low trunk of a tree. Shit! Who could that be?

"Speck, come," I yelled, hurrying toward the truck. "Speck, come here."

Speck walked a few steps toward the tree, wagged her tail, then turned, ran to me, and jumped into the back seat. I opened the front door and started to get in. A person stepped from behind the tree and waved to me. I could see that it was a woman.

"Help us!," she cried out. "Please help us!"

I hesitated for a moment, not knowing what to do. My first instinct was to jump in the Toyota and race back up to the highway. I could call 911 and send help. That's what I would do. This could be a trap. I'd heard of such things. Or maybe seen them in movies. I wasn't going to fall for some trick. I climbed up into the seat and pulled the door closed. The woman walked out from the grove of trees and hurried toward me. She was dirty, and her clothes were torn. She was crying out with her arms extended toward me.

"Please help, please. My husband's been shot. Please, help us."

I don't know why I changed my mind. Here was someone who was asking, pleading with me to help her. She looked like she needed help. I guess I didn't really think. I got out of the truck and went to her.

"Thank you," she cried, "Oh my God, thank you."

She turned and motioned back toward the trees.

"My husband's been shot. They shot him. He can barely walk."

I followed her. A man was leaning up against the trunk of a juniper tree. He was struggling to rise. His shoulder and arm were covered with blood. He looked up at me and lifted himself up on one knee.

"Hijackers," he said. "They tried to hijack us. They're still looking for us. Please help us get out of here. I'll pay you. My company will pay you. Please."

He reached up with his right arm, took hold of a branch, and rose to his feet. The woman ran to him and supported him as he steadied himself.

"Come on," I said. "Let's get in the truck and get out of here." I hurried to the Toyota and opened the passenger side doors. The man was unable to walk on his own, and I ran to help his wife, who was struggling to move him. We boosted him into the back seat. Speck backed away and wagged her tail. She looked at me as if to say, "I'm OK with this."

* * *

Breaking News from Channel Nine News
Liz Nuñez reporting

"More supporters of the so-called Recapture Brigade have arrived in central Utah, much to the dismay of local officials, and to the delight of businesses. Channel Nine's Liz Nuñez reports from Price. Liz:"

"Thanks Allyson. Things are hopping here in Carbon County. As you can see behind me, the field across from the fairgrounds has become a sprawling campground for people coming to join in with the protesters who are occupying federal land just south of here. The police estimate that there are over two hundred here, with more arriving daily. Stores and restaurants are doing a booming business. The county sheriff and federal officials are trying to keep more people from joining the group already camped in the San Rafael Swell, but as some here will tell you, there are ways to get around those efforts. Bob Miller, for example, says he has been in and out of the protesters' camp several times. How have you been doing it, Bob?"

"Well, you don't expect me to tell you, do you? I just know my way around these parts, and, well, there are ways. Let's just leave it at that, OK?"

"All right then, Bob, but tell our viewers, how are things there in the camp? How many are out there, and how are they holding up?"

"I can't say how many's in the camp, but they're doing just fine. These are outdoors people. They're hunters, campers. They've got latrines, and kitchens, you know, they're organized."

"How about supplies? Since the sheriff isn't letting people in, how are they getting food?"

"Well, a couple semi-drivers pulled their rigs right in and donated their cargo, so there's lots of camping gear and food, don't you worry 'bout that. Oh, and, well, we've got a supply line going, so they've got what they need. Everything they need."

"How long do they plan to stay out there, Bob?"

"As long as it takes. All summer, all year if need be. This is our country we're fighting for. We're taking our country back, and we'll keep at it as long as it takes."

"Thank you, Bob. Well, Allyson, as you can see, the protesters are in for the long haul, and so far, no end is in sight."

"Liz Nuñez, Channel Nine News, *reporting from Price, in Carbon County, Utah. Back to the newsroom."*

A RUSH OF LUCIDITY

The woman closed the rear door behind her husband and climbed in the front passenger seat. I went around to the front, got in, started the engine, and put it in gear. I turned around in a wide spot and we headed back up the hill toward the highway.

As we approached the intersection, a tan Ford pickup with a red camper shell pulled off the pavement and onto the dirt track we were on.

"God, no!" the woman cried. "It's them. It's the hijackers. They're the ones, the ones who shot us." She turned and looked at me. I could see the terror in her face. "They've been looking for us all night."

The truck came straight toward us, then turned slightly and skidded to a stop, blocking the road. There was no way around them. The driver's door opened and a man got out. He was dressed in combat fatigues, and I could see that he had a sidearm strapped to his waist. He motioned to me to stop.

I glanced over at the woman. "Turn around," she motioned with her hands. "Please. Go! They're after us. They'll shoot us. They'll kill us all! Go! Go! Please go!" She looked up. The man from the truck was striding down the gravel road directly toward us. The passenger side door opened, and another man stepped out. He was holding a rifle.

I took a breath, and somehow a rush of lucidity came over me. I moved quickly and methodically. I knew what to do without thinking about it. I gunned the engine and headed straight toward the hijacker, who dived to the side as we approached. At the last second I spun the truck around, and with tires spinning and spitting gravel, we fishtailed down the road we had just come up. I heard shots ring out. A dust cloud rose behind us, and I couldn't see anything in the rear view mirror. I hoped it would keep the hijackers from seeing us well enough to shoot accurately. After a few hundred yards, I turned to the right on a small two-track road that looked like it went nowhere, but I knew, from somewhere deep in my memory, that it looped over the side of the hill, across a gully, and met up after a mile or so with a maintained gravel road leading to a railroad loading facility several miles west.

I drove fast but not recklessly. I watched in my rearview mirror to see what the tan truck would do. I couldn't see it as we went around the hill and across the gully, but as I turned on the coal road, a dust plume came up near the top of the hill. The tan truck was following us, and it was coming fast. On the better road, I floored it. I would be able to put a little space between us as our pursuer made his way down the rougher section and across the gully.

I looked over at the woman. She was in her late twenties, probably, with short, light brown hair, slim, tall, pretty, and athletic-looking. She was watching the rearview mirror, and had a frightened, intense look on her face. She looked over at me and shook her head.

"They hijacked us last night. Our semi. We were hauling a load for Family Grocers. Canned goods, shit, who knows. Grocery store stuff. We were at the rest stop, and we overslept a little. That turd," she motioned with a nod of her head toward the mirror, "he banged on the door and said, 'How about you donate your rig and cargo to the militia? We're taking our land back from the liberals,' something like that. Craig, he was in the driver seat, said very politely, 'No thank you, we've got to be going.' Then that jerk started hollering and pulled the door open and yelled for us to get out, that he was 'liberating' our cargo. Jesus. It was a nightmare. We should have been out of there before then, we know, but it wasn't even really dark yet, and we thought we could make it to Green River and get on the Interstate heading east and everything would be fine."

She shook her head and looked back at her husband, who appeared to be dozing.

"Craig, my husband, he shoved the guy away, slammed his door, and we took off. He said, 'Hang on' and started going as fast as he could. They had a car—an SUV—blocking the way out of the rest stop, and Craig just veered to the edge of the road and caught it in the front quarter and sent it spinning off the pavement. We hauled ass to the highway. That pickup—that tan and red one—it roared past us. That's when they started shooting."

She looked down and put her face in her hands. "I can't believe it. They were shooting. At us. Craig said to duck down, and I did. They were swerving all over and firing like crazy. They hit the windshield a couple of times. Craig was trying to run them over, but we started slowing down on an uphill grade, we couldn't catch them. They kept shooting, bam, bam, bam! and that's when Craig got hit. It got him in the left shoulder, but he didn't pay any attention. He told me to get his pistol out of the console, and I did." She looked down at the revolver and rolled it over in her hand. "Never used it. Never had a shot."

"How'd you get away from them? How'd they get your truck?" I asked.

"Well, when their pickup went over the hill, up ahead of us, Craig slammed on the brakes, stopped, and we jumped out and ran into the trees. We ran for a long way. A long way. Nobody followed us, but we could see that tan truck and a couple more. They got in the semi and took it away. Then they started driving up and down and back and forth on all the roads. I guess they were looking for us. All night. We didn't have any food or water or anything, just Craig's pistol. I'm so glad you found us. And now, shit, they're after you too. Jesus Christ, what is going on? Who are these people?" She started to cry, then looked again in the mirror. "They might be gaining on us," she said.

They were. I was driving fast and hard, but they were really pushing it. Maybe they'll crash, I thought. Hoped. Hoped we wouldn't. If we could make it to the rail loadout, I could turn onto an even better road, and then it would be only a few miles back to the highway. I glanced in the mirror and tried to become one with the truck and the road.

We have to trust each other

When we crested the rise just above the railroad tracks I could see that my planned escape route was blocked. Two wrecked coal trucks blocked the road completely, leaving only one way to go—deeper into the backcountry and away from paved roads, civilization, and help. I was pretty sure there was no phone coverage here and checked my phone. Nope. No choice but to keep running.

"Here, have a drink," I said, handing her a water bottle. "How badly is your husband hurt?"

"The bullet went into his shoulder, missed the bone, we think," she said, pointing to her upper arm. "It bled quite a bit. I think that's the worst part. He bled a lot before we could get it stopped. Now he is weak. And woozy." She turned and looked back at him. "I'm Lily," she said. Lily Clark. We're from Kentucky."

"Stan," I said. "Stan Watson. I'm from Salt Lake City."

As we raced along, across silvery-blue sage-covered flats, through deep green piñon and juniper forests, across washes, through rocky outcrops and over rolling hills, we seemed to be keeping the tan truck at a pretty constant distance behind us, about a half mile, maybe a mile. Not bad, I thought. Far enough that if nothing changed, in about a dozen miles we would come to a place where we could get on the interstate, where the sheriff and state troopers would be patrolling, and we could get help. That would take us a half hour or so, I calculated. We could do it.

And then it dawned on me. He was just keeping me in sight, not trying to catch me like he had been before. He was following us because he knows something. He knows that there will be others to help him. I tried to think. Where would that be? And then I knew. They probably had a camp. A fort or something. The most important resource out here is water, and we were heading right for one of the few permanent streams in the area, Dancing Water Creek. Not that far ahead. We're probably heading right for the pirates' camp. We'll drive right in and they'll have us. I envisioned something out of a Mad Max movie. Shit.

"We are going to have to do something. I think we're heading for more trouble," I said. "They're chasing us toward their camp. Their friends. Pirate City. We have to do something."

"What could we do?" Lily asked. "Turn around and try to get past them? I have Craig's pistol. We could shoot at them."

"Maybe, but they have more and bigger guns than we have," I said. "Let me think."

As I drove, another moment of lucidity swept over me.

"OK, I think I have it," I said. "A plan. When we go over this big hill ahead of us, the road swings to the left, then goes into a pretty deep wash. They won't be able to see us for a while. I'll get out with my rifle and hide. You drive on, and when they come over the edge of the wash, I'll ambush them. Try to shoot them. Make them wreck. I have a good rifle and plenty of ammo. They won't have any idea. You drive ahead a ways and if you don't see them following you, come back, pick me up, and we'll be out of here."

"Wait." Lily said. "What if you just hide and let them chase us down. Why should I trust you?"

"Look," I said. "I'm going to stop in that wash and try to ambush them. If they see the truck here they will stop and we'll have a gunfight. Maybe I'll hit them, maybe they'll blow me to smithereens. Us. Shoot us all. I think an ambush will be the best. I have to trust you too, you know. Trust you to come back and get me. We have to trust each other."

She looked at me, back at Craig, then back at me. She nodded. "OK."

I DESTROYED THAT POOR BOY'S SOUL

I stepped on it to put as much distance between us and our pursuers as I could. We crested the rise, went left along the ridge, and swept back to the right toward the wash. If we played this right, after I got out they would see my truck going over the ridge on the opposite side of the wash. They would never know that I was waiting to ambush them. Just above the wash, I braked sharply and stopped. I got out, opened the back and got my rifle case. Speck jumped out and stood by me. "OK, you can come," I said. "But you have to listen. Lily—get in the driver's seat. Take off. Go! Go fast!"

She climbed over the console, slammed the door, put it in gear, and roared off, not looking back.

"Come on, Speck," I called, and we ran away from the road and ducked behind a rock outcrop along the edge of the wash. I found a place where we would be concealed until the truck was just about to drop into the wash. They would slow down a little before the curve, and I'd have a pretty good chance for a clear shot. I called Speck and made her sit by me. The tone of my voice told her I was serious, and she leaned against my leg. I got the rifle out and slid the magazine in. My hands were shaking. Don't panic, I told myself. Shit, what do I do now? How do I get a round in the chamber? I should have practiced more. Might be easier if I wasn't shaking so much. Might be easier if my life didn't depend on it. I could hear the truck coming. Where's the safety? Safety off. Take a breath. Be sure to duck down. Get in position. Here it is. One, two, three, fire. I could see two silhouettes in the windshield.

Pop pop pop. The gun worked. By the time I fired the fourth round I could see the windshield spidering out and shattering. With the fifth shot, the truck lurched sharply to the left and launched off the edge of the road. It became airborne and made a dusty, roaring arc before it struck the rocky hillside just above the bottom of the wash. The truck, which had been flying, stopped instantly, seemed to shudder, and fell back, landing on its wheels. Steam erupted from the radiator. Speck pressed close to my leg and trembled. I waited a moment to gather my thoughts, then, after telling Speck to stay, crouched down and approached the steaming, sputtering pickup. I cautiously rounded the driver's side. I could see the driver, his head open, bleeding, smashed against the windshield. My God. I was transfixed for a moment. What have I done? Then I remembered that there were two of them. I edged around the back of the vehicle. The passenger's door was open, and a person was sprawled on the ground beside the truck. He was twitching and groaning. Oh no. It's a kid. I bet he's only seventeen or eighteen. Wearing camouflage pants and a blue BYU Football tee shirt. Blood, bubbles, and foam were oozing from a wound in his throat. He groaned and his right leg stiffened, then relaxed. Barely an adult. Good God, what should I do? Could I save him? I reached for my bandanna to cover his wound, when his eyes popped open. His eyes blinked and looked straight at me. His hand started to move toward the large pistol strapped to his leg. In an instant he had it. He was going to shoot me! I raised my rifle and destroyed that poor boy's soul. The bullet made only a tiny hole in his forehead, but I could see pieces of the back of his skull break apart and splatter around on the ground. My God. He was going to kill me. I had no choice. I had to.

Did I? Did I have to? Yes, yes I had to. Was the guy driving the truck his dad? Did I just wipe out an entire family? Why were they trying to kill me? Why did they force me to do these awful things?

I had to. I must remember that.

Speck came and leaned against my leg. She looked up at me and wagged her tail cautiously. She's as confused as I am. Thank God she didn't panic and run when the shooting started. I reached down and stroked her head, and for a moment we shared a look that seemed to me to assure each other that we were together, whatever might happen.

And now what? I looked around and remembered my Toyota and the girl who drove it away. Lily, her name's Lily.

Where is Lily, I wondered. She should be getting back here pretty soon. Come on Lily, where are you. I walked down across the wash and up the other side. She left me. She just left me here. I kept walking to the top of the ridge, where I figured I could see a larger area. When I got to the top I could see a dust plume in the distance. Sure enough, it was my truck, hauling ass. Dammit, she did leave me. Then I saw the other plume. Another vehicle came into view, and it appeared to be closing in on her. Oh no, they're going to get her after all, all because of my dumbass plan. And her husband too. Craig. Shit. Well, maybe we'd all be goners if I hadn't gotten out. We'd have the guys I killed, plus these new guys to contend with. Jesus. Maybe she can get away, or crash into them or something. The vehicles disappeared over the top of a hill.

Don't outsmart yourself

Well, what should I do? My thoughts raced. I need to get away from this wash and the dead guys. Their friends will find them and come looking. OK then. Where would be the easiest way to run? Up or down the wash? I was standing on the top of a ridge that angled away from the road. I'll go up the ridge. Stay out of view, below the top. Try to get at least a mile or two away from the road, or any place where they can drive. And stay hidden. I'm glad I'm wearing tan today. Maybe I should tie some bushes on me for camouflage. I should head down the wash for a few hundred yards, then hide my trail, to make them think I went that way. OK. Think clearly. I mean it.

I decided I had better head back to the wrecked truck and see if there was anything I needed. I looked around in the cab. Several rifles and pistols were scattered around. I found some things I could use—two additional clips and some ammo that fit my rifle, a hunting knife, a pair of binoculars and a water jug. I stuffed the smaller things in the canvas rifle case, slung it onto my back, adjusted the shoulder straps, picked up the water jug and my rifle, and set out.

"Come on Speck, let's go."

I headed to the wash and walked down it, not worrying about leaving a trail. Moving helped to calm me down. It gave me something to do other than panic. Whether anybody would try to track me, whether anybody would care, I had no way to know. Don't outsmart yourself, Stan, I thought. I told myself that all the time, and now I really meant it. I might be walking down the wash trying to outwit someone when I could be just wasting time, putting myself in more danger. Everything's a compromise. Compromise between making a diversion and just heading out. Compromises are part of decision-making. Even when the consequences are life or death. A compromise might mean death. Or life, actually.

Stop thinking and just do. Just do. Move. I jogged down the dry wash, hurrying, secure in knowing that I was out of sight of the road and that anyone who followed me would have to do so on foot, since the wash bottom was strewn with boulders that would make driving impossible. After maybe a half-mile, the drainage passed along a massive exposure of sandstone, which provided me a way to leave the wash. I headed west on the slickrock, and went up toward the ridge. I stayed on the exposed sandstone for as long as I could, then skipped from stone to stone and outcrop to outcrop when possible, walking daintily and lightly when I had to walk on softer sediments. I decided that it was good training and practice. As long as I was trying to evade the pirates or whoever they were, treading lightly, leaving little trace, was a good philosophy.

I had a gallon of water, which wouldn't last long in this heat. I knew that there were few streams in this region and that water was a primary limiting factor in foot travel. I headed for the crest of the ridge so I could get a little rest and take a look around.

The road through the wash where I had ambushed the pirates was empty in both directions as far as I could see, which I reckoned was about a mile each way. No sign of my truck and Lily, no sign of pirates or anyone else. It was comforting in a way, although I realized then that no information about the dangers you may face can be more disconcerting than some information, even if the knowledge is frightening. Real dangers are somehow better dealt with than imagined or anticipated ones.

The ridge I was on rose higher and higher, eventually cresting on the edge of the San Rafael Swell, a grand and spectacular geological structure of uplifted sandstone that defines a vast and rugged area, a region that boasted a significantly larger population one thousand years ago than it has since the arrival of the Europeans. I figured I could hang out where I was through the heat of the day, then head up the ridge in the cooler evening and perhaps be in striking distance of Milky Creek in the morning. Seemed like a plan.

I sat in the shade of a piñon tree and made myself comfortable. I decided to take inventory. One rifle—Tegra Arms .223 caliber, 104 rounds of ammo, four magazines. One Israeli Military Industries 9mm pistol, 43 rounds of ammo, and two ammo clips. One CRKT hunting knife. One pair of Steiner compact binoculars. One Arizona Iced Tea gallon jug, about three-quarters full of water. One canvas military-style rifle case with storage pockets and backpack straps. I had on a pair of brown Carhartt cargo pants, a tan long-sleeve shirt, a Salt Lake Bees baseball cap, a wallet with sixty-three dollars, several credit and business cards, my driver license, and tickets to a Stringdusters concert we were planning to attend on Chris's birthday. In my pockets I had a folding pocket knife, a Leatherman mini pocket tool, a pen, a small notebook, a bandanna, and a ChapStick. Wish I smoked, I thought. Then I'd have a lighter. Wish I had some sunscreen. Or a satellite phone. Then I could call in the troops. Jeez, who would I call? I don't think the sheriff would come get me. Maybe nobody would. At least I could call Chris and tell her that I was screwed and that she should call our insurance agent and tell him to get ready for some claims. Hell, maybe it's best that I don't have a phone. How could I tell her about what had happened today? That I had killed two men? That I was probably being hunted, and some people I tried to help were probably dead? I can't even believe it myself. Breathe, I told myself. Breathe.

Speck sat close to me. I gave her a little water from the jug in my cupped hand and took a drink myself. "Let's just rest, girl." I put my arm around her, and she nuzzled my neck. "We may have a long hike tonight."

* * *

Breaking News from Channel Nine News
Liz Nuñez reporting

"The story of the protests near Price has taken a new twist. A bad automobile accident that left one woman in the hospital with life-threatening injuries may be related in some way to the conflict. The woman, LaNae Prusser, was injured in a violent collision last Friday night, and has been in a medically induced coma ever since. Her Jeep Wagoneer SUV was apparently broadsided by another vehicle sometime in the late evening near the Bear Creek Rest Area along Highway 6. The perplexing thing is, the other vehicle was never found. Carbon County Sheriff Cortland Hackney thinks the other vehicle fled the scene, but others say there is more to it. It happened on the same night that the tractor-trailer driven by Craig and Lily Clark of Rosine, Kentucky, disappeared. Spokespeople for the protesters assert that the Clarks drove their semi into the protest area, to donate the food and other cargo they were hauling. Relatives and co-workers of the Clarks dispute that claim and assert that the couple would never have voluntarily given up their truck, trailer, or its contents, to the protest."

"We have here Mr. Art Davis, of Art's Texaco in Price, who towed Mrs. Prusser's vehicle into town after the accident."

"What kind of damage did her vehicle show, Art?"

"Massive; massive's all I'd say. The whole front end was nearly sheared off. It was hit from the side, almost T-boned. Bad. About as bad as I'd ever seen."

"Do you think the vehicle that hit her could have driven away?"

"Like I say, well, no. Except maybe if it was a semi or something. Something really big. Really big."

"Thank you, Art. There you have it, questions about what happened to Lily and Craig Clark, and speculation that they may have been involved in an accident."

"We will continue to follow this evolving story. Liz Nuñez, Channel Nine News, *reporting from Price, in Carbon County, Utah. Back to Dick and Allyson at the station."*

CaCaw, CaCaw

We rested until early evening, then headed up the ridge. The going was fairly steep but not too rough. Soon we reached the crest. From there I could see a long way in all directions. The Book Cliffs looked for the first time to me like volumes in an ancient library, stratigraphic profiles streaked deep orange tinged with violet, punctuated by steep drainages. The parting burst of the sun's energy as it was pushed away by the rapidly deepening darkness gave the stark landscape a strikingly beautiful and foreboding presence.

I could see the interstate far to the south. It should be full of vehicles, trucks, buses, vacationers, business people, but no. No night travel was permitted on these roads. The only signs of civilization I could see were the lights at the intersection of the interstate and the road toward Price that I had been on, and the faint lights of the town of Green River in the distance. Man, it sure would be nice to be having a beer and a cheeseburger at Ray's Tavern right now, I thought.

No more of that kind of thinking. Focus. Focus on what you need to do. Look for lights in the other direction. See if you can spot the pirates' camp. I got out the binoculars and scanned the vast darkness to the north and west. Nothing. Wait, there's a tiny bit of light. Maybe a lantern or some headlights or something. Yep, it's a light. Right near Dancing Water Creek. So, I know where not to go. It must be where the road crosses the creek. Nothing along Milky Creek though, and I scanned the area where it flowed. "That's where we'll go in the morning, Speck. We'll have all the water we want." We each took another drink and tried to rest. We both seemed wide awake and energetic enough to continue on, but we needed to navigate some treacherous cliffs and steep slopes, and the dark of night is a mighty dangerous time to travel.

The stars were intensely bright and crystal clear. What an incredible place. I realized that I was seeing this area in nearly the same light as people one thousand, two thousand, or many thousands of years ago saw it, without artificial light. A satellite scooted across the sky, and an airplane blinked its way from east to west, reminding me that outside this little bubble I was trapped in, the modern, real world, the world that makes sense to me, the world I am familiar with and know my way around in, still exists. Speck twitched slightly in her sleep, and I lay back. I need to rest. Tomorrow will be a big day. I had trouble relaxing, and the image of me shooting the young pirate could not be dislodged from my mind. Every time I was able to relax a bit, the reality of my having killed two men, one of them barely an adult, leapt out at me and made me race with a rush of adrenaline. I had no choice. I had no choice. I kept repeating it as if it were a mantra. I did a breathing exercise Chris had taught me, breathing in for a count of five, out for a count of five, resting for a count of five. It seemed to help. I curled around Speck and was grateful for the comfort being next to her brought. We are a team. Even a small team is better than none. I thought of walking through the sage and junipers with her leading the way, step by step, and when sleep came, it was deep and restful.

We awoke early, when light was just starting to arrive, and we headed over the rim. A nice crack in the rock wall led us down to the first ledge, then we followed a rockfall that took us to the second ledge. We followed the ledge for several hundred yards and came to a slight overhang that contained just what I was hoping for. A seep. A layer in the sediments that carried and held water, and which at its exposure partway down the cliff, seeped moisture. The layer was caked white with mineral deposits, and dependent vegetation, the kinds of plants that cannot grow anywhere else in this arid environment, clung to the face, creating what is often called a hanging garden. We would be able to drink.

I found a spot where a small amount of water trickled from the side of the mountain and scooped out a basin to catch it. Within minutes, a tiny pool of water, perhaps a quart or so, had formed. I cupped my hands and brought some to my mouth. It tasted strongly of minerals and slightly salty, but it was going to be a life saver. Pure, filtered through stone, cool, refreshing, life giving. "Here you go, Speck," I said, inviting her to go to the water. "Drink up, girl." I stroked her back as she lapped away and looked around. This was a perfect little spot to hole up for a while. Very well hidden, inaccessible except on foot, and a difficult hike, or perhaps climb, at that. I could see clumps of Indian ricegrass growing along the slopes of the ledge, some prickly pears, needle-and-thread grass, and scattered clumps of wild rye. Up in a crack in the sandstone above the seep was a pretty substantial pack rat nest and midden. We would be able to survive for at least a few days here. I found a level spot and took off my pack. I arranged a flat stone at the seep so it would fill my water bottle, and, when full, would keep the small basin filled. Good. Now what? It was still early in the morning, so I decided to go back up to the rim where I had a great view in all directions and see what I could see. I took the binoculars, the water jug, and my rifle. "Come on, Speck," I called, and headed back up to the top.

I reminded myself to try to stay hidden, since a figure on the horizon— on the highest point around—was conspicuous. More conspicuous than the people and things I was going to try to see. I crouched down when in exposed areas and worked myself in behind trees and bushes when I could. I found a pretty good path as I neared the crest and was able to crawl under a piñon tree at the top of the rim that provided cover and a good, shady viewing spot.

First, I looked toward where I had seen the light the night before. I scanned the area with my binoculars. Sure enough, there was a group of campers, trailers, and tents down where the road crossed Dancing Water Creek. And yep, there's the semi and trailer. No, two of them. Two semis. They're all set. I bet those hijackers are praising God and Ronald Reagan for their manna from heaven in that Family Grocers trailer. Stolen, stolen at gunpoint. Stolen by shooting a man. He could be dead, for all I know. So could Lily. I turned my glasses in the other direction, toward where I had last seen my vehicle. After a few minutes, I spotted it. Looks like it might have rolled. Shit, there's an ATV by it. Somebody's there. I watched it off and on for several hours, and at one point, another ATV with a single rider arrived, and stayed. Strange. People must be staying there. I wonder if Lily and Craig are still alive. I decided to go down to the truck that night.

In the heat of the afternoon, I went back down to my camp. I explored a little bit and found that I was not the first one to use that camp. On the wall of the cliff just a little way down from the seep was a large painted ancient Indian rock art panel. One nearly life-sized figure, sort of like the "ghost" figures from Barrier Canyon dominated the smooth stone face. A complex set of designs—wandering maze-like white lines—decorated the interior of the vaguely human ghost-like body. Next to it was a small quadruped—a dog? And hovering near each shoulder were two figures that looked kind of like light bulbs with streamers coming from them. Upon closer examination the light bulbs had eyes and hands. And among the figures were several birds.

On the ground in front of the rock art was a slab of smooth stone—a grinding slab used by prehistoric people to grind seeds and roots. And beside it was a mano—a hand stone. To the side of the rock art panel was a small beehive-shaped stone and mud structure, about two feet high and two feet in diameter. A granary. A place for storing seeds and other food. It had a slab of stone covering the top, and when I pulled it back, I could see that rodents, probably the remote ancestors of the pack rats who lived nearby, had gotten into the granary and consumed whatever might have been stored there.

The findings made me feel even better about my little home, temporary though it might be. I sat down in the little flat spot, pulled over my pack to use as a pillow, called Speck, and lay back to rest up for a night of planned travel and exploration.

I thought of the painting I was going to pick up and bring to Chris. I could see the blues and oranges of the background and the magpie perched on the upthrust single trunk of a twisted, stunted juniper tree. The magpie seemed to be peering straight out from the canvas, and I had fallen in love with the painting at first sight in the Chesley Art Studio in Moab. I have always loved magpies, perhaps one of the most intelligent inhabitants of the desert, and my admiration for junipers, the most resilient citizen of these harsh environments, was deep and heartfelt. The painting gave me a feeling of power and strength, and I hoped Chris would love it.

As I slid from daydream to sleep, I saw the painting, and dreamed of floating in my little camp, with Speck floating near me, looking more like a big red wolf than a dog. Magpies sat on branches and spoke to us, "CaCaw, CaCaw," they said, and I kept thinking that there was something looking over my shoulder, but when I turned my head to look, nothing was there. Then I realized that I shouldn't look, I should just listen, and feel. I was being helped along, shown how and where to float, and I floated up and down the canyon and over the rim and down below, and I saw creatures that looked like long-legged badgers, with big gaping mouths and beady, yellow eyes. I saw a young antelope surrounded by the badgers, and I swooped down and picked her up and took her to a grassy field where she ran away with the magpies swooping and diving above her, cheering.

When I awoke, the faint orange glow of the approaching sunset washed the sky above the high mountains to the west, and I sat up. Speck was gone. Maybe she just got up to go pee, I thought. "Speck," I called. "Speck, here Speck," It's not like her to run off for long, I thought. Well, she knows how to find me. I got my water jug, shouldered my rifle, and headed up the hill. I had taken only a few steps when I heard some crashing in the brush below. I stood still, rifle at the ready. As the sound came closer, I could see a black and white form in the shadows. "Speck," I greeted her. "Where have you been?" She ran up to me, wagging her tail. In her mouth was a nearly complete hindquarter of a deer. Desiccated and disgusting, but still a treasure for a hungry dog. "Good for you, girl. Now leave that here. We have some traveling to do."

Road-Closure Protesters Disregard Sheriff's Orders

by Blaine Willis
The Salt Lake Tribune

Dozens of new arrivals driving pickup trucks and all-terrain vehicles have joined a small group of protesters in Utah's San Rafael Swell, overwhelming law enforcement personnel from the Carbon County Sheriff's Office and the Bureau of Land Management (BLM). Cleal Redd, spokesman for the sheriff's office said that approximately fifty protesters arrived in a group, apparently by design, and rode through temporary roadblocks set up to mark the boundary of the closed area. Dozens more have joined the protesters since then, with more arriving each day. The original protest consisted of a group of local ranchers and outdoorsmen, led by longtime conservative activist Drew Peacock of Price, Utah, who contested the closure of the Dancing Water Creek road as part of a new wilderness designation. Peacock and six others rode their vehicles through the barricade and set up a small camp early last week, calling themselves the Recapture Brigade. Law enforcement personnel surrounded the group but allowed them to remain, pending a planned meeting with delegations from the Governor's Office and the Department of the Interior. The arrival of reinforcements changes everything, according to Redd. "We are not prepared to deal with such a large group. We are pulling our officers back to the highway in order to avoid any further confrontation."

"This is a situation the BLM brought on themselves by disregarding the locals and locking up this land," said Travis Dmitrich, a spokesman for the protest. "The Recapture Brigade is made up of patriots who are tired of Washington and its thieves. They will stay out there as long as it takes."

Governor Norman Anderson is sending a representative to meet with the protesters next week, and Secretary of the Interior Starla Booker indicated that they were studying the matter. Meanwhile, a call for reinforcements has gone out on several antigovernment websites, and officials are increasingly worried that escalating tensions and more protesters will allow the situation to get out of hand.

"We are hoping that cool heads will prevail," said Carbon County Commissioner Elmo Kuykendall, speaking to reporters assembled at a hastily organized press conference. Dmitrich, speaking for the protesters, indicated that many inside the Recapture movement think that this could be "the start of a revolution." Utah Highway Patrol spokesman Mike Phelps responded that "order will be maintained, and there is nothing for the traveling public to fear."

LET'S GET THE FUCK OUT OF HERE

We made our way quickly but cautiously up to the rim, then down the long ridge, dropped over into an adjacent drainage and followed it down to where it opened into the main valley. A substantial open sage flat left us exposed, so we scurried across it and dropped into the gully that would intersect the road where my apparently incapacitated 4Runner sat. The steep-sided wash provided cover until we were within a couple hundred yards of the vehicle. I climbed a rise that would afford me a view of the area and the truck and found a small grove of junipers to hole up in. We ducked down under a spreading tree and rested quietly until I dozed off and slept fitfully and in short spurts. Just as dawn was breaking, Speck rose, a deep growl rumbling in her chest. I careened into consciousness and reached for her collar. Good thing she is not a barker, I thought. One bark and she could get us killed. Loud clanging erupted from the direction of the truck and disrupted the stillness of the morning. Several magpies burst from the trees nearby, calling loudly. I could see a wisp of smoke rising in the still morning, then heard shouting. It sounded like two men arguing. Maybe they are distracted enough that I can sneak up a little closer.

"OK, Speck, let's go," I said. "Heel."

We walked down the slope and into the gully. Cautiously I peered around the rising trunk of a juniper tree toward the SUV. I saw two men standing face-to-face, clearly in the middle of a heated argument. Where is Lily, I wondered. I moved cautiously a little bit closer to where I could see my Toyota.

It was indeed wrecked. Sitting on its badly bent and broken wheels, sides and roof crumpled, the windshield smashed out. Shit. Next to it was an ATV. At the rear of the SUV was my folding camp chair and cooler next to a smoldering fire. Lily was tied to the bumper, her hands over her head as she sat on the ground, facing toward and watching the two arguing men.

"Don't, Phil! Don't!" One of the men cried out. "We can work this out. Come on, be reasonable!" I could see that he was backing up, nearly on top of Lily. A shot rang out, and he fell backward, against the bumper of the truck.

The shooter held a pistol out in front of him with both hands. His features were exaggerated by his excitement and rage. "What do you have to say now, motherfucker?" He shrieked. "Want another one?"

The fallen man slumped sideways to the ground. I could see blood pouring from a wound in his back. The bullet had gone completely thorough his chest.

"Well, now I'm in charge," the shooter shouted, still standing over his victim. He looked over at Lily. "I'll get to you in a minute, sweetheart."

He laid his pistol on the roof of the SUV, reached down, and took the dying man by the shoulders. He lifted him almost effortlessly. I could see that the shooter was a very large, powerful man, with long blond hair and a full red beard. He dragged the still convulsing man away from the truck. I decided that it was time to act. I stepped from behind the tree, raised my rifle, and pointed it straight at his chest.

"Hands up," I shouted, "and on your knees. Now"

The shooter dropped his victim and made a slight move in my direction as if he were about to leap toward me. I squeezed off one shot that went only an inch or so from his head.

"Down," I ordered. "Now."

This time he complied. I made him lay face down and spread eagled. I kept the rifle trained on him as I went to Lily.

"Lily," I said softly, "Lily, it's Stan."

She looked at me as if she didn't recognize me. Her eyes were wide and her mouth tense, teeth clenched. She took a deep breath, looked at me, then at the man who had been shot, at the shooter, then back to me.

"Lily, it's me, Stan. I gave you and your husband a ride. This is my truck. Where's Craig? Are there any more pirates here?"

Lily stared at me wide eyed. She looked around, then back at me. "You're the guy? The guy in the truck?" she asked.

"Yes, it's me," I said. "Is anyone else here?

She shook her head. "Craig's dead." She stared straight ahead for a moment, then looked at me.

I took out my knife and cut the nylon cords that were binding her. The big man on the ground turned his head to look at us, and I fired another round into the dirt.

"Don't move. Don't move an inch," I shouted.

Lily stood and rubbed her wrists. She seemed to be gaining her bearings.

"Can you handle a rifle?" I asked. She nodded. I handed her the rifle. "Shoot him if he moves or tries anything. Right in the back." She nodded.

I found some nylon cord beside the ATV, got it, and bound the killer securely.

"You're lucky, asshole, that I didn't blow your head off," I said to him. I turned to Lily

"Let's get the fuck out of here," I said.

I ran to the 4Runner and grabbed a small emergency backpack I always kept in the back, an extra water bottle, a small plastic tarp, Speck's food, and my 9mm pistol. "Come on," I said to Lily, as I went to the ATV. I pulled down a flexible rod that flew a triangular red and black flag with a black bird on it from the ATV, climbed on, and called Speck to sit between my arms.

Lily didn't speak but came right to me and boosted herself on behind me. I pulled out on the road. We would head straight for the highway. After about a mile, I saw a dust plume coming toward us. I slowed and stopped on a rise where I could see what was causing it. Shit, a jacked-up pickup roared straight down the road toward us. Pirates. What to do now? I couldn't continue on the road going toward the highway, and when they found the pirate by the truck they would start looking for us. I could only think of one thing to do. Go back to where I had been.

I spun the ATV around and headed back down the road. I turned down a ridge that ran parallel to the wash and followed it, staying just over the edge so the coming truck couldn't see me. The ridge was thick with trees and rock outcrops and difficult traveling for the ATV. It would be very difficult, or impossible, I hoped, for a truck. After about a mile I dropped down into the wash and stayed down in it until I was just below the drainage I had walked down the night before. I left the ATV in the wash, in a tight bend where it was fairly well hidden. I took the key, gave Lily a drink from the water bottle, took one myself, and gave her a nod. "Let's go." We walked up and out of the wash. We hurried, keeping low and in good cover, and climbed the drainage. Partway up, we ascended the ridge, and followed it to the top. I could see the pirates' truck next to my wrecked vehicle and hoped the pirates thought Lily and I had escaped back to civilization on the ATV. We hurried over the rim, down through the crack and over the rockfall, and made our way to the little overhang and seep. I took the pack off, laid out the tarp, gave Lily some water to drink, and helped her lie down.

"I, I, I mean, my uh. . ." she stuttered, half crying.

"Just rest," I said. "You're safe here. We're safe. Just rest. We can talk later."

I wanted to hike back up to the top and look around, but thought Lily would need the assurance that she was protected so she could sleep, so I leaned up against the back of the shelter, stretched my legs out, called Speck to my side, and tried to relax.

They're Crazy Enough

Lily fell asleep quickly and deeply. She's exhausted, I thought. I bet she hasn't slept in days. She had told me on the way up how Craig had died from his wound. Seeing her husband die, and suffering through who knows what. What a nightmare.

I watched Speck chew on the deer leg and was reminded that I was hungry. I looked in the little knapsack I had gotten from my vehicle and was happy to see a tiny butane stove, a small aluminum cooking pan, a few utensils, salt and pepper, some tea bags, several packages of ramen, and a small package of dried beans. I put some beans in the pan with water to soak. Need to conserve fuel, I thought. Two canisters, good for a few meals at least.

What else was there? A coil of nylon cord, a small first aid kit, a windbreaker, and a lighter. OK, this helps.

As I sat there, I wondered what Chris and Bill were doing. Surely they had filed a missing person report. Probably by Saturday evening when they hadn't heard from me. And Craig's company would be searching for its missing semi. I had seen a small plane flying overhead, maybe they were searching. I'm sure they would have spotted the semi and the pirate camp, and maybe even my wrecked truck. I wonder what they will do? Local search and rescue surely wouldn't come out here. State and local governments mostly sympathize with the Recapture movement. They would like to take over federal lands for themselves. They probably hope the Recapture people succeed, or at least open the door for them to step in. The state and counties certainly won't go up against the protesters. Would the federal government? I don't know.

How could our government let things like this happen? It's political. But the politics of leaving law-abiding citizens at the mercy of criminals goes bad pretty quickly. Surely somebody is doing something. Surely they haven't given up on us. I know Chris wouldn't. I know my other friends wouldn't. Crazy bastards are probably gearing up to come out and find me. Bill and Ron and Andy and Joel—they're crazy enough. They'd love to go at it with some of these so-called patriots. They'd love it.

Bill and I had talked about the places we knew of to weather some shitstorm. Like a war or disaster or something that broke down normal cultural operations and institutions. Like what was happening to me now. He always said I could find him at Warm Springs Cave. A good spot with a spring, cover, shelter, and seclusion. A place where the Anasazi hung out when times got rough. We talked about Range Creek, about Floating Island, and about Dark Lord Cave. Shit, that's it. Dark Lord Cave. If Bill was stuck out here, I bet he'd head there. And I bet he thinks I will too. How far is it? Ten, fifteen miles? Mostly roadless, rugged terrain. It would be rough. Rougher than staying here. But then, it might be our only way out. That old ATV was about out of gas when I parked it. Might only make it partway to the highway, and the pirates were patrolling that area. They might even have found it by now. Better forget about going that way. Dark Lord Cave. Water, great shelter, really far from a road, a place where a person with the right skills could live for months. Years, even. That's what we should do. Head for Dark Lord Cave.

With Lily sleeping, I set about building a small fireplace. I figured we could make a fire at night when our smoke could not be seen, as long as we could keep the light from being visible. I gathered flat stones, which were plentiful on the ledge just below the camp and selected a spot up against the back wall of the shelter. I made a small box of stones with an opening in the front and in the top, which would be the cooking area and the smoke hole. I used a large flat stone to cover the front and to shield the fire from view. Then I gathered wood—mostly small pieces that would burn quickly in the firebox and not make too much smoke. I walked all around our little camp to see if there was a direct line of sight to any of the roads I knew of, or the pirate camp. We are pretty well hidden, both by the orientation of the cliff and by the trees that rise in front of our little rock shelter. Good.

I noticed that some clouds were building in the west, so I gathered a fairly substantial pile of firewood. The rock ledge overhung our camp area by quite a bit, so I was not too worried about rain wetting our gear or sleeping area. I found two long branches that I could lean against the back wall of the shelter to support the tarp just in case things got really nasty with wind blowing rain into the shelter.

I also decided to gather some juniper bark to use for tinder and bedding and found some good trees a hundred yards or so along the ledge beyond our shelter. I stripped a fairly substantial amount and carried a double armful back to the camp and was just picking up a second load when I heard a call from our camp, followed by another. I whistled for Speck and urged her on. "What is it? Go see what it is, Speck." She ran ahead of me toward camp. I dropped the juniper bark and ran after her. Damn, I thought, I should have brought a gun.

Call for Support Brings Resources to ATV Protesters

by Brandon Bringhurst
The Provo Daily News

Postings on social media and sympathetic websites asking for donations to support the occupation of central Utah's San Rafael Swell by off-road enthusiasts and antigovernment activists have apparently been heeded. Accounts set up in several banks have received significant cash donations, Travis Dmitrich, spokesman for the protesters, told reporters on Saturday. In addition, supporters have driven past barricades and roadblocks to take vehicles, including semi trucks loaded with camping gear, food, fuel, water, and other supplies to the Recapture Brigade's camp on Dancing Water Creek. "They're in there for the long haul," Dmitrich said. "This is the first step in taking back control of our lands from the federal overlords."

Environmental activists have criticized the county sheriff's office and the Bureau of Land Management for not doing more to curtail the protesters. "This is nothing more than a bunch of criminals blatantly violating federal law," said Lindsay Caster, an attorney for the Utah Backcountry Hikers Association. "The first group should have been arrested and charged, and it wouldn't have gotten to this point," she added.

"The closure of these lands is unconstitutional," countered LaMar Scoggins, of the Western States Land Rights Coalition. "The feds are trying to enslave us with their abuse of the constitution. They are depriving us of access to our God-given lands, and the days of submission are over. We're taking back this country, and Dancing Water Creek will go down in history as a key turning point."

Federal, state, and county officials refused to comment, citing the planned meetings with the protesters as a possible solution to the crisis.

THEY AREN'T ALL PIRATES

When I arrived, Lily was sitting up, hugging Speck, who was licking Lily's face. She had been sobbing.

"I woke up and didn't know where I was. My hand was asleep, and for a second I thought I was still tied up and that big pirate Viking asshole was coming after me. Jesus, I'm sorry. Then I saw your dog and she ran right up to me, and oh my God I can't believe the crap that's been happening." She let go of Speck and wiped her face with her hand. She ran her fingers back through her hair, looked at me, and shook her head. "Jesus," she said, and shook her head some more.

"You don't have to be sorry," I said. I stood at the edge of the shelter. "I, I don't know what to say. That guy's gone. We'll never see him again. But, but, shit. I keep telling myself to just focus on getting out. Do anything I need to do to get out."

Lily looked up at me and slowly shook her head. She took a breath and looked out from the shelter, as though she were looking through the trees and past them. "I can't believe it," she said. "What the hell's going on?"

"We're caught up in something, some big freaking nightmare. A nightmare."

"Are we just screwed? Is there any chance we can make it? Get away? Back. Back to, back to the real world?"

"We have to think so. We have to, to just plow ahead and get back. We can do it. We'll do our best. And, well, crap. That's all we can do. Speck here, she'll help too. I have a kind of a plan. All I'm doing is trying to stay alive and get out. We can. I don't know what else to do but try to get away." I looked at her, looked around at our spot, and realized how desperate we were. "I can't imagine what kind of hell you've been through," I said. "All I can do to help is try to get us out. That's all I can do."

"I don't even know you," she said. "I don't know anything. You and your dog. Is this it? Are we on our own?"

"Uh huh," I nodded. "Just us. We're in this together, like it or not." I walked over to the woodpile and got some sticks and loaded them into the fireplace. "Are you hungry? I'll cook some ramen, and I'll build a fire when it gets dark, and we can cook some beans for tomorrow. At least we have water and some food."

"Where the fuck are we?" she said. "What are we going to do, sit up in this shithole and eat ramen until those bastards find us? You know what they'll do, they'll kill you and fuck me to death." She twirled her fingers in Speck's fur. "That's what they'll do, you know."

"We're not going to just sit here and wait. We've got guns. I know this place, probably at least as well as these pirates. I've worked here and hiked here. We'll get out. We will."

I poured water in the pan and started the stove. "We have to eat. We have to be sharp as we can. That's how we'll get away. Not think about what will happen if they catch us. We can't. Don't. Don't think about what happened to you. Let's just think ahead, think about getting out."

Lily sighed. Tears came to her eyes. "I, I, never thought. I mean, I can't believe it. I can't." She took a breath and looked up. "You're right. We can't let fear beat us. If we do that, we'll lose. I learned that from my Grammy. If you think about messing up, you will. Screw these assholes. We need to get out of here so we can send all these fuckers to jail. For what they did to me. For what they did to Craig. And to you. Screw them." She pulled Speck close and hugged her tight.

Rain came in waves of varying intensity through the night. Lightning struck all around us after about midnight, starting a tree on fire on a ridge down along Milky Creek that lasted only a few minutes before the rain quenched it. Our shelter kept us dry and secure. I built up the fire and cooked the pot of beans. Lily and I slept or lay quietly for most of the night, which was punctuated by the shockingly bright flashes and explosions of the electrical storm. Speck fared the worst and tried to be as small as she could be, curled between my rifle bag and the back of the shelter. I took comfort in knowing that any tracks we had made would be obliterated by the rain.

The drumming of the rain reminded me of the last vacation Chris and I had taken to Oregon around five years ago, shortly after we were married, and the night we spent in a cabin on the coast. It had rained all night, and we had cuddled in the bed, warm and happy to be with each other, and we'd talked much of the night about making our home and the great adventures we would have. It seemed like that was a long time ago, and we hadn't had a vacation since, and we'd hardly done any of the things we dreamed about. Chris had always wanted kids, and I had resisted. I don't know why. Afraid I'd be a poor dad, partly. Maybe just selfishness. Was that it? Was I just too selfish to share? I realized now that I had been an asshole, keeping Chris from being a mother and depriving myself of having a real family. What a dick I've been. I do want kids. I want two or three. Chris had always wanted three, the same-size family she had come from. Maybe being an only child kept me from wanting kids. I don't know. I do know that if I get out of here, the first thing I want to do is to talk to Chris about babies. If I die in this desert, if some pirate shoots me down, I'll never have the chance. I want the chance. I want somebody to call me dad. I put my hand in the warm curl of Speck's belly and felt her move a bit, to accommodate the intrusion. I love Speck, and I know she loves me, and I know I want something more, and I vowed to live to make it happen. To make it up to Chris. To live. To have a reason to live. I imagined pushing a child, my child, in a swing set in our backyard, and we were giggling and Chris was smiling, and it was the happiest feeling, and it overwhelmed me, and I slept.

Dawn came quietly, and the rain lessened, until as the light grew enough for us to see beyond the confines of our shelter, the only sound was of droplets falling from the needles and branches of trees, rushing when the breeze came, slowing to near silence when the air was still.

"They aren't all pirates," Lily said, poking at the ashy coals with a small stick. "That one the big guy shot. The guy with a black beard. He tried to protect me. He buried Craig and treated me like a person. That other turd, that guy Phil, the one that looks like a wannabe Viking, he was a real dick. He didn't care about their cause, whatever that is. He wanted, well, if you hadn't shown up, he would have, man, how fucked up can it get?"

She put her face in her hands. After a few minutes she ran her hands through her hair and straightened her shirt. Her clothes were bloody—her own blood, Craig's, who knows who else's. She looked up at me.

"When I drove away after you got out, an ATV came after us. I didn't know where to go so I just drove, and when it got kind of close, I braked hard and swerved and hit him and he wrecked. And then I wrecked too. Fuck, it was an amateur move. I hit the little ditch along the road and overcorrected. That's when I rolled. When we stopped, I was trying to see if Craig was OK, you know, talking to him and trying to hold him, and well, he was about done for. That guy with the black beard, his name was Gus, he made me get out and took my pistol, but then he helped me with Craig. There was nothing we could do, and he dug a hole for him. That fucker Phil, the big one, he came up the next afternoon when Gus was out getting firewood. He saw that Gus was gone and started grabbing my tits and humping me and saying all kinds of weird shit. When Gus came back, he made him stop."

"He was like, 'Cut that crap out, let her go. We'll take her back to camp. She's not yours to mess with, she's a prisoner. We're not rapists, we're revolutionaries,' stuff like that. He came up and pulled the blond guy away from me."

"He said, 'Don't worry, we won't hurt you.' Since we only had one ATV, he wanted to wait for someone from the camp to come and take us back. We would just all wait, but Phil, he was totally nuts. He paced and swore and looked at me like he wanted to tear me to bits. Phil said his ATV was fine, and he was going to take the prisoner—me—to the Patriot Camp. That's what he called it, the Patriot Camp. Gus said he was the officer and it was his job. He said he would send somebody back for Phil when he got to the camp. Or he said we could all just wait. I think he thought that was the best way to get Phil to be calm."

"Well, Phil, the Viking one, he woke up that morning in a wild ass mood. He didn't want to wait any more. He said he was taking me to the camp and Gus could just wait. He went to the ATV and moved some things around on it and was going to take me, and I think Gus knew what Phil would do, and he wasn't going to let him leave, and well, you saw what happened. Phil shot Gus in the chest. Shot him right in the chest! I was thinking some more patriots had come. That's what I had been hoping for. I couldn't believe it when I saw you. I thought you were dead. I didn't know what to think. Jesus."

She shook her head, poked the fire, and threw a few more sticks in. "Well, here we are." She looked around. "Now what?"

LET'S JUST KEEP
BEING LUCKY

"I don't know. I had kind of a plan, but now that I see where their camp is and where they've been driving and patrolling, we can't go that way. We are in a pretty good spot here for a little bit. We can watch the roads and their camp and see if we can figure out what's going on— where they send vehicles, that sort of stuff. Maybe they'll think we got away. Think we made it back to the highway. That would be the best—the highway's less than ten miles away. And the interstate's not much farther." I was pacing. Lecturing. Shit. I always do that when I'm nervous. Anxious.

"Why don't we, then?" Lily asked. "Leave now. Let's go. Get the hell out. Back to the world."

I made myself stop moving. I sat down on a low juniper branch and faced Lily. "I don't know," I said. "I mean, it's tempting. If nothing happened, if we didn't run into, well, those pirates, we could walk out in less than a day. But they'd see us. They would, and we'd be screwed. Too open, too obvious. I'm thinking we should head north. More walking—like fifteen miles or so, but no roads or trails. Well, a few, but not many. And I know of a spot we can head for where my friends might try to look for us. A spot that, well, a spot kind of like this, with water and shelter but a long way from the pirate camp, and a place my friends might stake out in case we go there."

I stood and walked toward the trail, up and out of our little shelter. "We could go up to the top and look around with the binoculars and just see what we can see. Watch the enemy. We can take turns. Lay low and just watch. We'll let things settle down a bit and plan to take off, say, in a day or two. What do you think?"

"Why not just head out now?" Lily said. "Why wait? What are we waiting for?"

"Well, we could. We don't gain that much by waiting. Seems like it might keep raining for a while, and traveling would be rough in the mud. And we'd leave a big trail. Maybe they'll start to forget about us after a day or two. If they are even looking for us now. I don't know. I mean, it's just an idea. I'm not telling you what to do. We're in this together. I'm just making it up as we go. But hell, everything I can think of seems flawed." I sat down again and shrugged. "What do you think?"

Lily looked down and took a deep breath. She shook her head, pursed her lips, and looked at me. "You're probably right. I mean, the faster we get out of here and back to the real world the better. But, well, if we do something stupid and get caught, that won't be good. Might be suicide. Avoid bad moves. That's the most important thing. Avoid mistakes." She turned and looked toward the fire. "Can we eat some of those beans?"

We ate the beans in silence, passing the aluminum pan back and forth.

"They're not bad," Lily said. "Filling. Could use some tabasco. Or Sriracha."

"I think we're stuck with pretty plain food for a while. Lucky to have this," I said.

"Ummm hummm," Lily said, finishing the last few bites. "I think I'd like to rinse out these clothes. See if I can get some of this, this blood and stuff out of them."

"I'll go on up and see what I can see," I said. "I'll come back down for you in a couple hours." I took a water bottle, the binoculars, my rifle, and started out, then walked back to my pack. "Here, you'd better take this," I said, handing her the 9mm. "Do you know how to use it?"

Lily took the handgun and looked it over. "Israeli Military. A Baby Eagle, right?"

I nodded, surprised at her familiarity with the handgun.

"I know how to use it," She said. "Craig, he was into shooting and guns. He wanted me to know how to use all kinds of weapons. 'Course I grew up around hunting—me and my brothers shot .22s and shotguns all our lives. Yeah, this is a good weapon." She released the magazine and saw that it was full, then pulled back the action to see if there was a round in the chamber. She slid the clip back in, looked the handgun over again, and slid it into its holster. "Hasn't been shot too much," she said. "Is it new?"

"No, I've had it for a while. I don't really shoot very much."

"Seemed like you knew what you were doing with that black rifle of yours," she said, nodding toward my AR-15.

"The first time I used it I was close, and the guys I was shooting at didn't know I was there. I got lucky," I said. "And at the camp where you wrecked, I was shaking so much I almost blew that guy's head off."

"I wish you would have," Lily said. "That guy is the worst. I hope we never see him again. Well, unless he's in chains and we're testifying against him. Only then."

"Maybe I should have shot him," I said. "I don't know. Maybe an act of kindness will help us. Or, hell, I don't know. I don't know anything anymore."

"Well, let's just keep on being lucky," Lily said. "Um, when you come back down, holler something so I know it's you. Just say 'CaCaw CaCaw' or something."

I smiled. "That's exactly what me and my friend Bill always joked would be our secret call. 'CaCaw' it is. See you in a while."

✳ ✳ ✳

Breaking News from Channel Nine News
Liz Nuñez reporting

"Tonight we have more on the story of the protests near Price with Liz Nuñez, reporting. Liz?"

"Thanks Dick, We have uncovered more in the evolving story of the protests and the disappearance of truck drivers Lily and Craig Clark of Rosine, Kentucky, along with their truck and cargo. But the official story from Sheriff Cortland Hackney and the protest camp's spokesperson is that the Clarks are safe in the camp and that they donated their cargo to the cause. We reported yesterday that the horrific accident that left LaNae Prusser in a coma may have involved a semi-tractor like the one driven by the Clarks. Channel Nine has learned that Mrs. Prusser was not simply traveling along the highway but was indeed an active participant in the protest. Family sources have told Channel Nine News *that Mrs. Prusser had joined in the protest, along with her husband, Clive, and their eighteen-year-old son, Braxton. The Prussers have long been active in the 'Right to Ride' organization that advocates for off-road vehicle access in rural areas. These sources tell us that the Prussers joined in the original ride with Drew Peacock and others, beginning late last month. She was injured in the accident on Friday, June third, and remains in critical condition at University Hospital in Provo. Family members tell us they have not heard from Mr. Prusser or their son since they left Provo to join in the protests. Sheriff Cortland Hackney tells us that Mrs. Prusser was in the driver seat of her vehicle when it was involved in the accident and that no others could have been in the vehicle with her. The Prussers had another vehicle with them when they joined the protest, a tan Ford pickup, but it has not been seen since and is assumed to be with Clive and Braxton Prusser in the camp with the rest of the Recapture protest group."*

"We will keep you updated as we obtain more information on this continually evolving story. Reporting live from Price, Utah, Liz Nuñez, Channel Nine News. *"*

Is anybody looking?

The clouds appeared to be breaking up over the mountains to the west, but I could see some larger thunderheads building behind them. Probably an hour or two until they get here. Enough time to look around. Even though the rain had stopped, I was soaked from the wet leaves and branches I brushed up against by the time I reached the top of the ridge. Staying low and keeping Speck close to my side, I slipped in under the limbs of the piñon tree at the crest. I scanned in every direction and could see traffic moving steadily on the highway in the distance to the east. Smoke came from several spots in the area of the pirates' camp. I could see that it consisted of a cluster of what looked like camp trailers, trucks, and tents in a fairly large meadow near the bridge over Dancing Water Creek. Lily and Craig's semi and trailer were on the near edge of the camp. I figured it was about five miles away. Seven or eight miles if you walked, taking into account the ridges and steep canyons you would have to circumvent. Too far to easily see a person unless you had a good telescope or binoculars and were looking directly at them. I felt fairly secure in my vantage spot under the tree and knew that our little rock shelter down under the second ledge was not visible at all from the camp or the road.

About mid-morning a pickup and two ATVs left the camp and came east on the main road. I spotted them shortly after they left the camp and followed their progress as they came toward the ridge I was on. They stayed on the main road as it wound through the dissected canyons and hills, up toward the edge of the uplift, finally crossing the rim about two miles south of my position. I lost them for a few minutes when they reached the rim, but I figured they stopped there to scope the lowlands to their east, between them and the main highway. After a short while they made their way east along the same road I took when fleeing the first pirate truck just three days before. It seemed like an eternity ago. I watched them closely and could tell that the roads were very muddy and slick, as the ATVs slid and threw up high muddy rooster-tails behind them as they made their way toward the more well-maintained county gravel roads. They turned north and passed below me, about a mile away, apparently heading toward the spot where my truck was wrecked. When they reached the truck they stopped for about ten minutes, then left, one ATV heading north, and one east, toward the highway. The pickup headed south, and another pickup headed back along the road toward their camp. They're leaving guards out overnight. And they're looking for us. The ATVs swept back and forth, covering an area about ten miles by five miles, each stopping occasionally, apparently to check something on foot for a few minutes, then continuing on. They kept this up for about two hours, and then came together with the pickup near the wash where I had shot the first two men who were chasing us. They spent a few minutes there, then the ATVs headed back toward the main camp. The pickup stayed, keeping watch. They were surely looking for us, or anyone. Waiting to ambush some unsuspecting fool like me. Maybe they decided that we escaped. With the rain obliterating any tracks, maybe they will stop looking. Maybe they will forget about Lily and me and go back to whatever they usually do. Planning the revolution, praying, saying the pledge of allegiance, declaring war on the federal government, who knows?

I thought about Chris. I wonder what she's doing. Is Chris pestering everybody she can think of to come out and look for me? Have they decided that I'm dead? Is anybody looking for Craig and Lily? Have they spotted their semi and my truck and concluded that we're goners? Will some special forces team come helicoptering in and rescue us? How would they know where we are? Shit. I really don't know what to do other than to stay hidden. Stay hidden as long as possible, and maybe we'll have a chance of being rescued. I hope Lily and I can get along and work together. We need to. We really need to. A clap of thunder told me that it was time to come down from the ridge. I looked at my watch. One thirty. I headed down toward our camp.

The path on the way back down was not as muddy as before, and the brush and grasses were not as drenched, but the moisture made the going quiet, as if the vegetation was hushed by the humidity. I could hear an airliner high overhead and wondered, as I often do, about the people in it, heading for some business meeting, vacation, adventure, family visit, or even perhaps a funeral or a birth or a wedding. My mind did not dwell on the occupants of a fleeting plane but returned with a snap to the reality of the moment. I was amazed, and had been since this whole nightmare began, at how my mind took control, and I did as it instructed, as new and terrifying things unfolded around me.

I had never shot and killed anything in my life, but when it became necessary, I did as I knew I must, as directed. Somehow the indecisiveness that characterizes nearly every moment of my life was swept aside, vanquished, banished as unnecessary and counterproductive, damaging even, when seconds count. I had noticed it on several occasions, first when driving, and later, nearly every time action or quick decision-making was needed. Somewhere deep inside of me there was a control center that was taking charge, determining what needed to be done, and seeing that it was undertaken with complete dedication and concentration.

I thought of the ancient figure painted on the wall of the rock shelter that had become my, our, home. Two little creatures hovered over his shoulder. Maybe they were looking after him, instructing him, telling what he needed to pay attention to, what he ought to do. In a way, I felt that there was something like that following me around, helping me out, watching, seeing, guarding. Speck, too, seemed to have a special kind of attentiveness. She knew that things had turned serious. Usually her consciousness was dominated by her obsessive devotion to her profession of chasing and returning anything thrown and doing it over and over until she dropped from exhaustion, or her thrower, usually me, hid her ball, or ignored her long enough that she resigned herself to waiting until the next opportunity. Speck seemed to be a different dog, one with a different profession. She stuck by my side, alert to everything around us, not a playful companion looking for a toy or asking for a treat; she had become a partner, a teammate, a comrade. I knew now how and why people and dogs had evolved together. When life became meaningful, when knowing what was going on around you was critical, we enhanced each other. At this moment I felt a bond with Speck like I had never felt with another creature, human or otherwise. Maybe she was the watcher I had been thinking about. Or maybe both of us were being watched and helped.

Nestled like spoons

As I came within shouting distance of the camp, I stopped and called out "CaCaw, CaCaw." I immediately felt foolish and a bit embarrassed. Speck looked at me and almost seemed to smirk, then she looked ahead toward camp. We both listened. Nothing. We walked a little farther. "CaCaw, CaCaw." Nothing. I looked at Speck and shook my head. We walked a little closer, nearly to the camp. I didn't want to just barge in and startle the girl. What was her name again? Lily, that's right. And she had a handgun. No, I didn't want to startle her. "CaCaw, CaCaw." Nothing. I looked at Speck. "Go ahead," I said. "Go see." I nodded toward the camp. Speck headed straight ahead. I waited a minute, and called again, "CaCaw, CaCaw." This time I heard something in the brush. Speck came charging back at me. What? Speck, what? I could see that she was excited, her tail wagging, eyes bright. She jumped up, hit me with her paws on my chest, turned, and ran back toward camp. "Follow me," is what I think I heard. Then I heard something else. "CaCaw, CaCaw. It's OK, come on in." It was Lily.

When I entered the shelter, I could see Lily sitting on the tarp next to the pack. She was petting and kissing Speck. "Your dog woke me up with a big kiss." she said. "It was," she shook her head and sniffed, "it was the best thing. It was the best. She is the best." She hugged Speck close. Speck wagged her tail and nosed Lily's hair. Speck knew. Lily was part of the team.

"I was so dead. I must have been in the deepest sleep I've ever had," she said. "Man, I'm glad it was you. A bear could have walked in and eaten me and I would never have known it. I was dreaming about my mom. And Craig. I dreamed he was calling me, like he was coming for me. Kind of weird. Not a fun dream. Jesus." She released Speck from her hug and looked up at me. "And now, here we are again. I guess I didn't realize how exhausted I was. Am. I could sleep all day."

"Maybe you should," I said. "It's about to rain, and I bet it goes all night. No reason not to rest. You need it, I'm sure. We both do."

I looked around. Lily had piled the juniper bark on one end of the tarp and had been using it as a pillow. Her clothes were damp, but they were no longer blood and dirt-stained. She appeared to be shivering.

"Let's get a little fire going," I said, picking up some twigs and piling them in the firepit. "We can warm up, have something to eat, get some sleep tonight, and head out in the morning if the weather clears. Head away from these, um, pirates. Get away from them."

Lily nodded. We looked at each other, and I felt a little like I had when I looked at Speck earlier. I realized what cooperation and teamwork were really all about. I understood altruism. I wasn't helping Lily and Speck, I was helping myself. We all needed each other. I could feel it. I could see it in their eyes. I felt strength. I felt courage. And I knew that it was not much, but it was all we had.

The rain blew in sheets, blasting through the brushy piñon and juniper trees that fronted the shelter and under the overhanging rock. We piled the packs against the back wall, heaped the juniper bark I had gathered earlier against the packs, and made a nest. Speck was already staking out a place against the rifle bag when Lily and I sat down, backs against the packs. We piled juniper bark around us, covered ourselves loosely with the one windbreaker, and pulled the plastic tarp over us all. It took us a while to get everything right—pulling the tarp this way or that to stop leaks, wiggling ourselves into more comfortable positions, and closing drafts. Finally, as the gray light of the stormy afternoon faded into the dull black of the night, we settled in, all three of us succumbing to the exhaustion that we had fought, letting ourselves relax to the sounds of the storm, knowing that we would be safe from the outsiders, since the storm would keep them pinned down as well. They are probably playing cards and drinking coffee and smoking big cigars in a camper, or maybe the semi-trailer, I thought. Fuckers. I turned on my side and felt Lily snuggle back against me. I moved into her and we lay nestled like spoons. I reached my arm over her and felt Speck curled up in the curve of Lily's belly. This is the way Chris and I sleep most every night, I thought. Lily is longer and more angular than Chris, but the way we nested against each other felt right, and I did not feel any qualms about being this close with a woman I hardly knew. I realized that I wasn't thinking of her as a woman. Well, clearly she is a woman, but I guess I was just seeing her mostly as another creature, a person, an ally, someone who, like Speck, was in this predicament with me, and we were going to help each other find a way out of it. I felt a great comfort having someone to hold, to touch, to share warmth with, to support each other.

I thought of a photograph I had seen somewhere of two baby chimpanzees in a cage, hugging each other in terror of what kept them captive and what might await them. The vision of that photo had haunted me for years, and now I felt a great kinship with those chimps. I hugged Lily and Speck tighter, and I was comforted, and I felt as though I might be giving them some security, the knowledge that someone was offering to help them, to protect them. And I also felt strength, the strength of being needed, and also of being cared for, being part of something. This is my family now, I thought. For now. And now seems like it is everything. Like this now is everything I have ever experienced, or ever known. Or ever will. Now.

I remember people telling me how the principles of Zen taught them to live in the moment. To be present. To be conscious. I realized at this moment that those kinds of thoughts are luxuries, the dalliances afforded to those whose actions are not critical, whose lives are meaningless, who have to play tricks on themselves to get themselves to concentrate on just being. I had none of those difficulties now, and I knew that Lily and Speck did not either. We are here, now, and we have to throw everything we have into it, or there might not be a tomorrow. I knew I should sleep, and the warmth of Lily's body, the soft fur of Speck's belly around my hand, the rushing sound of the wind relaxed me and took me to a deep, restful, and comforting sleep, and dreams of good things, things not at all related to the wretched present.

Breaking News from Channel Nine News
Liz Nuñez reporting

"In light of recent revelations by Channel Nine News *that the violent car accident that left one woman in a coma may be related to Lily and Craig Clark, the missing Kentucky truck drivers, the wife and colleagues of another missing person, Salt Lake City geologist Stan Watson, have raised questions regarding the circumstances of his disappearance. Chris Haywood, his wife, told us he was driving to Moab last Saturday (June 4), and after buying a gyro sandwich at the Greek Stop and gas at Bassett's Pit Stop in Wellington, he called a friend in Moab and said he'd be there in a couple of hours. He has not been heard from since. His vehicle, a silver Toyota 4Runner, has not been seen, and his cell phone has disappeared from the service grid. Chris Haywood fears her husband may have somehow become entangled in the protest. The truck drivers have been missing since the evening before Stan Watson was last heard from, the same evening the car accident involving LaNae Prusser took place. Sheriff Cortland Hackney says his office has heard nothing about Mr. Watson's whereabouts, and that with so little to go on, has no reason to begin an investigation. The sheriff speculated in a phone conversation with me this afternoon that Mr. Watson may have joined in the protest, or may have simply 'flown the coop' so to speak."*

"The families and associates of the missing people think the sheriff is shirking his duty and worry that the lives of their loved ones may be in danger."

"Channel Nine will continue to follow this story and will report as new developments are available. Liz Nuñez, Channel Nine News, *reporting from Price, in Carbon County, Utah."*

EVEN THE BIRDS WERE QUIET

My eyes popped open as I bolted to full consciousness. Speck and Lily tensed too, as though we had all been simultaneously awakened by something—a noise, a gust of wind, a movement. I listened. Nothing. Maybe I had just jerked myself awake fleeing a startling dream and had broken the others' sleep. I lay quietly. I could tell that Lily and Speck were listening too, all of us having returned to consciousness, to the reality of our situation. We listened. The sounds of the storm had abated. The wind wasn't whistling and rushing through the branches. It had stopped raining, and the only sound was an occasional droplet released from a leaf or branch where it had been stranded for a time, when the grip of its surface tension finally loosed, and allowed gravity to take it down. Even the birds were quiet. Perhaps they were listening, too. Just waiting, listening to see what the coming day would bring. I could see the stars now, the clouds having passed, and the dark sky behind them was lightening with the slightest hint of blue replacing the stark black. I took a deep breath and was readying myself to sit up and push back the tarp when we all heard it. A sharp report, dulled and diffused by the thick, humid atmosphere through which it traveled. And then two more. Then a dozen or so, in rapid succession. We all tensed and listened. Nothing. Silence. Eventually Lily turned slightly toward me.

"Gunshots?" she said.

"Think so," I said.

We sat quietly for a few minutes. Speck pulled herself up to a sitting position and poked her head around, trying to find an opening in the tarp. I reached over and pulled back the edge of the tarp so she could free her head. A stream of icy water dribbled down my neck. I sat upright to clear myself of the drip. I pulled the tarp away from Speck and Lily.

"There you go, Speck," I said. She rose, stretched, and stepped away from the nest. "I guess we might as well get moving. I wonder what's going on, over at—over there," nodding toward the pirate camp. "That's where the shots or whatever they were came from, I think." Lily sat up and looked toward the trees, in the general direction of the camp. She nodded. Speck shook and headed toward the edge of the rock shelter. She glanced back at us, then turned and ducked into the brush.

I sat the rest of the way up, rose, and slid out from under the tarp and the windbreaker. Lily was sitting quietly with her arms crossed. I reached for the stove, lit it, and placed the pan over the flame.

"Guess we'll have some tea," I said, reaching for the bag that held our meager supply of food. Lily looked at me and nodded.

"Then let's get the fuck out of here," she said, pulling the tarp up around her shoulders.

"as far from here as we can get."

Could the shots mean something is going on at the Recapture camp? Could the government be making a move to bring them down? There would be more shooting, probably. Or, maybe, maybe as my friend Brigham, who had worked for a defense contractor, told me, the military has weapons you won't believe, not big bombs and planes, but tiny little things. Like drones the size of a small bird or even a bumblebee that they drop from planes or release from a base ship the size of a suitcase disguised as a rock or a bag of trash that has solar panels and communicates with all the tiny soldiers and charges them wirelessly. And each tiny drone is programmed to do one thing, like find a person. Some are even controlled by soldiers sitting in air-conditioned command centers in places like Las Vegas and Punxsutawney, Pennsylvania. The tiny drones have cameras and can be used to watch whatever's going on, like a fly on the wall. Or they're explosive and can fly up a person's nose or in his ear and blow up, or spray a gas in someone's face or inject them with something. They might put a tiny chip on someone that looks like a burr or a button or a piece of fuzz that can be used to trace wherever that person goes. I'm sure they have all these things and more we can't even imagine. At least the government probably knows everything about the pirate camp. And they're having a grand time testing their deadly toys. I hope they're using them right now. I hope the Recapture camp is no more.

You never know.

When the water was hot I turned the gas off and added a yerba mate tea bag. We shared the tea, sipping it directly from the pot, which was our only container. The air was cool and humid, and the only sound came from Speck as she chewed and gnawed on the deer leg that had gotten rehydrated a bit by the rain, apparently making it more delectable.

"You always do that?" Lily asked. She nodded toward my foot. "Craig was like that. Always wiggling or twitching something."

I looked down and could see that I was bouncing my right foot against the base of a serviceberry bush that grew at the outside edge of the rock shelter. I nodded.

"I've always done it. My dad does, too. My mom calls us "fidgeters." Nervous energy, I guess."

"You keep looking over that way," Lily said, nodding toward the southwest, in the general direction of the outlaw camp. "What do you think's going on?"

"No idea," I said. "Absolutely no idea. Hope they're all shooting each other. Or the army is there teaching them a lesson." I reached down to pet Speck, and we all jerked a little in reaction to the sound of another volley of shots breaking the silence. We listened intently. I cocked my head to the side, the way Speck often did.

"Hear that?" Lily asked. "Like engines or something. Trucks maybe."

I nodded, then shook my head.

"Let's get ready to leave," I said. "I'll run up to the top and see if I can see anything, but I think you're right. We'd better get away from here. Far away."

At the top, I scanned toward the camp and saw nothing unusual, but I could still hear the sound of a motor humming. When I saw an ATV heading east on the main road, I followed its movement, then saw it turn off the road and head north along Milky Creek. I followed its path along the small road that paralleled Milky Creek until I saw it. Dammit. Another camp. A smaller one, only about a half dozen pickups and a few more ATVs, but it was just below us. Less than a mile away. Too close. Way too close. And high above one of the pickups, on a long pole flew the black and red triangular flag I had taken down from the ATV at the camp by my wrecked truck. Phil's ATV. The Viking. Maybe there's been a disagreement among the pirates and some split off. Or maybe they're just setting up a satellite camp. Now the Viking was closer to us than ever. We have to get out of here.

When I reached camp, Lily was sipping tea and watching Speck gnaw on what was left of the deer leg. She had packed up most of our camp gear and looked up with inquiring eyes. I told her what I had seen. She nodded resolutely, took one last sip of tea from the aluminum pan, turned it over to shake out the last drops, and slid it into the pack." Let's get out of here."

"Take a good big drink and we'll fill the water bottles," I said. "Might be a while before we're near water again."

I'M A RUNNER

Iscattered the firepit stones, tossed the juniper bark bedding over the edge, and kicked dirt over the ashes. We shouldered our packs, and as we exited the shelter, I made a rough broom from a branch and brushed out our footprints. I took one last look at the ghost-like figure painted on the wall of the shelter, the animal beside it, and the two figures hovering over its shoulders. Looking at it had a calming effect on me, as viewing rock art often did. I looked at Lily, who had also paused by the painted figures. Our eyes met, and I felt reassured, a surge of strength to persevere, to find our way together, to get back to the world we knew, a world that was safe, a world we understood.

We made our way along the ledge we had camped on, the second ledge from the top of the long, meandering rocky rise that divided the sage flats to the east from the rocky ridges and canyons, swales, and occasional gentle valley to the west. We were paralleling the course of Milky Creek, only a mile or so west of us, and would, after about ten miles, leave the Milky Creek drainage behind and enter a more dissected area with few streams, and only occasional springs or improved cattle troughs. I wasn't sure how far the road along Milky Creek was passable, but I kept looking down, hoping I wouldn't see a vehicle heading up the valley.

After a mile or so our ledge became blocked with heavy rockfall and steep slopes, and we moved up to the first ledge, just below the rim. I was moving at a pretty fast pace, and it was only after slowing to pick our way up through the rocky slope as we neared the top that I realized that Lily had stuck with me and had not struggled or gotten out of breath. At the top of the slope, as we started along the upper ledge, breathing heavily, I stopped.

"Whew. Steep," I said, reaching up to mop sweat from my forehead. "We've been moving right along. You must hike a lot."

"I'm a runner," she said. "I, well, Craig and I run a lot. Races too, even marathons. We've been training to run one back home next month. Craig's fast. I'm slow but steady." She stopped and shook her head. "Jesus," she said, and shook her head again. "How fucked up everything got, in no time at all. I can't believe Craig's dead. He's dead. I can't fucking believe it."

"Here, sit down," I said, indicating an appropriate stone behind her. "Let's take a little break."

We sat quietly for a few moments. The sky was streaked with high, ribbony clouds that were rapidly turning from pink to white in the intensifying sunlight. I looked at Lily and wondered how she could even manage to keep going after all she had been through. She must have been a lot tougher than I was. I felt like I was barely able to maintain. She was facing the same thing, but a hundred times worse. She saw her husband die. She was tied to a wrecked truck while armed men fought over her. Jesus. We had been thrown together by random events, not at all related, and here we were, dependent on each other, total strangers, for our lives.

Looking at her in the golden morning light, I saw a warrior, a fighter, a colleague, a comrade, not a liability or someone to pity. Speck sat between us. When she saw me look down at her, she made eye contact, then stood. She faced to the north and stood, her tail slowly wagging.

"Looks like Speck is raring to go," Lily said. "I'm good. Ready to keep moving?"

I nodded, and lifted the rifle bag to my shoulder. "Every step's a little closer to getting out of here. Let's get in a few more miles before it gets too hot."

We headed north along the ledge, which gradually widened into a 100-yard-wide gently sloping forested avenue between the cliff face on our right and the steep drop-off to the next ledge on our left. We could see the dissected terrain to the west, with the winding canyon carved by Milky Creek marking the lowest spot, a mile or two away. The forested mesas in the distance that defined the far horizon were misty mottled grays and purple. I knew that there were no developed roads in sight, but the many folds and creases of the terrain, and the piñon and juniper trees that coated the hills and ridges were sometimes sparse, sometimes as dense as moss on a rock, and could provide cover for any number of possible persons and all-terrain vehicles, motorcycles, or horses.

We hiked through the morning over the relatively level terrain. I figured we had covered four or five miles from our sheltered camp, when the ledge we were on started to pinch out. I could see that travel on the ledge would be difficult or impossible just a short distance ahead. The late morning sun shone brightly, rapidly warming the air and illuminating the valley, from the mesas in the distance to the rounded crest above us.

"Let's try to find a way down to the next ledge," I said to Lily. "This one is about to peter out."

We started picking our way along the sandstone outcrop above the drop-off to the next ledge below, and after a few moments, I saw Speck disappear down a cleft in the rock. We followed her, saw that she had found a well-used game trail leading down a steep but walkable slope through a break in the sandstone. Looking over from the top, I could see her down on the next ledge looking up at us, wagging her tail.

The Carbon County Drumbeat
Recapture update—Latest news from The Swell

** Recapture group establishes second camp*

In addition to the original compound on Dancing Water Creek, the group has established a second, smaller camp on the Milky Creek road, according to an unconfirmed report from sources in the sheriff's office. Recapture spokesperson Travis Dmitrich had no comment.

BE SAFE

"Crap," I said, walking to the edge of the drop-off alongside the trail. Two parallel grooves cut through the sandy residual soils where Speck was standing. "ATV tracks."

"Speck, come!" I called, just loudly enough for her to hear. I turned and faced Lily. I shook my head, quickly resigning myself to a new reality. "They're fresh. Made today some time since the rain. We need to get out of sight."

Lily turned and headed back up the narrow path. Speck raced to join us, and we hurried, staying low, back up onto the ledge we had just left, then headed up a shallow drainage to the cover of a clump of junipers. We ducked down behind a rocky outcrop, breathing hard. I tried to quiet my breathing so I could listen. Lily cupped her hand over her ear and faced the drop-off to the ledge below. Speck peered back in the direction from which we had just come, alert, head cocked slightly to the side.

"Hear that?" Lily said.

I nodded. I crouched forward and crab-walked up to the edge of the drop-off. At the far side of the ledge below us I could see two ATVs moving slowly toward the south. The lead rider had long blond hair, was dressed in military-type clothing, and had a rifle slung over his shoulder. A triangular black and red flag whipped back and forth in the breeze from a long flexible pole on the vehicle. The Viking. Shit. I motioned for Lily to stay down and watched as they made their way along the ledge and out of sight behind the sloping cliff edge. I scurried along the slope to another spot where I could see and watched them turn down a wash and apparently head down toward Milky Creek. I watched for about half an hour and saw no more of the ATVs or their riders, so I headed back to join Lily and Speck.

"Two ATVs and riders. One of them is the Viking. I'm pretty sure." I said. "They're armed. I think they are headed south along Milky Creek. Maybe going back toward the new camp, where I saw them this morning."

"Damn," Lily said. She shook her head. "He's after us. Jesus."

"Think it's OK to let Speck loose?" she asked.

"Let's keep her close, just in case," I said. "I think we should hang tight for a little while and watch and listen, in case there are more of them, or if they come back."

We sat quietly and could hear the light, gusting breeze vibrating the needles of the junipers around us. A pinyon jay's raspy call signaled some small conflict along the cliff rising above us. I could hear my heart beating loud in my ears, but no sounds of danger, no sounds of humans or their things. I turned my shoulders to remove the rifle case from my back and slowly slipped the canvas pack off and eased it to the ground. I looked over at Lily and saw her tense. She opened her mouth slightly and raised her eyebrows. I heard it too. A low rumbling. A motor? Shit. We sat quietly and it seemed to get imperceptibly louder. ATVs getting closer? I tried to think of what to do. Should I go to the edge of the cliff and look to see what was going on? I started to lean forward so I could rise and head for the edge when I felt Lily's hand on my shoulder. I looked back at her. As our eyes met, she glanced upward, then back at me. I looked up. The contrails of an approaching airliner made a bright pinkish stripe across the sky in the light of the still-rising sun. A plane. No ATVs. No pirates hunting us. For now. But they were still out there. Somewhere.

"I think I should go to a place with a better view," I said. "See what's going on, if I can." Lily nodded.

"Go ahead. I'll keep Speck," she said. "Be safe." She nodded her head. "Be safe."

I crouched low and, carrying the rifle and binoculars, headed down the gully toward the drop-off. Just a short way to the north were the first boulders of the rockfall that blocked our path on the ledge, forcing us down to the lower ledge to continue traveling north. I stayed low, shielding myself from any view from below, and headed for the cover of the boulders. Once there, I found a large rock that would conceal me yet provided several points from which I could look over the edge with minimal exposure. I leaned the rifle against a branch, took the lens caps from the binoculars, and started scanning the terrain below.

Two sets of ATV tracks, one pair going north, just below us, and one heading south; the ones made by the ATVs I saw earlier were visible on the ledge below. The tracks were at times on top of each other, at times partially overlapping, and at times completely separate. From my vantage point I could not tell if they were going in the same or opposite directions. I would need to go down and inspect the tracks before I could tell if they were made by the two ATVs I had seen or if there were more, some still down there. I continued scanning the ground below. I saw no movement or sign of any human activity other than the tracks. Scanning the far edge of the ledge, I caught a glimpse of some sort of disturbance on the ground. I moved to another vantage spot and trained the binoculars on the spot. It looked like they had stopped and maybe turned around there. I decided the tracks had likely been made by the two ATVs and that they had turned around, and there were not likely any others on the ledge below us. I hoped.

I sat and watched for about an hour and saw and heard nothing more. The sun heated the air and brightened the landscape before me, adding a crispness to my view. Nothing alarming. I decided to check back in with Lily.

I made my way back, and found Lily leaning back against the trunk of a juniper, Speck at her side. Speck rose as I approached, then ran to me, tail wagging.

"Anything?" Lily asked.

I shook my head. "Two sets of ATV tracks, looks like. Can't say for sure without going down, but it looks like just the two vehicles. They still could be close by, can't tell."

"What should we do?" Lily asked. "Go back to the other camp?"

"I don't think so," I said. "I think we should wait here and keep watching. They can't get up here with ATVs, so maybe we should just stay hidden up here and keep looking, to see if we can figure out who's out there." I shrugged.

Lily nodded. "Is there a better place to wait? Or should we just stay here?"

"Let's go down to where I was. It's out of sight, and we have a good view of a big area below us. Let's just go down there and keep an eye out. See if we can tell what kind of a mess we're in this time."

Lily nodded. "K," she said.

"There's only one way up from the ledge below, and from there, we can watch it, make sure nobody comes to visit," I said, picking up my rifle case.

Lily stood, shouldered her pack, and followed me.

∗ ∗ ∗

Breaking News from Channel Nine News
Liz Nuñez reporting

"Channel Nine reporter Liz Nuñez reports that some people are questioning the official versions of what is really going on with the Recapture protests down in Carbon County. Let's go to her now. Liz?"

"Yes, Dick and Allyson, while the spokespeople for the protesters continue to claim that all is well in the so-called occupied zone and that several missing persons, including a truck-driving couple from Kentucky have voluntarily surrendered their cargo to support the protest, family and friends,—including Pendleton Shuffler, business partner of Craig Clark— remain adamant that their loved ones would have never joined in."

"I know Craig and Lily, and they are not the kind to take part in anything like this, and especially not to risk losing their truck, trailer, and their entire business. They would never do such a thing. I think they've been hijacked, that's what I think. Craig and Lily aren't even Republicans."

"Carbon County Sheriff Cortland Hackney maintains that he has no reason to mistrust the protesters, but County Commissioner Elmo Kuykendall is not so sure."

"I want to give the protesters the benefit of the doubt. Heck, I've known Drew Peacock since we were kids, and I trust him, but we need to assure that people are safe traveling in the area, and those missing truckers raise some concerns."

"What are you doing to get clarification? Can you communicate directly with Mr. Peacock?"

"Well, I've tried, and I've been talking with his spokesperson, Travis Dmitrich. From what he tells me, the truckers are fine and are at the camp supporting the protest. I'd just like to confirm that. You know, see a picture, or get a statement from them or something. Their family and business partners are anxious, and they are calling my office and the sheriff's office too, wanting answers. Not to mention their insurance company. They claim they're out half a million dollars, and they're threatening to hold the county responsible."

"Can they do that?"

"Well, I don't know, government immunity and all, but missing people? Unaccounted property? We're concerned about that. And that geologist— his people are hounding us. People want some answers, and frankly, I do too. I'm doing all I can to get to the bottom of this, I really am."

* * *

"As you can see, there's more to this story than the official version we are hearing from the protesters and the sheriff. Commissioner Kuykendall is seeking answers, and so are we. We will keep you posted as we learn more."

"Liz Nuñez, Channel Nine News, *reporting from Price, in Carbon County, Utah."*

Sego lilies

We made our way down to the boulder field and settled in behind the large monolith that provided cover and a good view of the terrain below and to the west of us. I kept Speck on a leash because I was worried that she might be seen. Lily and I trained our eyes on the landscape before us, both the rock-strewn scrub-forested, wide, sloping ledge below us, the Milky Creek Canyon beyond it, and the gnarled, twisted, dissected terrain beyond the canyon that stretched to the jagged horizon. We took turns with the binoculars, and we memorized the landmarks, the folds, the flats, the sculpted sandstone firmament upon which all else was scattered. The forests and the rippled badlands both near and far held our interest, as they provided the mazes and camouflage that could hide potential adversaries, bringers of hatred and death. We looked with intensity and purpose, and I thought of soldiers on watch, alert to the details of the tableau before them so any change would be immediately registered and attended to.

We saw the tracks left by the trail machines below us, but no other sign of people. After a while I worked my way farther up in the rocks to the north, where I could see a larger expanse of the ledge below us. I could see that the tracks made a big loop just a few hundred yards to the north of us, halted by a continuation of the massive rockfall that blocked off our own ledge. The ATVs had apparently come from the south and turned around at the rocky obstruction before heading back toward the south.

I made my way back to our watching spot and found Lily still scanning the vista below and to our west. I looked up and down the ledge, and up to the cliffs above us. Someone could conceivably come up behind us. Unlikely, but you never know.

"Looks like they came from the south—down that way," I gestured, "turned around where rocks block it off, and headed back down-canyon. At least they're not around anymore. I don't think."

Lily nodded. "I've been looking across the canyon to see if I could spot any trail or road or anything. I can't see any place where you could ride one of those things. You'd have a hard time even walking over there."

"I agree. It looks like you'd have to walk a mile up and down and around just to go a few hundred yards. If we have to run from those guys—if we thought they were about to find us—maybe we ought to head over there. Kind of a convoluted rat maze of hidey-holes. I'd never want to chase someone into a place like that. Never."

"I think Speck's getting hungry," Lily said. "And thirsty. We're kind of running low on water."

"We're good on water," I said, handing her a full gallon jug. "There's a pothole in the rock over there that caught a lot of rainwater. It's clean and clear and there's plenty."

I dug around in the pack and fished out a ziplock bag of dog food. "There's not a lot here, but if we ration it, we'll have enough for a few more days." I scooped out a handful and put it in my hat. "Here you go, girl. We'll let you loose when it gets dark. Maybe you can find some mice or something." I put the hat down and Speck dived into the food, sucking it in like a vacuum cleaner.

"She's actually a pretty good hunter," I said. I've seen her go through a field and catch and eat mice just like a fox or coyote. She'll fare better than we will once her kibble is gone."

"Well, we're about to find out," Lily said. "What do we have, two packages of ramen left? Not a lot."

"Three," I said, digging through the pack. "Maybe it's time for us to start thinking about supplementing our ramen."

"You mean with mice?" Lily asked, scrunching up her nose.

"Well, maybe," I said. "Maybe not right away with mice, but, well, look here, see these?" I reached into my pocket and pulled out a couple of brown bulbs. "These are sego lily bulbs. They're all over, and they're pretty good to eat." I placed one in Lily's hand. "See, you peel back the stringy outside, and inside is a crispy morsel. Tastes kind of like a potato. They're better cooked. We could pick some and see how it works for our dinner tonight, if you're up for it.

"Shit, yeah," Lily said. "Lilies. I love lilies, for obvious reasons. Are they the little white ones I've been seeing?"

"Uh huh. They're all over these slopes. They're the state flower. Indians ate them. I think it's illegal to collect them now, but, well, we're not likely to get a ticket."

"Can we find a place to get some where we'll be out of sight?"

"Up where I got these," I said. "You have to dig them out. Wanna give it a try?"

We got a couple of sticks and sharpened them for digging. There were dozens and dozens of blooming white sego lilies on the rocky slope above us, hidden from below by a thick stand of junipers.

"Just dig down under the flower. The bulb's about six or eight inches down," I said. I knelt over a flower and plunged my stick into the soil. After about a minute I lifted the bulb, cool and moist, from the earth.

We foraged for about a half hour, taking turns so we could keep watch. The sun was starting to drop to the horizon as we returned back to our camp behind the boulder. We kept up our vigilance, and as dusk deepened, prepared our dinner. We peeled the bulbs, put them in the pan, boiled them with a little salt until they were tender, and after a while, shared our first foraged meal.

"You know, these are really good. Kind of sweet. A little unusual, but not awful, for sure, and, well, I could eat them, if it was all we had. Better than starving. A lot better." Lily said, smiling as she chewed. "Lilies. I'm eating lilies. Sweet."

"I agree," I said. I looked at her, sitting on the ground, eating a foraged meal of sego lily bulbs, full of grit and fiber, and not complaining, even complimenting the food. "And, well, you're amazing," I said. "You're really amazing."

Lily looked up at me, pushed a piece of fiber from one of the bulbs to the end of her tongue, blew it off, and took another bite. "Whatever," she said. "Whatever."

Local Protest Gets Nationwide Attention

by Frank Saccomano
The Carbon County Drumbeat

When local rancher and former county councilman Drew Peacock organized an ATV ride down the Dancing Water Creek road to protest the newly designated San Rafael Swell Wilderness Area, most people thought it would be an opportunity for some venting and maybe a shouting match. Peacock is known for such demonstrations, as he and a growing group of supporters have stood up against the federal government and its land management policies. What most did not foresee was the explosion of interest from the news media, and the resulting outpouring of support from like-minded individuals and groups nationwide. The only times this area has seen this kind of attention in recent years have been the Price River flood of 1992 and last years' East Carbon Rodeo Days demolition derby scandal. (Just kidding about the last one!)

Drew Peacock has found himself in the center of a back alley brawl between big government and locals who've had enough. Usually happy to provide a quote or an on-camera interview, Peacock has remained at the Recapture Brigade compound on Dancing Water Creek (by the old suspension bridge) and has designated Travis Dmitrich, former drama teacher at Dorman Hills High School, as spokesperson. All sources indicate that the group at the camp has grown from the original half-dozen or so to over 100, and despite the efforts of law enforcement to keep the area closed, supporters keep finding their way to the compound. Observers close to the site report that at least two semis full of supplies have reached the camp in recent days. Dmitrich's claim that the occupiers are prepared to stay all summer seems at least possible now that a significant supply chain seems to have been established.

Federal, state, and county officials are working together to try to keep the number of protesters from growing, and also to keep members of the general public from wandering into the disputed area. A perimeter has been set up, and officials are warning people to avoid The Swell in general. Travel is prohibited in the area bounded by Highway 191 on the east, I-70 on the south, the Broken Hills road on the west, and the Van Deusen Trail on the north. Travelers are advised to avoid any of these roads after dark.

A small group of wilderness supporters has set up a camp at the Buckhead Wash campground and has been handing out fliers supporting the wilderness designation, along with peanut butter and jelly sandwiches and lemonade, to anyone passing through. "This land belongs to all of us," said spokesperson Margene Hagstrom. "Some of it needs to be protected, so our kids and grandkids can have a place to go and not see roads, oil wells, mines, and general destruction."

Dmitrich insists that it is a constitutional issue, with ramifications for all citizens. "This is about a lot more than just an ATV trail," he said. "It's about the Second Amendment, the right to bear arms, the right to free speech, and the right to life, liberty, and the pursuit of happiness. Without those things, we are nothing more than slaves."

Bureau of Land Management spokesperson Juanita Smith-Perkins asks the public to stay away from the area while the BLM works with local and state officials to achieve a peaceful end to the protest. "We would like to give the protesters an opportunity to air their grievances while at the same time maintaining public order and enforcing the laws of the land. We are asking the protesters to avoid brandishing arms. The last thing we want is bloodshed."

Big freakin' deer

We kept watch well after the sun had gone down and the moonless night darkened the entire region, with only the intense brightness of the stars and planets to illuminate the earth. We saw no lights or other signs of human activity, and readied our camp for sleeping. Lily nestled back against the packs, holding Speck close.

"How about this," she said. "I'll go down to that next level in the morning and check things out. You can stay here and cover me. If you see anything, well, let me know somehow. Or start shooting. I'll see where the tracks go, and whatever else I can find out."

I thought for a minute. "I was thinking we would both go down together, you know, just kind of head out, like we've been doing. I worry about us getting split up."

"Yeah, but you can see so much from up here. You might see something we couldn't see from down there. I don't know, it's just a thought."

"It's not a bad idea. Or I could go down. Let's think it over, make up our minds in the morning."

"K," Lily said, and pulled the tarp up to her neck, turned to face and curl around Speck. "Night."

We slept fairly well, although I kept dreaming and half dreaming that awful raiders were riding ATVs around our camp shooting at us with shotguns and flame throwers, and Lily and I were trying to shoot at them, but we couldn't find our ammunition. We awoke with the first hint of dawn and had tea.

"I dreamed about Craig again last night," Lily said. "Like he was coming for me, to take me with him. It was awful. Awful."

I sat for a minute and thought about how she must feel, losing her husband and now fearing him.

"You know," I said. "Some tribal people believe that sometimes people who die are lonely and try to get their loved ones to join them. So they leave the area. Leave them behind."

Lily closed her eyes and nodded. "That's kind of what it seems like," she said. "It's weird."

"I, uh, I had a strange thing happen when I was a kid," I said. "My grandfather lived with us, in the back bedroom, and when I was about six he died, and I started having nightmares about him coming down the hall for me at night. I'd wake up screaming. It seemed so real."

"Maybe he was there. Maybe Craig's here," Lily said. "Seems pretty real to me. At least it did when I was asleep."

"It stopped though," I said. "My mother would come and stay with me when I had the nightmares, and she reminded me of how much Grandpap loved me and told me I should be happy to see him, that he would never hurt me, and I knew it was true. She told me how much she missed him, and she stayed and slept with me after the nightmare and told me she wanted to dream about Grandpap because she missed him so much."

"Did you stop dreaming about him?" Lily asked.

"Eventually, but it all changed, you know, what my Mom said was true, I loved Grandpap and he loved me, and I started dreaming that he was coming to visit me, not hurt me. It worked."

"Well, maybe Craig is coming to visit. Maybe I should try to dream about him, and, well, just spend some time with him." Lily looked at me and shook her head. "Christ, what a mess, what a mess."

I wiped the pan clean and stashed it in the pack. The cloudless sky was growing light, and magpies and jays were flying about excitedly, readying themselves for a spectacular day.

"I really do want to go down and check things out," Lily said. "Maybe I could take Speck. We could look out for each other down there, and you can watch from up here."

"We'd better wait until it's light out. Light enough to see, at least," I said. "What do you think, Speck. Wanna go exploring with Lily?"

Speck stood, jumped around, and wagged her tail.

"I guess that's settled," I said.

"What do you think I should look for?" Lily asked. "I mean, try to figure out where the ATVs came from and where they went. Anything else?"

"Maybe you can follow their trail around and see if they stopped anywhere. See if they were hunting, maybe, or who knows. Maybe they stopped and left some trash. Maybe a cooler full of beer fell off their ATV."

"Now you're thinking!" Lily said, smiling. "Or maybe they crashed their bikes and croaked and all we need to do is ride away. That would be good."

We both laughed a little at our silliness. Speck barked at me as if to remind me that she had been promised a walk.

"Here, take some water, and put the pistol on your belt. Make sure it's ready." I said. "And stay low. You never know."

"Come on, Speck," Lily said. "See you later, um, Stan. I almost forgot your name. I never knew a Stan before. See you, Stan." She turned, clucked her cheeks to Speck, and walked toward the path down to the lower ledge. Speck ran after her a few strides, stopped, looked back at me, wagged her tail, and ran after Lily.

I got the binoculars and my rifle and found a good spot to watch as Lily and Speck searched below. When they reached the ledge, Lily went north, following the set of tracks. I moved to keep her in sight and kept scanning the distant slopes and forests for any sign of others. She traced the tracks as they went north, then followed them as they turned toward the west. She took quite a bit of time looking around at the north end of the tracks, then turned and followed the tracks where they turned south. She was in a much more exposed position as she headed south, being closer to the edge of the drop-off. Speck scampered ahead of her, looping around and checking back with her every few minutes. From my vantage point they seemed to be taking forever, but I had to remind myself that they were covering quite a bit of ground, and the territory was rugged and their path winding, with lots of ups and downs. The afternoon sun was hot, and I was starting to get thirsty, so I turned and got the water jug. I took a long swig, set the jug down, and scanned the ledge below for Lily and Speck.

Where are they? I couldn't see them at first. They were near the edge of the drop-off, and Lily seemed to be moving very slowly, looking over the edge. Speck was right by her side, heeling. What's going on, I wondered. Then Lily dived to the ground. Shit! I scanned the area in front of her and reached for my rifle. What is it? What is it? Lily crawled toward a large bush and seemed to use it for cover. She slowly rose to her knees, cautiously peered over the bush, then rose and walked to the edge and looked over. She turned to face me and kind of shrugged and waved. I took that as a sign that everything was OK. My heart was beating so fast I could barely keep the binoculars still.

They continued working along the edge of the drop-off to the south until they passed around a bend in the canyon and I could no longer see them. I thought about running along the ledge I was on to get a better view but decided that it would take me too long to reach a place where I could possibly spot them, so I sat tight and waited.

About a half hour later they appeared again, walking north toward our camp. The sun was dropping and turned the bottoms of a few wispy clouds lingering to the west a bright pinkish purple that contrasted with the deep blue of the sky. That would make a great photograph, I thought.

Speck entered camp first and ran to me with a wild greeting as if we had not seen each other for weeks. Lily followed a few minutes later. She walked into camp, took a big drink from her water bottle, smiled at me, and flopped down.

"Wow," she said. "This country is incredible."

"Yeah, it is," I said. "But what about the ATV people? The Viking? And what happened when you hit the dirt and were crawling around? Scared the crap out of me."

"Oh, that," she said. "Deer. I saw some deer down by the creek. Didn't want to spook them. Three does with fawns. And they were huge. I mean huge!"

"Well that's a relief," I said. "I was worried that you'd seen someone."

"Nope, just deer," she said. "Big freakin' deer."

Mule deer," I said. "You're probably used to seeing white tails. They're teeny compared to mule deer."

"Anyway, the ATVs came from the south and went back to the south. They got up on the ledge below us because they couldn't go any farther up the creek. Big boulder fields on both sides and clogging up the streambed, too. They jumped up on that ledge below us and turned around when they couldn't get past the boulders. I think they came from that new pirate camp and found out they were blocked off."

"That's good," I said. "Really good. It means we can head north and not be as worried about somebody coming up behind us. And we can safely go down to the creek. Well, safely-er, I guess."

"Yeah, and we can get something to eat to go with our lily roots. Venison. Mmmmmm."

"Well, we're having roots again tonight," I said. "And ramen. A real feast."

"Good, I'm hungry," Lily said. "Oh yeah, Speck got something down in that field—a mouse or something. She kind of cocked her head, jumped in the air and pounced down on something. She got it in her mouth and gulped it down." She reached down and petted Speck on the head and scratched her ears. "Was that a yummy mouse, Speck? Mmmmmm."

"Did you see anything else?" I asked. "Or did they just ride around?"

"No, they stopped and took a little hike up on the north end. They walked up to the top of the rock pile that blocked them. Looked around to see if they could find a way through, I guess. Didn't leave any trash or anything, that I saw anyway. Oh yeah, I did see a cigarette butt. Some kind of a filter, like a Marlboro, maybe. It was empty, like he'd field-stripped it—you know—put it out and shook all the tobacco out to keep the butt to throw away later. Maybe it fell out of his pocket."

"I wonder if they are looking for us. Or if they are just patrolling, checking different places out, you know, gathering intelligence about the territory," I said.

"Or just riding around looking for shit to break, people to mess up," Lily said. "That Viking dude, Phil, he scares me. He's a psychopath. Total freakin' psychopath"

We pondered our situation as we prepared our meal. We took turns eating from the one pot, passing it back and forth until it was nearly finished.

"Mind if I give the last little bit to Speck?" Lily asked. "She looks like she could use some roots and ramen."

"Sure," I said, "I've had enough."

Lily put the pan down in front of the dog, who sniffed it a couple times before diving in.

"The flavor pack from the ramen made the whole meal pretty tasty. I mean, as awful and salty as that crap is, it seems, I don't know, almost wonderful that we have something that good out here. It's amazing how things change. Priorities change. In a hurry. Christ, this whole thing just blows my mind. I mean, it's nuts. Thinking ramen is good. Ridiculous." Lily picked up the pan from where Speck had been eating. "Licked clean," she said, holding it up to show me.

* * *

Breaking News from Channel Nine News
Liz Nuñez reporting

"This is Liz Nuñez reporting from Price on an unfolding set of events related to the Recapture protests taking place in the San Rafael Swell Wilderness southwest of here. Sources close to the protest tell us that a second camp has been established on Milky Creek, several miles from the original protest camp. Those sources maintain that the camp was set up to facilitate the search for several protesters, including Clive Prusser and his son Braxton, husband and son of the woman badly injured in an automobile accident last Friday evening, who have been missing since the night of the accident. These sources tell us that while the official statements from the protest organizers through their spokesperson maintain that the two men, along with the missing truckers, are at the main camp, that is not the case. We have been told by two independent sources that the Prussers and another man named Rosenberg have been absent from the camp since that night. They also tell us that the missing truckers, Craig and Lily Clark, have not been seen in the camp, nor has the geologist Stan Watson."

"A written statement issued this afternoon by Travis Dmitrich, spokesperson for the protest, claims that the missing protesters, along with the truckers and the geologist, are at the second camp, which was established on Tuesday, four days after the accident involving LaNae Prusser and the disappearance of the Clarks. Dmitrich has not been available to reporters and has not responded to email and phone messages asking for clarification."

"Carbon County Commissioner Elmo Kuykendall continues to pursue answers to questions about the missing persons and expressed frustration with the apparent disagreement between the official statement and what he calls rumors about the whereabouts of those missing:"

"I've been hearing that all is not well in the protest camp, and that there may be more to the story of the missing truckers and the geologist than we are hearing. We're also concerned about the Prussers, as their family has expressed concern about their whereabouts. They tell me that they would never leave their wife and mother alone in the hospital with such grave injuries. I've asked Sheriff Hackney to dig deeper into these matters, and he has told me that he is doing what he can. I don't think it is enough, frankly, but this is a ticklish situation."

"The families of Lily and Craig Clark and Stan Watson are likewise frustrated with the lack of information about their loved ones, and have

told me that they are seeking federal investigation into possible civil rights violations as well as urging all involved to take the case of their missing family members more seriously."

"We will keep you informed as more information becomes available surrounding what started as a few local men on ATVs protesting some closed roads, but which is now seeming more like a Wild West adventure tale. Reporting from Price, in Carbon County, Utah, Liz Nuñez, Channel Nine News. *"*

Nighthawk hunting

I put the pan and stove away and got the binoculars. Evening had descended and most of the color had gone from the western sky. I scanned the terrain as far as I could see in all directions, but saw nothing of concern. Suddenly a bright shooting star streaked across the sky to the west.

"Wow," Lily said. "Man, the stars sure are bright out here. Brightest I've ever seen."

"Mmm hmmm," I muttered.

"It always makes me feel tiny to look at the sky like this," Lily said.

"Mmm hmmm," I said.

"Are you religious?" Lily asked.

"Not really," I said.

"I'm not. Craig and I, we're kind of the black sheep in both our families because we don't really go for that kind of stuff. Well, the church and preacher kind of stuff. We both think there's something that ties us all together, though. Some kind of energy or something, not so much a god, not with rules and sins and heaven and hell kind of stuff."

"That's kind of where I am, too," I said. We don't go to church. We consider coming out to places like this as our church. We—Chris and I— we've talked about what to do if we ever have kids, whether we should take them to church and all that. I don't know. If we have kids I'll probably take them camping a lot and just forget about church."

"Chris is your wife?" Lily asked.

"Yep, married five years," I said.

"Me and Craig too. Well, six almost. Got married on the Fourth of July. We always said everyone had parades and lit fireworks to celebrate our anniversary."

"Well, I always do," I said. "I looked at Lily and saw that she was blinking her eyes and shaking her head. "I'm sorry," I said. "Really sorry."

I leaned on the boulder with my elbows and steadied the binoculars, sweeping back and forth in the general direction we would be heading in the morning—to the north. Nothing to draw my attention. I listened, and heard only the sounds of a few night creatures—frogs from down near the creek, crickets nearby, and the sudden pulse of fluttering wings that signaled a nighthawk hunting above us. Out of the silence came a high-pitched yip followed by a chorus of shrieks and quavering yelps.

"Is that coyotes?" Lily asked. They sound close."

"They're down below. Probably near the creek," I said.

"Sounds like they're having a big party," Lily said. "They're really yak-king it up."

"Probably got something to eat. Killed or found something, and they're celebrating," I said. "Sometimes it's kind of beautiful when they howl, mournful and harmonic, but when they're yapping like that it's, I don't know, it sounds kind of scary. Like cackling ghouls or witches or something."

I felt Lily step close to me. Her warmth felt good, and I moved slightly toward her, until we touched. I felt her put her arm around my waist and pull in close. I turned to face her, and we embraced.

"It feels so good just to be close to someone," she said. "It really does."

I nodded my head. "It really does."

There's killing, and then there's murder

We went to sleep early and did our best to sleep. The coyotes sang, quarreled, and partied off and on throughout the night, and their cries were comforting, as I knew they would not be that talkative if there were intruders down closer to them, along the creek. We left our camp before dawn and found a way through the rubble and tumbled rocks that obstructed the ledge we had been traveling on. We wanted to stay above the ledge below in case the ATV riders returned. I worried that if they did return they would see the tracks Lily had made yesterday, but there was nothing we could do about that now.

We made our way north, and after a few miles, the ledged uplift we had been hiking along veered to the west and constricted the valley we were following, narrowing into a tight canyon through which Milky Creek flowed. We were able to hike down to near the creek and follow it up through the canyon. There was no actual path or trail, but we picked our way along. The light of the rising day warmed us as we searched for a way through the rugged and steep-sided canyon. We traveled without too much concern, as we knew no one had passed this way recently, and in fact, I doubt that many people had ever hiked this portion of the Milky Creek drainage. No ATVs or other vehicles could even enter the canyon, let alone negotiate its challenging jumble of stone.

The canyon widened a bit a mile or so upstream, and the going became easier. Cliffs rose on both sides of the narrow valley, and the stream flowed quietly, meandering somewhat through willow-thicketed glades strewn with towering cottonwood trees. Vegetation choked the canyon, and game trails were narrow and winding. This place hasn't seen cattle in some time, I thought. There's little evidence of grazing, and I haven't seen any cowpies at all. The stream ran clear and cold. I wondered if there might be fish hiding in some of these holes.

A ridge coming down from the east side of the valley ended in a raised promontory that would give us a view of the terrain.

"Let's go up on that rise and take a look around," I said, pointing. Speck could see where we were moving and charged up the slope.

At the top was a low ring of stones that encircled the end of the ridge.

"Whoa, check this out," I said, indicating the stones. "It's an old house or fort or something."

"Um, I see these rocks, but what?" Lily pondered, tapping her lower lip with an index finger.

"It's a foundation, to a kind of a house, from way back. Like a thousand years or so. Before any Europeans got here," I said. "The Fremont culture, probably. They were all over this country a thousand years ago or so. It's kind of a big deal in this area. People are fascinated by these old ruins."

"Well, it doesn't look like much now," Lily said, sliding her pack off and taking a seat on one of the stones. "Makes a good chair though."

We took a drink and rested for a few minutes while we looked around. The secluded valley seemed peaceful and quiet.

"I think this little valley goes for about three or four miles more before the creek dies out. Then if we keep heading mostly north, we'll hop over a little divide, cross some sage flats, and drop down into a steep canyon that will take us to the cave I was telling you about," I said. "Dark Lord Cave."

"Weird name," Lily said. That's the hideout your friends know about?"

"Yep. We should be able to reach there in a few more days, if we keep hiking," I said. "Not too far, really. Though it gets rough dropping down into the canyon."

"Rougher than what we came through today?" Lily asked, pulling her pant leg up and rubbing a nasty-looking scrape.

"Not really rougher," I said. "That was pretty sketchy going today. Just more dangerous. Bigger drop-offs. Farther to fall."

"At least Mad Max and his boys won't be riding their machines on these trails after us," Lily said. "I doubt those turds ever walk more than a hundred feet from their little scooters."

But they might be able to get to the tops of the cliffs on either side of our canyon, I thought. No reason to worry Lily, though.

"Maybe we should just camp here," I said. "The Indians did. Might not be a bad place. And we can go down to the creek and bathe."

"Yeah, and maybe get something for dinner," Lily said.

"There are a lot more sego lilies on this ridge," I said, "and Indian ricegrass too."

"Not that," Lily said. "There are lots of deer in this canyon. I saw tracks and sign all over. Bet we could get a deer pretty easily."

"I guess so," I said. "Did you say you and um, Craig, you hunt? I don't. I've never hunted."

"Really?" Lily asked. "Heck yeah, I've hunted all my life. I can teach you." She looked at me. "You do eat meat, don't you? You're not a vegetarian?"

"No, I'm not. Well, I don't really eat lots of meat, but no. And I don't have anything against it, I've just, just never killed anything. Well, shit, that's not true. I shot two people. Jesus. What kind of freak does that make me—afraid to kill an animal but killed two men this week. Hell, one of them was only a kid. The idea of killing an animal just to eat it, well, kind of upsets me."

"You could probably kill an animal that was attacking you or your family," Lily said. "That's different. That's what you did. Those people were attacking you. You had no choice. But if you eat meat, you kill things. Well, even worse, you pay people to kill for you. That's not very kind or humane. Not to put you down or anything, but I've always thought that if you're gonna eat meat, you've gotta face the fact that something had to die for your meal. And someone had to kill it."

"I know, I know," I said. "I'm a hypocrite, I know. I guess I'm just too weak to stop eating meat, and too weak to actually kill something. Or even to face up to the issue of death as a necessary part of meat eating."

"Well, there's killing, and then there's murder." Lily said. I think keeping an animal in a factory farm and killing it in an assembly line is murder. It is hideous. Hideous. That's why I hunt. That's why my family has always raised our animals. We know what they ate. We know how they lived. We know they lived good lives. The ones we raised, we even know their names."

"I couldn't do that, I know I couldn't," I said. "Kill an animal I knew. Couldn't do it."

"Well, it isn't easy," Lily said, "But life isn't easy. I learned a lot about life and death from my grandmother. She's an old farm girl. Raised a big garden to feed her family, and chickens and hogs and lambs and calves, too. And she named each one. She loved all her animals. When it was time to kill one, say, a chicken, she would feed it and call it to her. And she would pet it and call it by its name and tell it she loved it and kill it before it knew anything was wrong. She said that we eat meat, and are born to eat meat, just like cats and foxes and hawks, and there's no getting around that. And she always said she wanted to treat her animals well, to make them feel loved, and when the time came, to have it come fast, so their last thought was a happy one. She always said that was how she would want to go, being held by someone she loved." Lily looked at me. "That's the way I was brought up, and that's the way I live. And as far as hunting goes, I only hunt for food, and I only kill an animal that looks happy, or at least is content and quiet. Kill it while it's eating. No chasing, scaring it, running it down, none of that." Lily looked at me and shrugged.

I was speechless. I slowly sat down on a rock facing Lily. I had never heard anything like what she had just said. Finally, I managed to speak, in a croaky voice.

"I, uh, I, well, I've heard about tribal hunters thanking the soul of an animal for its sacrifice after killing it. And I've heard about the rituals around kosher killing, but not like that. Not about taking it to a personal level. That's really incredible. And beautiful."

"Well, it's kind of wrapped up in her religion somewhat. She's really a believer. A Christian. She goes to church and all that, but I think her philosophy is all her own," Lily said, looking off into the distance.

"You see, she really believes in God. She says God is all around us. She says God created everything, so He is everything. Basically, she thinks that God *is* everything. She asked me once, 'What if that chicken is God? What if he took the form of that chicken? How would you treat it? What if He was a dog in the street, or a deer, or a worm?' Grammy used to say that God is all of those things. He is the worm, or the moth. He feels what they feel. He is the chicken. He is you, and He knows you have to eat to live. That you have to kill to live, just like the fox has to kill to live, or the owl, or the snake. He made them all, and he knew what he was doing. Those animals don't hate the ones they eat. And they don't torture them, the way some people do. The way they do in feedlots and factory farms. Animals don't kill for fun the way some people do. Grammy said we should behave as though God was that animal we were going to eat, because He is. We should treat all animals with respect and kindness, and only hurt and kill them when we must. She says that when people like to kill, when they like to hurt animals and people, that's the devil in them, that's evil. She's killed a lot of animals in her lifetime, and I think she loved every one. And I think it's a pretty good way to live your life. I love her and miss her. I don't believe in God, really, but I do believe that my Grammy is on to something. Something that makes sense. Kindness. That's what it is all about. Kindness. Not a bad way to live, I don't think."

"I'd really like to meet your Grammy someday," I said. "She sounds like an extraordinary woman."

"Shit, you know it," Lily said. "And you should hear her play the fiddle. Plays the crap out of it, and she's the toughest and kindest person I have ever known. I'd love to introduce you. We'll plan on it. Soon as we get out of this fine mess. Right after that."

The sun had passed below the horizon and the cloudless western sky was lit orange fading to blue overhead. I arranged some stones in a small circle and started gathering sticks for a fire. "Guess we'll have some ramen tonight," I said. "How about that?"

"Our last," Lily asked.

"There are two packages. I figured we'd eat one more, then try to get by until we really need the last one."

"Oh, we'll be livin' high on meat and roots by tomorrow," Lily said. "You'll see."

* * *

"Donations" to Recapture Brigade Questioned

by Joe Bachman
East Desert News

Pioneer Trucking of Sparks, Nevada, confirms that one of its drivers, Mr. Darrel Simms of Austin, Nevada, voluntarily drove his semi-truck and contributed it and its contents to the antigovernment protesters in Utah's San Rafael Swell. According to Simms's wife, Darlene, her husband phoned her shortly before leaving Green River, Utah, last Thursday and told her he was taking his semi to donate it and its cargo "to the patriots." The semi, owned by Pioneer Trucking, and its contents— sporting goods and survival gear originally destined for a distribution center in Reno, have been missing, and Simms has not been heard from since Thursday. According to Darlene Simms, her husband agreed with the protesters, and while he realized that it could cost him his job and send him to jail, he assured her that "it was worth it to support the cause."

Pioneer spokesman George Coy said his company had no knowledge of Simms's plans or political leanings and that it was working with its client and insurance companies to make things right.

While Simms may have sided with the protesters, the driver of the other semi in the hands of the protesters, Craig Clark, most certainly did not, according to Pendleton Shuffler, president of Blue Grass Express Trucking of Rosine, Kentucky, the owner of the missing semi. "Craig would never have sided with the protesters, and he would never have participated in a theft of company equipment or his cargo," Shuffler said. "We have every reason to believe that Craig and his wife, Lily, have been harmed or are being held against their will."

Shuffler told the Rosine, Kentucky, Daily Sounder, *"We do not think the sheriff is doing enough to recover our property and look after the safety of our employees and family." Craig Clark is Shuffler's nephew and a part owner of the trucking firm. "Craig has been driving long-haul trucks with us for over ten years and has never had an accident or any kind of an incident. We are very concerned."*

Carbon County Sheriff Cortland Hackney said that his office is doing everything it can. "The protesters tell us that Mr. Clark drove in of his own accord and that he and his wife support the cause. We will continue the investigation as best we can, given the unusual circumstances."

In another developing story, a man from Salt Lake City who was traveling to Moab last Saturday is missing, and his family is concerned that he may have run afoul of the protesters. Stan Watson, 35, picked up a gyro sandwich at the Greek Stop in Price and purchased gas at Bassett's Pit Stop in Wellington at 12:30 p.m. on Saturday. He has not been heard from since. Family members are concerned for his safety and ask anyone who has seen him, his white and black border collie, or his silver Toyota 4Runner, license number 10YR52, to please call the Carbon County Sheriff's Office at 435-867-5309. Travis Dmitrich, spokesperson for the Recapture Brigade, told reporters that Watson and the two truckers are at the second camp set up by the protesters.

We'll hunt in the
morning

Lily settled into the bed of bark and duff we had fashioned under the branches of the massive, multi-trunked juniper tree that rose just inside the upper wall of the ancient stone ring. "Um, I don't mean to get all personal, but I was just wondering. How old are you?"

"I don't mind," I said. "Thirty-five." I adjusted the heap of juniper bark we were using as a pillow. "Gettin' up there. You?"

"Twenty-nine," she said. She sniffed. "Twenty-nine. A widow before I turned thirty. Jesus, that's the first I've thought of that. That word. I'm a widow."

We lay quietly under that tree. I could see the north star through a break in the overhead branches. I wondered if Chris would soon be a widow too.

"So you're a scientist or something." Lily asked. "Is that what you do?"

"Well, kind of. I'm a geologist. A geomorphologist, really."

"What do you do then?" Lily asked. "Study rocks?"

"Yeah," I said. "I studied geology in school—you know, all about rocks and minerals, but I concentrated on things like how hills and valleys and modern landscapes were formed, how soils and sediments are laid down. Now I mostly work on environmental impact statements and things like that. Try to see what effect things like mines and highways will have on the land. It's for planning. The theory is to try to make developments less damaging, not so ugly, to not wreck scenic or historic places too much."

"So, what's that have to do with a highway or something? You plan where to put it? Do you work for the highway department?"

"Well, I try to make suggestions about how to make things better. Not the engineering of roads and pipelines, but how they change the landscape, how they can damage other things. And I work with other geologists and water scientists and archaeologists, historians, all kinds of people. I help them with their studies—help them understand the land, how it was formed, things like that. We make recommendations. To the government mostly. Sometimes they listen, sometimes they don't. I worked on studies for that big pipeline that runs right down the middle of that valley by the highway over there. Kind of where you were hijacked. Where I found you. That's how I know my way around here a little bit."

"You?" I asked. "Have you always been a truck driver?"

"I'm only a part timer," Lily said. "Well, I do have my license, and I do drive sometimes, but Craig, he's the trucker. I work in my family's landscaping business. And I'm a potter. I make ceramics and sell them at art festivals and in little shops. And I'm a substitute teacher. I kind of mess around at a bunch of things."

"That's quite a mix. Landscaping, art, teaching. I'd like to see your ceramic pieces. Chris collects bowls and platters. We'll have to come see your work. After, well, after all this is over."

"It's what I really love, what I studied in school, but, well, I've never made much money at it. Landscaping and teaching pay pretty well. I might go into teaching full time one of these days. I like it."

"That's gotta be rewarding," I said. "Working with kids, helping them learn about the world."

"Yeah, mostly," she said. "Kind of depressing too, when you see how neglected some of them are, what shitty parents they have."

"I admire teachers," I said. "My mom was a teacher. She taught my third grade class for a while too. Kind of weird, having your mom for your teacher. Weird, but good, too, I guess."

"What about your wife," Lily asked. "What's she do?"

"She's a lawyer," I said. "Works for a big firm. Mostly tax law. Stuff I know nothing about. I guess she's pretty good at it. Works hard. Works all the time."

We lay quietly. The branches we had cut to augment the needle and bark duff under the tree gave off a comforting, gin-like aroma. I turned on my side and wiggled to move the duff away from under my hip and shoulders. Lily and Speck cuddled in close to my back.

"We'll hunt in the morning," Lily whispered.

* * *

The Carbon County Drumbeat
Recapture update—Latest news from The Swell

* Drumbeat *reporter embedded*

Drumbeat *reporter Frank Saccomano, a long-time friend and confidant of Recapture Brigade leader Drew Peacock has embedded himself with the protesters. Frank will be checking in by satellite phone to provide a more "up close and personal" side to the reporting. Stories about the protest have to date been dominated by carefully edited statements from spokespersons. Our Man in the Swell, Frank Saccomano, will get the real scoop. Stay tuned.*

I FELT A GREAT RELIEF

The thought of hunting sent a twisting pang to my gut. Visions of sneaking around in the brush and tracking down and killing some animal ran through my mind. Shooting and crippling an animal, making it suffer and cry out in terror and pain as I walk up to it. I was worried about doing something I had never done, about being a completely incompetent idiot and making a fool of myself. Shit, I'm worrying about trying to impress this person I barely know, a person whose clothes are stained with the blood of her murdered husband. She is not just a person, I realized. She's the only person in my world. She may be the last person I ever see. And she is a woman. I would be embarrassed to be a bumbling fool of a hunter whether in front of a man or a woman. But it's different. She's not a man. She's a woman, and I am starting to have strong feelings for her. Not really sexual, I don't think, but kind of a dependence, a feeling of responsibility and vulnerability that makes me want to be my best, to be the best. Shit, what I need to do now is think about hunting. I'll make a fool of myself. Shit.

Then I thought about how good some roast meat would taste. As I drifted off to sleep, I kept the thought of a good meal in mind, and it drove the fear of the unknown away. Thoughts about the ancient house we slept in and its original inhabitants entered my mind, and I dreamed Lily and I were in a large domed room, and Speck and Chris and Craig were there too, and we had a fire and were cooking meat on a rack and we were laughing and telling stories, and the morning came quickly.

"Let's go," Lily said. "Put a leash on Speck so she doesn't spook any game." She threw back the tarp and sat up. The faintest indication of an approaching dawn appeared in the eastern sky. I grasped Speck's collar and held her while I fished in the rifle bag for the cord I was using for a leash.

"Is the mag in your rifle full?" she asked.

"Yeah," I said.

"That's all we'll need. Too bad you've got military rounds in it," Lily said. "Hollow points would be a lot better than these metal jackets, but we'll be OK. Bring your knife too, and that cord." She licked her finger and held it high above her head. "We'll move upstream. The air is moving downstream. Game won't smell us. As soon."

"Why don't you carry the rifle," I said. "You know what you're doing. Why don't you take it."

Lily reached out and took the rifle. I felt a great relief.

Lily led the way along the edge of the ridge and kept us at about the same elevation above the stream. We moved slowly and carefully, her in front, me leading Speck a few paces back. The light gradually increased, and we carefully studied the land in front of us as we made our way north. Lily used the binoculars occasionally to examine something ahead or down below, but mostly she and I just scanned the meadows and openings in the vegetation. After a short while Lily stopped in the middle of the path and motioned with her hand for me to stop. She dropped to one knee and lifted the binoculars to her eyes. After about a minute of looking through the binoculars she let them hang on her chest, raised the rifle, adjusted the rear sight, sat motionless for several seconds, then fired. She stood quickly and fired again, then relaxed. She turned toward me and nodded. "Let's go see," she said.

A buck mule deer lay at the edge of a small, grassy clearing just above the stream. Blood came from its mouth, and feces oozed, steaming, from its anus. Just a moment ago it had been standing in this beautiful spot, eating grass or thinking about getting a drink, or dreaming of the rutting season, and in an instant it was gone, nothing but a body remaining. Could happen to us, too. A heart attack or lightning or an asteroid or a bomb or pirates could take us out, and we would be gone before we could even contemplate death. I know some people think that would be the way to go, but I don't know. I think I'd like some time, even a minute, to think things over. Or just freak out completely. Who knows.

"Let's get to work," Lily said, pulling the deer by its hind legs away from the tangled brush it had landed in. "Come on Stan, get out the knife. I'll show you how to process a carcass."

Breaking News from Channel Nine News
Liz Nuñez reporting

"Channel Nine has learned that at least one witness has come forward to report gunfire and unusual activity in the vicinity of the Bear Creek Rest Area on Highway 6 on the night of Friday, June third, the same night the tractor and trailer being driven by Craig and Lily Clark disappeared."

"Eldon Dorfman, an electrician at the Horselily Mine, just east of the rest area, told sheriff's deputies that he heard a number of gunshots and several vehicles traveling at high speeds on the highway late Friday evening as he was leaving work and driving home."

"Mr. Dorfman, what can you tell us about what you saw that night?"

"Well, to start with, we've been told to be extra careful driving that road at night because of the protests and all, so I try to pay attention, you know, to the cars and such. Well, that night I left the mine at around eight, and just before I got to the highway I could hear some vehicles coming fast, and I heard what sounded like gunshots. Could've been backfires, but I don't think so. Anyway, at least a couple of vehicles roared by, I couldn't really see them because of the hill and trees right there, but they were really going. And I heard some more shots, too, I think. Kinda got my blood racing, you know."

"So you heard shots and some vehicles going by pretty fast. Could you tell which way they were heading?"

"Oh yeah, that's where the road comes off the plateau and drops down to the flats. Big hill, you know. They were coming down the hill. Heck, you can get going eighty down that hill even if you're not trying. I bet they was over a hundred. Sounded like a jet plane going by, that's how fast they was going."

"You reported this to the sheriff, didn't you?"

"Sure did. They wrote some things down and said thanks, that's about all."

"Thank you Mr. Dorfman. Channel Nine contacted the sheriff's office about Mr. Dorfman's observations, and they said that they were aware of his statement and were continuing to investigate. When we contacted the spokesperson for the Recapture protesters, we were told that Mr. Dorfman most likely heard backfiring and engine brakes, as big trucks often get going too fast on that steep downgrade, and they make a lot of noise trying to slow down."

"Friday night is the night the semi disappeared, and it is also the night LaNae Prusser was badly injured. Her husband Clive and son Braxton have not, to our knowledge, been seen since then, and may not even be aware of their loved one's trauma."

"Channel Nine will stay with this story as it unfolds. Reporting from Price, in Carbon County, Utah, Liz Nuñez, Channel Nine News.*"*

THE WATER'S FINE

Over the course of the next few hours, Lily guided me through the necessary steps of bleeding, gutting, skinning, and butchering the deer. We built a fire and roasted the liver and chunks of the tenderloin on sticks as we worked, stopping to eat in late morning. I had never liked liver, but this was one of the best things I had ever put in my mouth. Speck ate organ meat and whatever scraps we threw her, and when our hands and arms were sticky and bloody we walked down to the stream to wash them off. We worked quickly and cut the meat into long thin strips and hung it on willow poles we cut and suspended between the branches of exposed, south-facing trees and shrubs for good exposure to the sun. We draped the meat strands in rows and built small fires and waved branches every once in a while at the drying meat to chase away flies.

"If we can keep the flies away long enough for it to dry out a bit, the meat will be good, and won't get maggoty," Lily said.

I had seen a film in an anthropology class years ago of the Bushmen of southern Africa cutting giraffe meat in strips and drying it on bushes, just like we were doing.

"Look at my meat suit," Lily exclaimed, her arms covered with strips of meat as she headed for the drying poles. "I'm Lady Gaga."

"I like it," I said. "Mmmmmm, meat!"

We cooked ribs and roasts over the fire on a rack of green willows, and I went back to our camp to get the things we had left behind so we could camp nearer to the drying meat. When I returned, I did not see Lily for a minute, then Speck ran down to the creek.

"Come on down," I hear Lily call. "The water's fine,"

Lily had found a small pool deep enough to sit in and bathe. She had washed her clothes, which were hanging on nearby bushes, and she was lying back in the water swishing her hair back and forth in the stream. It looked refreshing and wonderful, and I followed suit.

"Sure feels nice to get cleaned off," she said. "It's been what, a week?"

"About, I think," I said. "Well, yeah, a week. You got hijacked on Friday night, I came on Saturday, and today's Saturday. A whole week. Seems like a lifetime." It really did.

We bathed, arranged our clothes on bushes and branches to dry, and napped in the tall grass, enjoying the warmth of the sun and the cleansing feeling it gave us. When Lily rolled toward me and looked me in the eye, we touched hands, and I felt a cool energy run through her slender fingers, and it was a perfect moment. I wanted to embrace her, to make love to her, with her, and knew that our simple touch had accomplished that, as if we had given ourselves completely to each other. We touched hands there in that grassy meadow not too far from where we had killed and butchered a buck mule deer, and it seemed like an affirmation of our commitment, a sacramental act that absolved us for a time of the horrors that had been inflicted upon us, that melded our emotional energies in a way that seemed perfect. At that moment I loved and needed her more than I had ever loved and needed anything in my life, and the feeling seemed reciprocal.

The Carbon County Drumbeat
Recapture update—Latest news from The Swell

** Equipment Problems Hamper Communication*

Apparent equipment problems have kept Drumbeat *reporter Frank Saccomano from communicating since he joined the protesters last Thursday. Attempts to reach him on his satellite phone have been unsuccessful. Stay tuned.*

SEE IF ONE OF THEM
IS A HORSE

We tended to our fires and drying meat, ate and took care of our camp duties and rested and enjoyed this respite from our horrifying reality, and when morning came we knew that we had to move on, so we made bundles of dried meat secured by nylon cord, packed up our belongings, and started moving north again, ever northward, toward Dark Lord Cave.

Our packs full of dried and roasted venison, and with strips of dried meat tied atop them, we left the ring of stones, the ancient abandoned home of some long-forgotten family of farmers, the place where we became hunters and carnivores and the spot where we had consecrated our partnership, and we headed north. Before the day began to lighten we hiked, scurrying, it seemed, like mice skittering from the grain bin, hoping to duck under cover before the cat arrives. When the course of Milky Creek headed west, we left the riparian streamside zone and climbed out of the valley, up its sloping and ledge-stepped margin toward the divide that separates the Milky Creek drainage from the labyrinth of canyons that make up the Badger Canyon Badlands. The badlands offered a safe haven of narrow defiles, slot canyons, drop-offs, uplifts, potholes, hoodoos, goblins, cracks, and holes that we could disappear into as we made our way toward Dark Lord Cave and possible rescue.

At the crest of the rise leading away from Milky Creek, the land flattened, and we began to traverse a gently sloping, relatively open area of rolling hills and patchy scrub forest that in about five miles would drop away into the badlands. In a small clump of trees on a hill that provided a good view of the terrain ahead, we stopped to rest and have a look around.

"The main east-west road across this part of the Swell crosses this open land ahead of us, down there," I said, pointing. "See that line across that reddish hillside? That's the road. We have to be extra careful along in here. Until we drop down into the badlands, over there past that far line of trees, we could run into bad guys. Patrols, who knows."

"We could stay in these trees, kind of skulk around the edges of these hills for a ways," Lily said. "And maybe cross the road tonight, or in the morning. In the dark."

"Definitely cross in the dark. Maybe do most of our traveling when it's dark," I said. "We need to be careful. We'll be kind of in the open until we're in the Badger Canyon area. Tomorrow some time."

The day was clear and the air clean, and it seemed that we could see in perfect detail all the way to the horizon. The terrain rolled and swooped in front of us, devoid of the sharp angles and rakish uplifts we had been passing through, as though the tense and flexed muscles of the buckled sandstone had relaxed, and for a time, the land had reclined, smoothing out the wrinkles and folds, easing the tension that held it in such harsh angularity elsewhere in the Swell. We could see a substantial open space, stretching for several miles in each direction, through which the lone road in this area, the Quorum Pass road, ran straight and purposefully, as though made by a single stroke of a massive sword.

"That's the road?" Lily asked, pointing to the light line that bisected the sage and shrub-covered expanse.

I nodded. "It comes through a little gap in the uplift over to the east and goes across these flats and up through a pass over there, where the pinkish hills rise up in the west. Quorum Pass road it's called. This little park we're in is called Raven's Flat. We're heading up that way, straight north across the flat, then down over a big drop-off into the Badger Canyon area. This is probably the most dangerous place for us, with the road. Good place to be spotted. No place to hide."

We sat for a while, taking turns looking through the binoculars, familiarizing ourselves with the flat.

"What's that darkish spot down there?" Lily asked. "The road runs right by it."

"It's a little marshy place by a spring," I said. "There's a cattle trough and some cattails and things where the water trickles down and away from the spring. There are some cattle down near there—see those brown and black spots?"

"Yeah," Lily said. "I see them. There's eight mamas and seven calves. And, um, well, I can't tell for sure, but I think it's a person. It looks like somebody's sitting under that tree, that little one just past the stock pond," she said, handing the binoculars to me. "He's wearing a blue shirt and a white cowboy hat."

Sure enough, somebody was sitting under the tree. I looked all around to see if I could see anyone else, or any sign of a vehicle, but saw nothing.

"That's really weird," I said, lowering the binoculars and looking at Lily. "I can't imagine how he got there or what he's doing down there."

"Maybe they're his cows," Lily said. "Look at them all again and see if one of them is a horse."

"No horses," I said. "Nothing else. Just him. And no sign of anyone else. Just a bunch of magpies hanging out in the tree and around the trough."

I looked and made sure Speck was close by and not running around. "He could be a lookout. Maybe they left someone to watch the stock pond. He's probably got a radio and a gun. I bet he's there to watch things. Watch out for people like us."

Lily took the binoculars and looked for several minutes toward the tank. "If he has guns and things, they are probably somewhere else. It doesn't look like he's carrying one."

"Probably stashed someplace else," I said. "Let's just keep watching him and try to figure out what's going on."

LET'S DO THIS

We stayed put and kept a close watch on the man by the trough. He got up a few times and walked around, always returning to the shade of the tree. He went to the trough and appeared to fill a water bottle and get a drink, and he walked around the trough and the little marsh once, but always returned to the shade of the tree. We did not see him go to another place where he might have had tools or gear hidden. Late in the afternoon he laid back, put his hat over his eyes, and appeared to go to sleep.

"Looks like he's sleeping. I think we should go see what is going on," I said. "We could go down the gully and get close to the stock tank and stay hidden. You cover me with the rifle and I'll, um, I guess I'll just go over and see what his deal is. I'll take the pistol, and take him by surprise. If anything goes south, you'll have the rifle."

Lily shrugged. "Unless you just want to sneak down there and plug him. That would be the safest."

"Yeah, but, jeez, just shoot him? What if he's just some cowboy whose horse ran off?"

"I'm just talkin'," Lily said. "Just to see what you'd say. If he's not a bad guy maybe he can help us. If he is a bad guy we can maybe learn something from him." She dug into her pack, took out the pistol, handed it to me, and reached for the rifle. "You want Speck with you, or should she stay with me?"

"I'll keep her with me," I said, "She'll be good." I looked up at Lily. "Let's do this."

I looked one more time to make sure the cowboy was sleeping, and headed for the gully. When we had gotten to within about fifty yards of the stock tank, we stopped. Lily found a spot with a good view of the tank, the cowboy, and the tree and gave me a thumbs up. I crouched down and, keeping the galvanized stock tank between me and the sleeping cowboy, approached the tank. I lay on the ground, and used the tank for cover. I cocked the pistol and pointed it toward the prostrate man. I took a deep breath, glanced at Lily, and trained the sights on him.

"Hello," I yelled. "Hello!"

The man under the tree rolled quickly onto his side and looked toward the road, away from me. He leaned up on one elbow, and then sat up.

"What do you want now?" he yelled. "Why don't you just leave me alone."

"Stand and hold your hands up," I shouted. "And drop any weapons, or I'll shoot."

The man appeared to be muttering to himself as he rolled to his hands and knees and stood. He raised his hands, and looked over toward me.

"Move away from the tree," I said. He stepped forward a few steps and stopped.

"That's enough," I said. Keeping the pistol trained on him, I slowly stood.

"Who are you?" he asked. "Who the hell are you? Where did you come from? Are you one of the Recapture people? Who are you?"

"Just stay where you are," I said. "Who are you? Are you one of the protesters?"

"No," he yelled, "Hell no. They stole my truck and left me here. I'm not one of them. No." He faced toward me. I could see that he was tall and slender and had thick gray hair that stuck out in all directions from the way he had been sleeping. I started to walk toward him when I heard a whistle. Lily. I looked over toward her and saw her point. A dust cloud appeared just over the closest rise. Dammit, somebody's coming. I ducked down behind the galvanized trough.

"It's them," the man said. He dropped his hands, walked to the tree where he had been sleeping, stooped, picked up his hat, put it on his head and adjusted it, and stood and waited.

A tan Dodge pickup pulled up. I could see a triangular red and black flag flying from a pole behind the cab. A man stepped out of the passenger side. He had long blond hair and a full, long red beard. Shit, the Viking. He was carrying a pistol in his hand.

"Where are they," he said to the cowboy. "You must have seen them."

"I don't know," the cowboy said. "I haven't seen anyone."

"Don't lie to me," the Viking hollered. "They had to have come by here. Why didn't you call on the radio? What the hell have you been doing? You're supposed to be watching."

Another man stepped out of the pickup truck. He too was carrying a pistol. He walked straight up to the cowboy and shoved him in the chest, sending him back several steps before he caught his balance.

The man walked up to the cowboy and raised his pistol. He was going to shoot him! The cowboy pleaded, "Come on, what are you doing?" he said. "Don't do this, don't do this."

I trained my sights on the man who was threatening the cowboy, but the cowboy was between us, blocking a clean shot. Out of the corner of my eye I could see the Viking step around the front of the truck.

"You're a spy, old man, admit it! You're a spy," he hollered, and pointed his pistol at the man's head.

A slight gust of wind picked up a slender wisp of dust and twirled it in front of us. A single magpie pecked at something on the ground between me and the men, cocked its head, and burst into flight, straight up, and was joined by several others from the tree and they spiraled up, rasping in corvid harmony. Speck raised up, a low growl rising in her throat that seemed to match the cries of the magpies. I held my pistol in front of me as I lay on the ground, partially shielded by the galvanized trough, and waited. I had nothing to aim at, so I waited. The sun felt hot on my back and I tried not to breathe and my hands trembled, and I waited.

A shot rang out. The cowboy fell straight to the ground. The pirate dropped to his knees, then lurched forward onto his belly. The cowboy thrashed and crawled toward the tree. The pirate raised up onto his knees. The Viking ran a few steps forward, closer to me, raised his pistol, crouched, and started sighting around, looking for something. I fired at him, and heard another shot. He spun around and faced me. I could see the cowboy struggling to rise. The other pirate was crawling toward the truck. I sighted again on the Viking, and as I did I saw him face me with his gun raised. I pulled my trigger, and at the same time saw a bright flash and felt my head jolt back. I heard more shots and some screaming, but I couldn't see. Something's in my eyes, I thought, and I wiped at them with my hand. My eyes burned. They're all wet, I thought, something's in them. I rubbed harder. Then I realized that my entire face was wet and very warm, and I knew then that it was blood. I couldn't see at all. I heard the truck door slam and the motor roar. More shots rang out. I tried to scoot backwards, to shield myself from any further shooting. I covered my face with my hands, and I could feel throbbing. I knew I was in trouble, but I didn't know what to do. Press on your face, I thought. Maybe I can press on it and stop the bleeding. I felt hot, and the throbbing grew, and the blood ran over my mouth and the metallic taste of my own blood ran through me like an electric current, and I felt like I was spinning. I'll keep pressing on my face, and just rest a minute. Rest. I lay my head forward in my hands. I needed to rest.

∗ ∗ ∗

Breaking News from Channel Nine News
Liz Nuñez reporting

"Channel Nine News has learned that a new camp established by the Recapture protesters may not have been a strategic move, as the organizers contend. Sources tell us that a disagreement or series of disagreements led to a small group breaking away from the formal camp established by Drew Peacock and the other organizers of the protest. County Commissioner Elmo Kuykendall has received reports of trouble within the protest camp and is asking the Carbon County sheriff to provide answers. Commissioner Kuykendall, what can you tell us about the situation in the protest area?"

"The, um, the official word from the protesters is that the second camp was established to provide a presence closer to the main highway to facilitate security and communication, but we've had some information come to us that the second camp is actually a breakaway group that had some kind of disagreement with the protest leaders, so they made their own camp over on Milky Creek."

"How have you gotten this information, Commissioner? Are you in contact with people in the camps—either one?"

"No, well, not directly. One of my associates has a relative in the camp who has been passing information out to him. So, it's kind of second-hand, so to speak. But I believe it is factual. I know both the people involved, and don't think they have any reason to make things up."

"Have you heard anything else? About the disagreement, for instance— what is it over?"

"No, well, not too much. We do know with some certainty that there were arguments, loud arguments, and they lasted for a long time, like a day and all night. And when the group left the main camp, there was a lot of shouting and gunfire. Not gunfights, just firing guns in the air, that sort of thing."

"Do you think this indicates that the protest is falling apart? That they might be losing their resolve? Or at least their focus?"

"I really don't know, and the spokespeople for the protest aren't telling us much. They are staying "on message," so to speak, and only want to talk about all the support they are receiving from around the country, and how even congressmen and senators are behind them. They claim

the protesters are united and that they are staying true to their goals. And, maybe they are, maybe this is just a little glitch. I guess we'll have to wait and see."

"Commissioner, is there any additional information on the fate or whereabouts of the missing truckers Craig and Lily Clark, or the geologist Stan Watson?"

"No, not really, although my contact in the protest camp says he has not seen them, and in fact seemed unaware that they were supposed to have been there. He did confirm that the Family Grocers semi and trailer were in the camp. That's really all I know at this point."

"Thank you, Commissioner. As the commissioner has stated, there are still a number of unanswered questions swirling around this protest and through the region. We will do our best to keep you informed as the protest, now in its third week, continues."

"Reporting from Price, in Carbon County, Utah, Liz Nuñez, Channel Nine News. *"*

I NEED HELP

I was in a dark room, face down, and the room was hot. Open a window, I thought. I need to open a window. I could hear faint voices and tried to call out to them, but nothing seemed to work. I could not make a sound. I felt something pressing between my hands and my face as if forcing me to move my hands. I fought it but it would not stop, and I felt it wiping around my mouth and nose, and it was warm, and it felt familiar. Speck! It was Speck, licking me. Thank God for Speck, she would help me. Help me Speck, I need help. I felt someone lifting my shoulder and rolling me over. I was so hot, burning up. Speck kept licking me, and I felt something cool on my head, then something washing over it. I had never felt anything so good and cool on my burning head. I felt something cool pressing against my forehead, and the voices seemed closer.

"Stan, Stan," I heard a distant voice say. "Stan, can you hear me? Are you awake? Stan, please Stan, please say something."

I felt something touch my lips and I opened my mouth slightly. Water. I wanted water. More than anything in the world. I took a sip and held it in my mouth. "More," I said, but no sound came. "More," I said again, trying to shout, but all that came out was a whisper. I heard the voice say

"Here's more. Thank God, you can hear me. Here, have some more. Try not to choke." Speck continued to lick at my face, and I reached out to embrace her.

"Lie back," Lily said, and I thought it was the most beautiful voice I had ever heard. Lily and Speck would help me. "Lie back and let me see how badly you're hurt."

I rolled onto my back. I could feel a hand pressing a wet cloth to my forehead. Lily was taking care of me. I've been shot. Damn, it just dawned on me. Shot in the head. I'm conscious, so maybe it's not too bad. Lots of blood though, it seems like. Head wounds always bleed a lot. I have a head wound. I was in a gun battle with the pirates. I started to sit up.

"Bad guys?" I asked. "Bad guys?"

"Calm down," Lily said. "Lie back down and don't move. You're badly hurt. Just relax and try not to move."

Lily held the cloth on my forehead, and when she wiped around my eyes, a grating pain ran through my face, as though she was rubbing sandpaper across my eyeballs. I flinched and whimpered.

"Sorry," she said. "Your eyes are a mess. I'll just drip some water over them."

The cool water felt good. I tried to flutter my eyes a bit, to see if the water could clean under my lids, but the slightest amount of light entering them seemed blinding.

"You've got two pretty deep wounds," Lily said, continuing to wipe my face. "One in the middle of your forehead, one over your eyebrow. They're like deep gouges. I don't know what's in them or if a bullet hit you. The wounds are full of dirt and gravel. Maybe bullet fragments, hard to tell."

I could hear Lily talking with someone, but couldn't make out what they were saying. I felt like I was drifting in and out of consciousness. I could feel the warm sun shining on me, and the light looked red through my closed eyes. Both of my eyes seemed to be sensitive to the light, so that's a good sign, isn't it? I felt heavy and drowsy, but I thought that I had better fight the urge to sleep. I tried to focus. What did I need to do? I wiggled my hands and feet and took a deep breath. It's just my eyes. Maybe it's just my eyes. And my head. I wondered how much blood I had lost. Then I remembered what had happened, and where we were. I could hear more talking.

"We need to get out of here," I blurted out. "We can't stay here. We need to get to a hospital."

"Just stay down," Lily said, still holding her hand on my forehead. "We need to take care of you, make sure you are not bleeding too much. Then we'll think about moving."

"Did they get away?" I asked. "The Viking. The bad guys. Did they get away? Who's there with you?"

I realized that I had no idea about what had happened. Were we prisoners of the Viking? Was the cowboy dead? Speck licked me again, and lay against me. I put my arm around her and pulled her close. "What's going on," I asked.

I could feel Lily sitting beside me. She put something over my face to shield it from the sun, and put her arm around me "Everything's going to be OK," she said, whispering into my ear. "You need to just lie here and rest. Hug Speck and try to relax. I'll make sure everything is OK. You just rest."

I had been fighting to stay awake, and the sound of Lily's voice and the comforting touch of Speck curled against my side helped me to let go, and I eased into the comfort of unconsciousness. I drifted up and down, nearly waking, then slipping back, waking at times when someone gave me water or when Speck moved a bit. I'm going to die out here. What a place to die. And I'm leaving so many things undone. Why have I been wasting my life? Why haven't I done all the things I wanted to do. What will Chris do? I'll never have kids. Chris doesn't have the kids she's always wanted. Why have I been so selfish? I never wanted kids, and now, well, now I'll never get to tell my kids all about the world, about the things I've learned, about Grandpap and my folks, and about this adventure, and about getting shot in the head and being blinded. Am I blind? Am I about to die? I drifted and drifted and floated about, lost, not knowing whether I was alive or dead, and my mind at times felt like I was in a spaceship entering hyperspace, where all things merge into a white light, and I felt a white glow and it covered me and I was part of it and I tingled all over and it was a good feeling, and once in a while I heard or felt something and realized that I was not dead yet but felt that if I was going to die, it would be OK, and then I'd remember all the reasons it wasn't OK and I'd panic. And then I'd drift off again.

When darkness came, I dropped further and further and dreamed of trying to find my house, but I couldn't see clearly and I kept going to doors and feeling for the door knob and trying to get in, but they were all locked and sometimes people opened the door and told me to go away. It seemed like the dream went on forever, and I only awoke when the sun was shining hot on my face and I could feel and hear Speck growling. I started to open my eyes, but the sunlight was searing. Speck rose to her feet but did not move. Her growl deepened, but I could not hear anything else.

"It's OK, pup," I heard a man's voice say. "I'll stay back. Lily will be here in a minute."

I had no idea who was speaking, and I didn't want to start talking and I realized that I really needed to pee, so I just stayed as still as I could. Speck calmed down, and a few minutes later I could feel her stand, and her body moved as though she was wagging her tail.

"Good girl, Speck," Lily said. "Good girl." She came close and put her hand on my chest and removed the cloth from my forehead. It stuck, and felt like my flesh was ripping and hurt when she pulled it off.

"Sorry. Sorry about that. You've been sleeping. You're probably awake now. Sorry."

"Yeah," I whispered. I coughed to clear my throat. "Yeah."

"Let's see if you can sit up. We need to get you moving."

Lily helped me sit up. She gave me a drink, then helped me stand. I used the side of the stock tank for support and with her help, stood. I had to drop right down to my knees for a minute or two, then tried it again. I felt a little shaky at first, but everything seemed to be OK. Except my eyes. I tried to open them but they were very sensitive to the light, and even moving them around with my eyes closed was painful.

"Need to pee?" Lily asked. I nodded. She helped me walk a few steps and went behind me and supported me under my arms while I undid my pants and peed.

"Think you can walk?" she asked.

"Think so," I said. "Except I can't see."

"I'll help with that," she said. "And I'm sure Speck will. She won't leave your side."

I could feel Speck pressed against my leg. I reached down and petted her on the head and scratched her ears.

"We need to get moving," Lily said. "We have to get away from this road. If you can walk, we'll get going. Even if we just go a little ways, it will be better than staying here. Stand here for a minute and we'll get packed up."

I put my hand on the rim of the stock tank and steadied myself. Keeping one hand on the tank, I walked around it, first one direction, then the other. I tried to breathe deeply and make the fog in my brain go away. I wasn't going to an emergency room, so I had better do what I can to be strong and get going. To help Lily help me. I had to find strength. No choice.

After a few minutes Lily handed me the leash cord. "Take my arm," she said, "and Speck will walk on the other side of you. We'll take it slow and easy. Ready? Let's go."

The Carbon County Drumbeat

Recapture update—Latest news from The Swell

** Volunteers turned back*

A group of about ten heavily armed men was apprehended along the Van Deusen Trail road late Sunday night as they apparently attempted to join the protesters. Officers at the Van Deusen check station were able to stop their vehicles and persuade them to turn back without major incident. "We discourage anyone else from trying to join the protesters," said Sheriff Cortland Hackney. Federal officials have stated that anyone seeking to join the protesters will be charged with violating a federal directive, a misdemeanor.

I THINK WE NEED SOME TEA

Walking was not too difficult at first, and it felt good to be moving again. I wanted to ask about who was with us but walking took all of my energy and concentration. Have I ever felt this weak and tired? Weary, I felt weary. I never really appreciated that word until now. I'm weary. Worn out, emotionally and physically. Weary. I'm weary.

My eyes were mostly OK as long as they were closed, but even the slightest attempt to open them brought fiery flashes of light and pain. At most, I caught strobe-like glimpses of the ground or my surroundings, discerning little but light and dark. The ground rose and fell, and caused me to stumble and fall a couple of times, and after a while Lily said the trail was too narrow to walk side-by-side, so she went ahead and I put one hand on her shoulder and Speck stayed beside me and that worked pretty well except that I stepped on the back of Lily's heels a time or two and caused us both to falter. I learned to walk by lifting the toes of my feet higher than usual with each step because I had no idea of what lay in my path and I didn't want to trip. Did blind people always walk this way? The sound of the low scuffling of our feet on the soil told me that the ground was soft and not rocky. A slight breeze blew against our faces, and from the warmth of the sun on the left side of my face I knew it was after noon and that we were headed north. A branch caught me in the forehead and must have hit one of my wounds because I felt blood running down my face. I called out to Lily and we stopped and sat down while she wiped my face and put pressure on the wound to stop the bleeding.

"We've gone far enough," she said. "We are almost to where we'll drop off into the canyons. We can stop here for the night, then head down in the morning."

"The badlands," I said. "The Badger Badlands."

The Badger Badlands, long infamous as a hideout used by outlaws on the lam, named for Cletus "Badger" Brosky, who hid out in the badlands for weeks following his execution-style killing of Sheriff John Perkins who had drunkenly shot Brosky's brother Sam in the chest the night before in front of Dick's Bar in Carbonado. Perkins was known as a corrupt bully, but he was the sheriff, and even though Badger was thought to be a hero by many, he was hunted down and eventually dragged back to town and hanged from a cottonwood tree. How odd, or maybe ironic, that we are heading for the Badger Badlands, hoping to hide from people who are trying to hunt us down and probably kill us. Hope it works out better for us than it did for Badger.

Lily helped me find a place to sit down and get comfortable. I took a drink of water and stroked Speck's head. I don't think she had gone more than two feet away from me the entire day. My body tingled from exhaustion, and my legs were just about used up. I drew Speck close and took a few deep breaths. Sitting with my arms around the most loyal friend I would ever have gave me a feeling of momentary wellbeing. Sitting in the dirt with an oozing head wound and wrecked eyes, and I'm feeling euphoric just hugging my dog. You take what you can get, I suppose.

"Well," I said. "Are we, um, OK? Wanna fill me in on what's happened—what's going on?"

"Yeah, yeah, sorry it's taken so long. It's, well, pretty good though. I mean, except for you getting shot. Except for that." Lily took my hand in hers. "You need to meet Frank. Frank, this is Stan." She lifted my hand and I felt another, larger hand grasp it. We shook hands.

"Frank," a man's voice said. "Frank Saccomano. I'm from Price."

"Stan Watson," I said. "Salt Lake."

"Frank was the man by the stock tank. Under the tree," Lily said. "The pirates had left him there, kind of to be a watchman, right Frank?"

"So you're one of them," I broke in.

"No, hell no," Frank said. "They stole my truck and everything I had. They said they'd let me live if I stayed by that watering trough with a radio and call them if anybody showed up. They were looking for you two."

"That long-haired guy—was he behind it? And the other one—the one who was raving and screaming at you? I thought he killed you. I thought you were dead."

"So did I," Frank said. "The long-haired guy's named Phil. The other guy, Marty, was his toady. Phil told me he was the leader of the Recapture Brigade. I knew that was BS, but that's what he said. He said you two had murdered one of his men and he needed to find you and bring you to trial. He was pissed because he thought you had gotten by me—past the road there by the watering trough—and I hadn't called him. He was about to have me shot, I guess, at least that's the way it seemed to me. I owe you my life."

"I didn't shoot him," I said. "Like I said, I thought he got you. Shot you in the head."

"It was me," Lily said. "I got a clean shot at him and took it. I worried I had waited too long when you both went down, but I got him, then he crawled away and I hit him again. And Stan hit the Viking, I think. Phil. He wasn't a leader of anything. He's a murderer. We saw him kill one of his own men so he could do what he wanted to with me. He's a scumbag. Nothing but a scumbag."

"Yeah, he wanted to find us, all right," I said. "We saw him murder another man. He wanted to shut us up. Asshole."

"I really didn't know what had happened, at first," Frank said. "When I heard the shot I just dropped. Instinct I guess. Then tried to get away. You know, when he was about to shoot me, your dog ran out and distracted him for just an instant. She helped save me."

"She sure did," Lily said. "She ran out at just the right time."

"I don't think I even saw that," I said. "I was focusing on the Viking. Seems to me like we shot at each other at the same time."

"Exactly the same time," Lily said. "I thought you were gone." She reached and took my hand again. "He spun around, and then he ran to the truck. I might have hit him, can't be sure. I fired a few rounds at the truck as he left, but it kept going."

We sat there in silence for a few minutes. "So we stayed there, by that trough, for the rest of the day and night?" I asked. "That was probably pretty risky."

"We didn't have much choice. You couldn't travel. Frank piled a bunch of branches and rocks at a couple places in the road so if anyone came they'd have to stop before they got to us. And he stayed up all night. Frank's been great."

"Well, I owe you my life." Frank said. "Both of you. Well, all three of you. I'll tell you, this is not what I had planned for this week. Nope. Not in the plans."

"Let's make camp," Lily said. "And have some tea. I think we need some tea."

The Carbon County Drumbeat

Recapture update—Latest news from The Swell

** Demonstrations support Recapture Protest*

Several groups sympathetic to the Recapture Brigade protesters have staged demonstrations and ride-ins in support of the occupation of the San Rafael Swell. A group calling themselves The Standard-Bearers has taken over a campground near Baggs, Wyoming, to protest wilderness designations in general, calling them "communist takeovers." And closer to home, an off-road motorcycle club that stresses disaster preparation has declared an area known as Starvation Flats near Fish Springs, Utah, to be an "environmentalist-free zone." The loosely organized group sometimes refers to itself as the Apocalypse Squadron and has many members who dress like actors in a Mad Max movie. Over the course of several days they built a large Burning Man type of statue representing environmental icon Edward Abbey, and after piercing it with arrows and spears, burned it to the ground Saturday night. The flaming effigy was circled by dozens of cheering motorcyclists popping wheelies and brandishing swords, clubs, and battle axes.

I JUST WANT IT TO END

We ate dried meat and shared the tea from our last tea bag. Frank gathered some Mormon tea branches, and when our tea was finished, we steeped the spiny leaves in hot water and sipped the bitter, grassy brew. Speck leaned against my leg the whole time except for when she went to get a drink Lily offered her, and once to pee.

"So, I take it you're the truckers. The missing truckers," Frank said. "You've been in the news. From Kentucky, right?"

"Well, kind of," Lily said. "My husband and I were hijacked. He's dead. Hijackers shot him. Stan here, he stopped and helped us. We'd never seen each other before that."

"People were saying you joined the Recapture movement. That you drove your truck in to support the protest," Frank said. "That's what's been reported. The trucking company says no, that you wouldn't do that, but, I don't know, the sheriff says he thought you joined them."

"Well, that lets the sheriff off the hook as far as coming after us," Lily said. "That's a bunch of horseshit. They shot my husband and stole our truck. Joined them. Jesus!"

"And you must be the missing geologist," Frank said. "Sheriff said you were probably just out looking at rocks somewhere and got stuck or something."

"This sheriff sure seems to have it all figured out," I said. "No need to bother the terrorists. No, they haven't done anything wrong. People are just running out and getting lost and joining them right and left."

"Well, they kind of are," Frank said. "Quite a few people have shown up wanting to join in. There are a bunch of them hanging out in trailers and RVs in the Walmart parking lot in Price. It looks like a Rambo convention. And at the KOA. The main thing the law enforcement people have been doing is trying to keep more people from going out there and joining the protesters."

"And what are you doing?" I asked. "How did you get caught up in this mess?"

"I'm just an idiot, I guess," Frank said. "I'm a semi-retired journalist. I do some part-time work at the local weekly paper—the *Carbon County Drumbeat*. And I know the guy who's kind of behind this whole thing—Drew Peacock—you may have heard of him. He's a big off-road activist, you know. He fights every time the government wants to close a road or designate wilderness. He got this whole thing going with the protest ride down Dancing Water Creek when the BLM closed that area to vehicles. He claimed it was a highway his family used to get to their mining claims, and he got a bunch of people to join him. It all spiraled out of control from there. Anyway, I thought I could just come on out and interview him—you know—tell the inside story. But I ran into Phil first, and it all went to hell in a hurry."

"He's the one we've been calling the Viking." I said.

"Yeah, and I can see why," Frank said. "Don't know anything more about him, except he said he was an officer in the Recapture Brigade and he had that kid Marty with him following his orders. The one she shot."

"All this so some dicks could ride their damn toys around in the desert," I said. "Jesus. Jesus fucking Christ."

"Well, there's a little more to it than that," Frank said. "They think local issues and rights are being ignored by the government. They want some say in how the land is managed."

"They do have a say," I chimed in. "All those decisions are made through a public process. There's always a comment period. What about FLPMA and NEPA, all those endless sets of steps the government has to go through just to make the tiniest decision? They have a say. Everyone has a say."

"It's um, well, it's a hot subject around here," Frank said. "People think all the decisions get made back east, that they don't care what we think out here. And we're the ones who have to live with it, every day."

"They're just pissed because they don't like the outcome," I said. "They should hire lawyers to challenge the decisions, not load their guns and shoot people. That's all I'm sayin'."

"OK, come on," Lily said. "We're in a tight spot here. My husband's been killed and I was about to be raped and I shot a man and Stan shot some people and some asshole shot him in the face and he's blind and we've got a long way to go before we can sit around and chat about what the government does or who needs a lawyer. Stan, lean back and I'll wash your eyes out with some clean water. Then we'll get some sleep, because we're heading off that cliff into those badlands first thing in the morning. I'm ready to get the hell out of here. I don't care why this happened, I just want it to end."

Giant cabbages and pumpkins

It seemed strange to me having this guy Frank with us. I guess I didn't have any reason not to trust him, but we had been alone for so long now, just the two of us. Well, three, counting Speck, and Speck didn't seem to like Frank. It just seemed like one more thing to keep track of. Lily and I were in this together. We knew we could count on each other. And now I was completely dependent on her. I couldn't see a thing. Hell, I was nothing but a liability. A huge liability. And even if Lily was committed to helping me, Frank might not be. He could just let me walk off a cliff. Or double-cross both of us if the shit hit the fan.

"Lean back," Lily said, putting one hand behind my head and another on my chest. "Lean your head back. There. Can you open your eyes just a little? Open them up and I'll drip some water in, clean them up a little. They're getting all oozy and crusty."

My eyes had been very teary and drained constantly. Whatever was coming from them dried and made them stick shut. I wiped at my eyes and picked the crusty bits away from them and leaned my head back. I opened my eyes a little. They didn't seem to want to cooperate, so I opened my right eye with my fingers and Lily dripped some water in. It was such a shock that I jerked my head back.

"Hurt that bad?" she asked.

"Yeah. They're tender, and the water's cold, like icicles. Feels better now, a little better. Do the other one."

The left eye seemed to be in a little better shape. The water felt good in it, and after I had wiped the excess away from my face with my sleeve, I sat up and tried to open them.

"I can see a little," I said. "I can open them for a second and get a little bit of a look before I need to shut them. Can't say that I can see, but I can maybe get a quick look if I need to."

I exaggerated. Opening them was very painful. My right eye throbbed after being open for just an instant. I could see only the most obscure outlines of what was in front of me, but for some reason, I wanted them to think things weren't so bad. I wanted to be strong, to be useful, to be able to help Lily and Speck. Maybe if I pretended to be OK I would get better sooner. And I didn't want Frank to know how incapable I was. I didn't want him to start thinking of ways to get rid of me. I wanted to be an asset for these people, not a liability. Not a liability that could cost them their lives.

"Let's get some sleep," Lily said. "I don't think we have too much to worry about, nobody's going to surprise us here. Get some rest, Frank. I'm tired. You too, Stan, I bet you're exhausted. Night."

I covered up with the windbreaker and settled in between Lily and Speck. I was drained, and almost as soon as I lay down and got comfortable, bright scenes and colored patterns began appearing before me, much brighter and with much greater detail than I was able to see when fully awake, and I drifted directly to sleep and dreamed, and in my dreams Chris and I were at the state fair and were eating corn dogs and walking through an agricultural hall filled with rows and rows of giant cabbages and pumpkins, and little children had made playhouses in the vegetables with tiny doors and round windows and we laughed and I thought how nice it would be to live in a giant pumpkin.

Breaking News from Channel Nine News
Liz Nuñez reporting

"We are live in Price, Utah, with continuing coverage of the protest against the U.S. government's closure of certain roads to vehicular travel, and the designation of a large wilderness area. What began as a protest ride on ATVs three weeks ago has grown into what some are calling an armed occupation. We have with us the spokesman for the protesters, Travis Dmitrich. Can you tell us, Mr. Dmitrich, what is known about the status of the three people who are missing in the area of the protests?"

"Well, first off, it is not an "armed occupation," for heaven's sake. It's a group of citizens exercising their lawful right to speak out against federal tyranny and to peacefully protest. That's what is going on—peaceful protest. You people in the liberal media keep trying to make this into something that it isn't. It's a peaceful protest, nothing more."

"Thank you for that clarification, Mr. Dmitrich. Now, what can you tell us about the truckers, Mr. and Mrs. Clark? And the geologist, Mr. Watson. What can you tell us about them?"

"OK, well, I told you before he was at the second camp. That's all I know. As far as the truckers, as I've stated before, they donated their truck and its contents to the movement. They are part of the protest. They're not missing, they are doing their patriotic duty and standing up to government overreach."

"The friends and associates of the truckers disagree. They say that the Clarks would not join in such a protest and would have never turned their truck and cargo over to them."

"Well, sometimes people surprise you. I can assure you that they did join in the protest voluntarily."

"Have you spoken directly with them about that? Have you heard them state that they voluntarily gave their truck and cargo to the protest?"

"Well, no, not me personally. But others in the protest, leaders in the movement, have assured me that they have joined in and are fully supportive."

"Where are they then, why haven't they contacted their relatives?"

"They're in the camp. Communication is limited, as you know. There's almost no cell coverage out there, and there are only a few satellite

phones. You city people think there's phone coverage everywhere, but there's not. There's just not."

"Mr. Dmitrich, we have on good authority that the Clarks have not been seen in the Recapture camp. Their truck and cargo are there, but nobody has seen them. Where are they, Mr. Dmitrich?"

"They were in the camp, I can tell you that. Maybe they're in the second camp. That's where they probably are, in the second camp."

"And why would that be, Mr. Dmitrich? Why would they be in the second camp?"

"I don't know why, but that's where they are, that's all. No more questions. This interview is over."

"There you have it, the spokesman for the protest says the missing truckers are at the second, breakaway camp and not at the main camp. Each passing day seems to turn up more loose ends."

"We will stay on this story as it continues to evolve. Reporting from Price, in Carbon County, Utah, Liz Nuñez, Channel Nine News.*"*

Drinking Jack Daniel's and smoking Bull Durham cigarettes

Speck was the first to move. I could feel her rise quickly and stand at alert. She growled slightly and moved away from me. I raised up on one elbow and tried to see, only to realize that my eyes were crusted shut. I rubbed and picked at the crystalline caulk that held my eyes closed, and when I was able to open my lids a little, I realized that it was still dark, and that my eyes burned when I tried to open them.

"It's OK, Speck," I heard Lily say. "It's only Frank. Good girl."

"You lie back down," she said, touching me on my arm. "I've boiled some water so I can wash your eyes out again. It'll be cool in a minute. Just hang loose."

"How's the fuel holding out?" I asked. "Probably not much left."

"Oh, there's enough for another pot or two of water," she said. "We're about out. Well, we're about out of everything. Out of tea. Out of ramen. Nothing left but dried meat and Mormon tea."

"Maybe we could gather some more sego lilies, or even ricegrass seeds," I said.

"Maybe we should just get the hell out of here," Lily said. "How far to that place where your friends are going to meet us?"

"Might meet us," I said. "About ten miles, I guess. Windy, up and down miles. Through the badlands. Not too far. We should be able to get there in a couple of days if everything goes well."

"Things are going to go well. Nothing is going to get in our way," Lily said. "We've crossed the hump. The Viking is behind us, and we're headed out of this shithole. Two more days. That'll be a what, Thursday?"

"I don't even remember. I guess so. If it even matters."

Lily washed my eyes out, and they burned. I found that my left eye was a little better than my right, and I could open it a tiny bit and see a little of what was going on in front of me.

"This one big wound in your head is getting a little infected," Lily said. "I'm going to pull the scab away from it so it can drain. I guess that's what I should do."

I shrugged. "Probably so."

One frightening thing about being away from modern amenities like soap, clean water, and antibiotics, was infection. We didn't even think about infections much anymore. But they used to kill people all the time. People who lived the way we were—without access to medicine and even clean conditions. "Yeah, two days. Let's get to Dark Lord Cave by Thursday evening."

I could hear footsteps. "Dark Lord Cave? You mean Muley Cave—that the big cave in Muley Canyon? The one the University of Utah excavated back in the seventies?" Frank asked.

"You're pretty good," I said. "Yep, that's the one. How did you know about it?"

"Oh, I've traipsed around these parts for years," Frank said. "I actually visited the cave when the crews were here excavating. Came with Doc Westfall on one of his rock art jeep safaris. He knew the professor. We spent the night down there. Doc Westfall and Professor Manson got shit-faced. Stayed up all night drinking Jack Daniel's and smoking Bull Durham cigarettes. Those guys were a real trip."

"So you knew Manson. Wow, he's legendary. I got to meet Doc Westfall once—great guy. But Manson. So you drank with them?

"Oh, no. They drank. In Manson's tent. I had to hang out with the students and wash and label artifacts after dinner. Actually, it was a lot of fun. I even majored in anthropology for a while in college. Changed my mind and went into journalism. Glad I did. Archaeology is a fun hobby. I got to write about it a bit but never became an archaeologist."

"Then you know what a good place the cave is, with good shelter and a spring. My friends and I always said that is where we'd go when the apocalypse came. Seems like a good place to head, and maybe, just maybe, some of my pals will go there looking for me."

"If the Recapture Squad doesn't have anybody posted there," Frank said. "Seems like a place they'd want to check on."

"But it's so far from the road," I said. "At least a couple of miles."

"You're forgetting that there used to be a road down there. It was closed when the BLM designated it as a Wilderness Study Area. But the Recapture people don't care about that. They'd take great pleasure in driving their jeeps and ATVs on all of those closed roads and trails. Their jeeps—shit. My truck is one of the vehicles they have now. The one those guys had when we had that shootout with them. That was mine. They stole it from me and left me there. Assholes."

Frank had a very good point. I was thinking that there were no roads to Dark Lord Cave because they were not legal, but of course, there had been roads into that area long before any closures or wilderness designations. And the pirates wouldn't have any problem driving wherever they wanted to.

"I still think it's worth going to. We can be careful, and there's a chance my friends will try to meet us there. Or maybe leave a cache of stuff. Like a satellite phone. Who knows? Maybe I'm just having a big fantasy, I don't know. I don't know anything anymore."

"Well, I know it's time to walk, and we had better head into those badlands before the Recapture people come following our tracks and drag us back with them. Can you see enough to walk? What if we found you a stick to use for a cane? Could you get along with Speck and a cane, or would you like to hang on to one of us?" Lily helped me stand.

"I'll give Speck and a cane a try," I said. "I can see a little bit. I'll give it a try."

ONE BLIND, ONE NEARLY CRIPPLED

The going was easy for the first half hour or so. The air was cool and still, and Speck was a very patient helper, keeping just enough ahead of me to lead the way, but not pulling on the leash or stopping suddenly or doing anything to cause me difficulty. What a great dog. I could almost feel the energy passing between us, like a field that kept us connected and attached to each other, but which held us at a certain distance apart so we did not collide or interfere with each other. I felt that I was both being pulled along and bounced back when I got too close. Amazing. And necessary. My eyes burned and watered constantly. I was pretty sure that they were getting worse instead of better. I wondered if Speck and I would need to be tied to each other for the rest of my life. Or hers, I guess, since she was already six and probably had less than ten years left in her. Wait, what am I thinking? Imagining myself walking around blind for the next ten years when I don't even know if we'll be around tomorrow. Positive thinking, I guess, but imagining a future of blindness seemed to me to be a rather bleak form of daydreaming.

"Here we go," Lily announced, and I knew she meant that we were about to head down, over the drop-off that separated the drainage basin we had been crossing from the Badger Canyon Badlands, a masterpiece of erosion, a maze of meandering cuts and channels, fins and cliffs, ridges and spines—a hiker's nightmare. The badlands occupied a stretch of the country where erosion cut through crumbly, soft clayey shales rather than the sturdier sandstone that made up most of the underlying deposits in this area. Erosion had cut hundreds of steep-sided channels that, because of the soft and unstable nature of the deposits, started and stopped randomly, unlike the usual drainages that were continuous and flowed downhill. In the badlands, slopes caved in and collapsed into washes, damming them, which altered the direction of the flow, sometimes causing water to drain backward, or this way or that way, resulting in confusing and dangerous terrain, terrain devoid of vegetation and water. Badlands is a most appropriate name for such a stark and foreboding place.

It didn't take long for me to slip, fall, and slide into Speck, taking her with me as we slid on a crumbly, loose bed of stones and gravel. We stopped suddenly when my feet hit a solid embankment, jarring us both.

"Damn," I muttered. "Sorry, Speck."

"You two OK?" Lily said, coming back to us.

"Yeah, think so," I said, reaching for my stick and the leash. "You OK, Speck?" I asked her, putting my arms around my most amazing and patient friend who sat quietly on my lap. "I'm gonna have to take it real slow," I said. "Little steps."

"Yeah," Lily said. "It's awful, even for me. And I can see."

We could hear some gravel sliding behind me, and I braced for a collision. Frank had slipped too. He slid to a stop beside me.

"You know, when I was a kid we used to come out here and do that on purpose," he said. "Not as much fun now. Things don't work the way they're supposed to."

"Did you hurt yourself," I asked, "other than your butt?"

"Skinned my hands a bit, no big deal," he said. "It's my knees. They're shot. No cartilage left. I'm going to get new ones next month. Didn't plan on any big hikes until after surgery, but, well, I don't have much choice, do I?"

"We'll take it slow and easy," Lily said. We'll be out of these badlands in what, Stan, a couple miles? And I think it kind of levels out a little ways ahead of us. Come on, let's keep moving."

I turned Speck loose from the leash, as there was no value in it for me and only danger of being stepped on or crushed for her. I used my cane mostly as a brake, dragging it behind me and digging it into the slope when it got too steep. I opened my eyes frequently. Each attempt to see was painful, but the little glimpses I got helped me reconnoiter the treacherous slope. We made our way down into the badlands. I could hear Frank behind me and Lily ahead of me, but fairly quickly they both became faint as we strung out, making our way down through the dissected plateau. We pushed forward, downward, and each step was an adventure.

I wondered how far Lily had gone ahead. She could just walk away, keep going. What value was it to her, helping two completely dependent men, one blind, one nearly crippled? She should walk on out, strike out on her own, I thought. We are just going to drag her down, hurt any chance she has of getting out alive. Maybe she could make it out and send help for us. I stopped and listened for footsteps—hers or Frank's, and heard nothing. I hoped she had just left us. At least then one of us would have a chance. At least she might make it out. I realized then that I was no longer dreaming of a future, even a blind future. I saw nothing. I saw a future that was not there for me. Nothing. Shit. And, for some reason, I knew that Lily would not leave me. Us. I knew it.

When Lily stopped for a break she called to Speck, and I could hear her talking to Speck and petting her. "I think we are past the worst of it," she said. "Everything is kind of leveling out, and the walking won't be so treacherous. I hope. Here, have some water."

I took a sip. It tasted a little green, like from algae. Water from the stock tank. Probably full of giardia. Oh well. "How's our water holding out?" I asked.

"That's it," Lily said. "Frank has some, but we're about out. Isn't there a stream or spring once we get out of these badlands? I thought you said we'd find water pretty soon."

"Well, there's a spring at Dark Lord Cave, but that's a pretty long hike. The closest would be one of the seeps at the foot of the Old Woman—it's a spire at the edge of the cliffs just past the badlands that looks like a woman standing there. Or I've seen some potholes in this area. Might be some in the slickrock where the badlands peter out. That'd be my best guess."

"How far would that be?" Lily asked.

"If we are down at the bottom where the badlands level out, then maybe only a mile or two. Not far. We can make it this afternoon. Easy."

I tried to be positive and optimistic, and I hoped it didn't sound insincere, but I really did not know exactly where we were, and I didn't know for sure that there would be water in the potholes, but I thought there would be. I hoped there would be. And I wanted there to be. And I wanted Lily to think so.

Frank came slipping and sliding along shortly. His water was almost gone as well, and he agreed that there was likely water in the potholes at the edge of the badlands. "My dad lost a calf in one of those holes once. Big enough that it couldn't get out and drowned. Spoiled the water for drinking for a whole year."

When we started walking again, the terrain was indeed less steep. We seemed to be weaving back and forth in the bottom of a wash, kind of like a slot canyon, with steep walls rising on either side of us. I guessed that it was midday, but the canyon walls were so abrupt that sunlight hit us infrequently as we wove through the area. We had been walking for about a half hour at a fairly good rate, and I was starting to think that we would be about to exit the badlands for more open country, when I heard Lily exclaim, "Oh, no!"

"Dammit," she said. "Stop, you guys, stop."

"What's going on?" I asked, trying to peek through crusty, teary slits.

"We're screwed," Lily said. "Canyon's blocked. It's like a landslide or something blocked off the entire drainage. Dammed it up. And there's a giant mudhole. Looks like quicksand. Pure gooey, slimy crap. Nowhere to go but up. Dammit."

The Carbon County Drumbeat

Recapture update—latest news from The Swell

** Four men arrested in San Rafael Wilderness*

Four heavily-armed men in two side-by-side all-terrain vehicles were arrested early Friday morning in Cottonwood Canyon, south of the Dragerton Road. They fled when approached by Bureau of Land Management agents who were patrolling the northern boundary of the San Rafael Wilderness Area. The men had crossed into the roadless area and were apparently attempting to join the Recapture Brigade protesters. They were arrested for fleeing officers after the agents attempted to stop them for driving in a designated wilderness area.

During the chase, one of the ATVs overturned, injuring both the driver and the passenger. Following the accident, all four surrendered. The injured were taken to Castle View Hospital, where one man underwent surgery for internal injuries. As of Friday evening, both were listed in stable condition. The men will be identified when formal charges are filed. Anticipated charges include trespassing, use of a vehicle in a restricted area, and fleeing an officer.

Christmas or Disneyland

I knew exactly what we had run into. It was not uncommon in badlands like these. A side slope had sloughed off and blocked the main channel. When rain came, like the big rains last week, it made a lake, which turned to mud. We couldn't go farther down the wash, we had to go up and over somehow and find another way out. I sat down and loosened the straps on my pack.

"Which way," I asked. "Which way do you think we should go?"

"We can't go any way but back the way we came, at least for a ways. The sides are too steep," Lily said. "We're screwed."

"There was a kind of little pass off to the west, just maybe a quarter mile back that might be a way to get into the next drainage," Frank said. "I looked at it when we came by. I bet I could get up and over it. At least that's what comes to mind."

"I saw that too," said Lily. "Looked like there might be a little game trail or something going over it."

"Yeah, that was it," said Frank. "Maybe that's where the deer started going after the cave in. Makes sense. We should check it out."

I stood and adjusted my pack. "Guess we'd better head back up the canyon. Come on Speck, let's go."

When we reached the spot where Lily and Frank had seen the trail, we stopped.

"OK, tell you what," Lily said. "You guys stay put. We'll divide the water up, and I'll head up and see what this pass or trail leads to. No reason for you two to come along, you'll just slow things down. No offense. I'll find a way out and come back with some water, how about that? Will you boys be OK by yourselves?"

It seemed for a minute that Lily was acting like our mom, about to leave us behind for a trip to the store, when she was really doing something incredibly brave. We knew her solution was the only feasible one and that we were completely dependent on her.

"Take most of the water," I said. "You'll need it. We'll just sit here in the shade and rest. Just take water and maybe a stick of jerky. And the rifle. Be sure to take the rifle. Thank you, Lily. Thank you for doing this. Oh my God, thank you."

"Yeah, whatever," she said. "I'll go up to the top of this little crest and see where the game trail goes. I'll holler down and let you know what I'm up to. I may not make it back tonight, so don't panic. If it gets dark on me, I don't think I'll be running around in these badlands. But I'll be back. You can count on that. She gave me a hug. We both breathed deeply and held tight for long enough to assure me of our common commitment and dependence on each other. Especially my dependence on her. She petted Speck, said goodbye to Frank, and headed out. After about fifteen minutes she shouted that the path went down into the drainage to the west and that she was going to follow it. We all called goodbyes, and the sounds of our voices seemed to linger in the empty badlands surrounding us. I took off my pack, scooped away some of the loose deposits to make a comfortable spot to sit, and settled in. I could hear Frank doing the same.

"We're damn lucky to have her with us," he said. "She's a godsend."

"Sure is," I said. "Sure is."

We sat for quite a while, letting the silence, the heat, and the situation we found ourselves in settle in. I wished I could be with Lily, leaving this dead-end spot behind, heading toward Dark Lord Cave. I had started thinking of Dark Lord Cave the way a child might think of Christmas or Disneyland, or a believer might think of heaven. My heart leapt each time I thought of the place, as though it would bring relief from the horrible reality of fear, death, and now blindness that enveloped me and those around me. This heaven, this dream land, is really no more than an arc of void in the sandstone, a place where ages and ages of desert people had made their homes, a place hot and dry, with graceful, haunting painted figures dancing on the walls surrounded by tiny floating creatures and birds that seemed to be talking to them, reporting to them, telling them what they needed to know. A place where a cool spring flowed into a tiny pool at the rear of the cave, a cave that had the same, pleasant temperature year round, a cave that had been ravaged by artifact hunters and thieves before Professor Manson, the Dark Lord himself, excavated the site and made it famous as the place where the keys to thousands of years of prehistory were unlocked and revealed. The official name of the site was, of course, the more mundane Muley Cave, but some knew it as Dark Lord, and for many reasons, that was the more appropriate.

Rescuing our state from the federal invaders

"You've been to the cave?" Frank asked, as though reading my mind. "Recently?"

"About a year ago," I said. "I've been there five or six times over the years. Did a documentation of the gully erosion out in front of it for the Park Service about five years ago. They were worried that their tamarisk control effort was going to destabilize the wash and damage the cave. The willows came right back and took care of that. Fun project. We did a little work in the cave, too. I spent about a month down there."

"So you think somebody might be there waiting to meet you? Or leave some supplies or something?"

"Well, one of the people I worked with on that project, my friend Bill, we talked a lot in camp about going there if we needed to, like if, oh, you know how you talk around a campfire when you've been away from civilization for a while. It seems easy to imagine the worst. Gives you something to think about."

"You think he remembers those conversations?" Frank asked.

"Oh sure, and, well, he's the kind of guy who would come here and look for me. I'd do the same for him. I don't know, it might be just a fantasy, but it's at least a place to aim for. A goal. A better goal than just running, just running away. A place to run to. I don't know. Gives me some hope, I guess."

We sat for a while. I could hear Frank moving, and I opened my eyes a bit and could see that he was flexing and working one of his knees.

"Really bothering you?" I asked.

"Yep." He said. "I really strained them scrambling around when all the shooting was going on, then hiking all this way really did a number on them, especially the right one. Every step is, well, every step hurts like hell."

"We're quite a pair," I said. "I hope we aren't attacked by a chipmunk or a lizard or anything while Lily's gone. It'd kick our asses."

"No shit," Frank said. "Hope she's OK. I mean, for her sake, but for ours, too. We're pretty much screwed if something happens to her."

"That's for sure," I said. "Well, you'll probably have a good story for the paper, if we make it out of here, that is. Not the story you planned on, but quite a story."

"Sometimes things happen, don't they," he said. "I thought I'd come out and interview Drew Peacock and write a story about how he and his patriot friends were rescuing our state from the federal invaders. Guess it'll be a little more action packed than that."

"Is that what you really think, that these Recapture Brigade people are heroes? That they are doing something honorable? Do you really think that?"

"Calm down a little," Frank said. "No, I don't think that, but a lot of people around here do. I do think that the environmentalists could learn a little by listening to locals though, and maybe we wouldn't reach the kind of standoff we're in now."

"What do you mean?" I asked. "These guys want to ride ATVs all over the place and strip mine half the west for tar sand and oil shale and who knows what else. Soon there won't be anything left."

"It's really a little more subtle than that," Frank said. "I understand the environmentalist side. I really do. I've published articles in backpacking magazines and *High Country News* and places like that, but there's a side to the conversation that the environmentalists don't seem to be hearing, and it's getting us, well, it's getting us to the point that people are pulling out their guns. Something's gone wrong."

"Sure has," I said. "Sure has."

"Environmentalists don't see the land the way we do," Frank said. "You see its beauty. You see its majesty, its grandeur. You love the wildlife. You appreciate the silence, the clean air, the flowing streams. You see it as a wonderful treasure. And when you go back to Salt Lake City or Phoenix or LA or Philadelphia to your job as a lawyer or a manager or a business owner or doctor, you want it to stay just the way it was, for you to visit and enjoy, to gain inspiration from. To have respite from your daily life, a life that may not have much beauty or majesty or silence."

"Well, yeah, of course," I said. "That's right."

"Yes, but when you live here, you see those things too. You love the beauty and the silence and the wildlife. We see those things. We love them too. Perhaps more than you do. We have connections to these places. When I visit Raven Flats I remember coming here with my grandfather, rounding up his cattle to take them to their summer range. My folks were here and my aunts and uncles and cousins, and we all worked hard and we had names for every gully and hill, and we camped and slept on the ground, and we ate wonderful meals and the sunsets were the most beautiful you've ever seen, and we sat around the campfire, and Grandpa played the guitar and sang Jimmie Rodgers songs and Uncle Lyman played the harmonica, and I thought I was the luckiest boy alive.

"While you see beauty, I see the condition of the range. I see places where we could cut cedar fence posts and get firewood. I see the condition of the deer herd. I can tell whose cows are fat and happy and whose are struggling. You see, this isn't just a pretty place for me, I am part of it. I see beauty, but I also see the details, the living, breathing details. You talk about the ecosystem as if it is something apart, something people are separate from. Well, just look a little deeper, and you'll see that people have been part of this place for a long time. And we will be forever. A thousand years from now, we'll still be part of this place. I agree it should be kept up and not destroyed. That's critical. But not as an imaginary magic kingdom for city people to come and look at. Not a place where cowboys are props for pictures you and the Jetsons take from hover cars and monorails and ooh and aah and go back to fancy hotels in Las Vegas and talk about your wilderness experience. No. Maybe cattle grazing isn't the best use of this land, but the land deserves more than to just be a pretty thing to look at."

"But what about oil wells and mines?"

"You may only see an ugly road or a pump jack or a drilling rig, but what a lot of locals see is hope. Hope their son can finally find a better job. Hope that they can avoid bankruptcy. Hope for the future. We'd probably rather they not be just oil and gas and coal. We like clean air too, but we do drive cars—you do too—and turn on our lights. And we know what powers those things."

"But they destroy so much land for the wells and pipelines," I said. "And fracking, what about fracking? And global warming. There are lots of reasons oil and gas and coal need to be on their way out."

"Well, sure, all those things are right, but what are the alternatives? I, for one, would rather see an oil well than a vacation home or a weekend cabin, that's for sure. An oil well produces energy, which thousands of people will use to drive to work, take their kids to school, go on vacations. It produces jobs, good jobs. And the wells around here will only produce for twenty, maybe thirty years, and even if they last fifty or a hundred years, at some point they'll be closed up and the ground smoothed over and revegetated, and things will start healing." Frank lifted himself up a little, smoothed the ground under his seat, and settled back down.

"And that cabin? That second home? It'll be there forever, and when it falls down another will be built, and who benefits from it? The owner, that's all. And they built a road and dug water and sewer lines and put in a septic system, all so one owner and his family and pals could have a place to escape to on weekends and holidays. Yep, I'd rather see an oil well."

"That's a good argument to keep the land in federal hands instead of private," I said. "And maybe what we should be working on is cleaner resources, like solar and wind, stuff like that."

Frank picked a spine from a nearby stunted greasewood shrub and used it as a toothpick. "What we need is alternatives that provide hope for locals. And I don't mean cleaning motel rooms and washing dishes for tourists. That's not hope, that's demeaning and demoralizing."

The Carbon County Drumbeat

Recapture update—Latest news from The Swell

Pledge Keepers vow to protect Recapture Brigade

Following the arrest of four men attempting to join the Recapture Brigade this week, Pledge Keepers founder Randy Stewart asserts that he and members of his group will protect the protesters should federal marshals try to arrest them. The Pledge Keepers, best known for participating in a standoff with federal marshals last year at the Clovis Brady ranch in Nevada, has a long history of antigovernment activism.

"This is not over," Steward told reporters and fellow activists yesterday. "The government is hereby put on notice that it cannot arrest people for speaking out. We will be there to stand up for the persecuted patriots."

Stewart went on to say, "We support the constitution and rise up against government tyranny. We will protect these patriots and stand by them and their rights to free speech and to bear arms."

Many civil rights organizations, including the Civil Rights Coalition (CRC), have labeled Stewart a "right-wing extremist" and the Pledge Keepers as a possible terrorist group.

The Pledge Keepers website claims its membership includes more than 12,000 law enforcement officers, soldiers, and military veterans as members," although the CRC considers those figures to be inflated.

Cockeyed is the Word for It

We sat quietly for a while. The sun had dropped below the rise to our west, and the air was cooler and starting to flow down from the south. I wondered about Lily, and as the afternoon progressed toward evening, I resigned myself to likely not seeing her before morning. I realized that I wasn't just wondering where she was, I was worrying, spinning stories in my mind, dreading the worst, hoping, longing really, longing to see her again. I'm completely dependent on her. And not just physically. She's my source of confidence and hope. And I long for her. I do.

I took the tarp from my pack, spread it out in the bottom of the wash, picked up and shook the water jug.

"Not a lot left," I said. "My dad always used to say that the best place to keep water is in your stomach. I don't know. Saving a little to wet your lips once in a while probably helps your state of mind."

"Tell you what," Frank said. "Not that we don't trust each other, but, well, for peace of mind and all that, why don't we divide the water up right now. Then we'll each have some to drink or save or whatever. Then we won't be tempted to cheat. Or accuse the other guy."

"Good idea, Frank. Why don't you divide the water up, and I'll choose which bottle to take."

"Deal," he said. "Looks like we might have about a quart total. Not that bad, really."

Frank divided the water between our two bottles and let me select the one I wanted. As far as I could tell, they were identical. I liked Frank's idea and was starting to think he might be all right.

Darkness came slowly. Several times I tried to look around, but my eyes still burned, and it seemed that when I looked through them, things were blurry. I cleaned away the crusty gunk from the corners of my eyes, and Speck nosed my face and licked around my eyes. I figured it couldn't hurt, and let her doctor me for a few minutes. I gave her a little drink in the water bottle lid.

"I'll save a little of mine for the pup too," Frank said. "I owe her that at the very least." He reached over and petted Speck. "Kinda wish I had my boy Bluey along. He's a good dog. You'd like Bluey, Speck. He's a good guy. I miss him."

"What kind of dog is Bluey?" I asked.

"Heeler," Frank said. "Blue heeler. As you probably guessed from the very creative name. He's got one blue eye, just like Speck. They say dogs with one blue eye can see better in the dark. I don't know if it's true or not, but that's what they say."

"I always thought it makes them look crazy, like they're, well, unbalanced," I said.

"Cockeyed, cockeyed is the word for it." Frank laughed.

"It really is a pretty sunset," Frank said. "Too bad your eyes aren't working too well. They'll get better. I got a bunch of sawdust packed into my eyes once. Couldn't even open 'em for a week. Turned out OK."

Our earlier conversation was still running around in my mind. "You know, I get what you're saying about environmentalists." I said. "I mean, it's not just about recreation and beauty, but, well, those seem to be the things that get people out to places like this. People who want to protect it. Seems like the rural people just want to use the land up to make some money now, and to hell with tomorrow. Sometimes it seems like that."

"Well, you're right. A lot of locals do think like that. And so do a lot of city folks. They don't care what or who they hurt, as long as they can get their two bits worth."

"And, you know," I said. "It's not like I have anything against ATVs either. Or mountain bikes or motorcycles. If people would use them respectfully, and stay out of some areas. Seems like there are tracks everywhere, straight up mountains, down creeks, all over. And that's what the ads show, too. You don't see an ATV ad with people riding carefully and enjoying nature. No, it's an adventure, jumping off of hills and doing wheelies and tearing things up. That's what I don't like."

"I agree," Frank said. "But the way local people see it, the problem is access. They want access to places that get cut off, and they resent that."

"That's a real issue," I said, "but it seems to me like the ones who want access are the oil companies and pipeline companies and outfits that make their investors money by tearing the shit out of places so they can take anything valuable out and sell it. They get the locals riled up and tell them that their rights are being violated when it's really the mega-conglomerates behind these Recapture people. Multinational corporations. And don't forget the motorcycle and ATV companies. They put a lot of money into these kinds of campaigns and the so-called associations that try to 'take back America.' They want to take it back *from* America *for* the oil companies."

"You know, those investors aren't just billionaires. If you have a retirement fund or mutual fund or anything, you might have oil or coal stock. Most of us do. And we like it when we make money and hate it when we lose. I do, and I ain't no rich man. No rich man's son."

"There are ways to invest that get away from dirty technology, but it takes work," I said. "I guess it is just the trajectory that needs to change. It's hard to get away from dirty technology because we have relied on it for so long. It built the modern world, but it's time to move on, move to better, cleaner ways to power our lives. Until we do, I guess we'll be arguing about what to do next, how to move along without killing ourselves and wrecking everything in our path."

"I'm not gonna argue with you on a lot of that," Frank said. "I do think we need more talking and less yelling, more listening. These local folks aren't all a bunch of anti-environment motorheads. They have some legitimate points. They really do."

We both seemed to realize that we had talked ourselves out and that we were not going to accomplish much more by debating environmental law in the bottom of a gully while our fate rested on a woman from Kentucky finding her way around in the Badger Canyon Badlands in the San Rafael Swell of central Utah, a place she had never even heard of until last week. I had only known her for a short time, and now my life was completely dependent on her. I worried about her and knew that it was more than just worry. Much more.

I dozed off pretty quickly after we stopped talking, and I dreamed of Lily walking across the desert, and pretty soon she was riding a camel and racing down sand dunes being chased by people who looked like the Viking in jeeps and then I was running alongside a camel holding on to its bridle and trying to keep up because I couldn't see and I could hear the jeeps behind me and I felt like I was sinking in quicksand and I rubbed my eyes and they burned and when I opened them I could see a crescent moon straight overhead. My mouth was dry, and I could hear Frank snoring. As I sat there, I realized that I had never been in such a dismal situation and that if I thought about things clearly I would know that there was almost no hope. No hope. That's a tough spot to find yourself in.

I was reminded of a book I'd read about the Shackleton expedition whose ship was trapped in pack ice. The crew endured unspeakable odds to survive. I remember thinking when I read the book that I would probably have just given up. I couldn't imagine having the strength to go on in the face of such incredible hardship. I recall that the men talked about their wives and families and gained strength through committing themselves to making it out to rejoin their loved ones.

And here I am, in a pretty tough spot. Shot, nearly blind, hungry, almost out of water, being hunted by vicious killers. What could be worse? So I started listing the things that gave me hope. Like thinking of Chris. And Lily. And Speck. And Frank. And Bill. And I knew that giving up was not a consideration because none of us was going to give up. We would all dig deep and do everything we could to get out. For ourselves and for each other. Just go to sleep. Save your energy and water, and Lily will come hiking over that hill in the morning. I imagined Lily coming over the hill with two big bottles full of water, and all was good, and I went to sleep.

An Overwhelming Stroke of Good Luck

My first clue that dawn was approaching was the smell. Something of an organic, grassy essence seemed to waft up from the north. Speck caught it too. She stood, shook, sniffed a bit, and walked up the gully to pee. I found the water bottle and took a sip. Very little left. Maybe only a cup. One precious cup. I hope Lily is holed up somewhere comfortable and close and that she has full jugs of water, and when she gets here we'll drink up and start walking and get to Dark Lord Cave by evening. Find Bill and the troops he'll have with him and be in my own bed by the next day. What day would that be? Wednesday? I realized that I wasn't sure. I'd need to work it out later, I thought.

Frank was moving, and I cracked my eyes open to look around. I couldn't see much, but it seemed like the sky had tiny flecks of blue and pink appearing and disappearing, a sort of teaser for the coming dawn. Lucky there are no clouds out. We'd be really screwed in the bottom of this gully in the badlands if we had any kind of rain. Even a little sprinkle can turn this clay into slick goop that's like walking on axle grease that globs on to your feet so that each step carries five pounds of muck along with it.

"Where's your dog?" Frank asked.

"What? Crap!" I turned and tried to look around. "She was just here. Maybe five minutes ago. You can't see her?"

"No," Frank said, standing to look around. "Not as far as I can see."

"Speck," I called. "Speck, come here girl." I whistled and made clucking noises with my cheeks. "Here Speck, come on Speck, here girl."

"Maybe she went to get a drink," Frank said. "They can smell water from a long ways away. She was thirsty and she smelled water. She'll be back. She's not the type to run off, is she?"

"No," I said. "Especially since I got hurt. She's stuck right by me. That's why this is kind of strange."

"There's some explanation," Frank said. "They're a lot smarter than we are sometimes. She'll be OK. And she definitely won't leave you. Hell, I've watched the way she looks after you, like you're her pup. She'd probably carry you around by the scruff of your neck if she could. She'll be back. All wet and muddy."

I sat back and tried to calm myself down. I'd wait, wait quietly, not waste energy or water, just wait. Wait for Speck, wait for Lily. Wait. Just wait.

But I fidgeted. I couldn't sit still. My mind wouldn't stop racing. I'd never been good at waiting. I hated waiting rooms and sitting forever at a government office waiting for your number to be called. I felt more anxious than I'd ever been, as if I was in a line waiting to jump off a cliff. Maybe that was exactly what I was doing. Waiting. Waiting for something to happen, something that would most likely be awful.

I'm hungry and thirsty and uncomfortable and I haven't seen my wife in weeks and might never see her again, and I'm sitting in the bottom of a gully and my dog's gone and now I just have to wait and hope Lily is OK and will bring us water and help us out of here, because if she is hurt or lost, or even, shit, I can't even think it, if she is dead, I'm dead. Frank is dead. And nobody will ever find us. A rainstorm will come sometime in the next week or so, the gully will run full and fast, and our dried and half-mummified bodies will wash like driftwood into the muddy pond dammed up behind the caved-in cutbank below us and we'll be entombed. Maybe after 100,000 years or so some hiker will see my bones embedded in stone, and he'll make a name for himself describing the fossil skeleton of some ancient human from the days when people still had these archaic bodies.

"You know, Frank, there's a good chance we'll die out here. Never be heard from again. I guess there are worse places to die."

"Plenty of them. Like in a hospital bed with wires and tubes stuck in every hole you have and some you didn't have, and nothing but machines and monitors and beeping and buzzing and alarms going off. I think I'd rather just drift off here in this gully. Or I'd rather not just yet, but when the time comes, you know. . ."

"I'm reminded of a hiker who died out near Moab that Abbey wrote about in *Desert Solitaire*," I said. "Abbey said he wanted to congratulate the man on his good taste in a place to die. Something like, 'To die in the open, under the sky, is an overwhelming stroke of good luck.' Something like that."

"Abbey had a keen sense of this country, that's for sure," Frank said. "*Desert Solitaire* is an incredible book. Everybody who ever comes to this part of the world should read it."

"I'm surprised to hear you say that," I said. "Abbey was a pretty rabid environmentalist. Ahead of his time."

"Oh yeah, sure. But *Desert Solitaire* is a love story. And I'm a sucker for a love story."

"What do you think of his other books?" I asked. "Have you read any of his other books?"

"Sure," Frank said. "Not all of them, he wrote a bunch. But I've read *The Monkey Wrench Gang* and a couple others. *Desert Solitaire* and *The Monkey Wrench Gang* are classics. I don't really care for some of his others. And his later work, like post–*Monkey Wrench*, are not even readable, if you ask me. I couldn't get through them."

"I tend to agree," I said. "But those two are incredible. Really something. I wish I could have met him."

"Are you sure?" Frank asked. "Because I knew him. Well, kind of, not well. I met him a couple of times through mutual friends. I thought he was kind of a jerk. Womanizer. Maybe he wasn't always like that, but I didn't enjoy meeting him. He was a great talent though. Out there, but a great talent."

"I think he inspired a lot of people," I said. "And that's a big accomplishment for anyone."

"Oh sure," Frank said. "I half expected somebody to make a serious attempt to blow up the Glen Canyon Dam. Or some other dam, like Flaming Gorge. I guess the Feds did a pretty good job of protecting them."

"Well, people have done a lot of monkey wrenching over the years," I said. "Smaller scale, like putting sand in the air intakes of heavy equipment, trashing survey markers, slashing tires, stuff like that."

"Yeah, there's been some of that kind of thing. Still going on," Frank said. "You know, what these Recapture Brigade people are doing isn't that different if you think about it."

"What?" I said. "What are you talking about? Abbey wanted to protect these places, these Recapture people want to wreck them."

"Well, what they all want is for government to make decisions they like, and whether it's monkey wrenching or Recapturing, it involves people taking things into their own hands. Maybe through frustration, who knows. But there's more in common between Abbey and the Recapture people than you might think."

"Maybe," I said. "Maybe. But there's a big difference between wanting to save something and wanting to use it up. Protect things as opposed to damaging and destroying them."

"Yes, certainly," Frank said, "but there's also a difference between those who make their living from the land and those who are removed from it. Those far removed from the land, and that's most people these days, don't realize that taking from the land is how we all make our livings. The land, and, of course, air and water and sunlight, provide everything, and we have to do something to them to get what we need. We plow up the land to plant crops. We dig to get minerals and gas and oil. Lots of people are several steps removed from the land and don't realize how we rely on the natural resources to keep us alive, and how we have to alter the land to make it productive. It's like the difference between a gardener and some-one who eats salad from a salad bar. Or between a rancher and a bologna eater. Bologna eaters think food comes from a store, gas from a pump, electricity from an outlet. Most environmentalists are bologna eaters, even the vegans."

Tribal groups demand action

Indian Country News

Leaders of Native Earth Guardians, a coalition of tribes that advocates for better protection of traditional lands, blasted government officials for their lack of action regarding the "ride in" currently being staged in Utah's San Rafael Swell. Board members Shedrick Chapoose and Vyrveen Serawop, both members of the Ute Tribe, led a rally in Salt Lake City Tuesday. Two hundred or so marchers chanted "Mother Earth, Sacred Land" and were accompanied by drumming, singing, and a number of dancers in traditional regalia. From a podium set up at the Indian Cultural Center, Chapoose and Serawop spoke passionately about the need to care for the land, and the responsibility the government has to protect it. "Native Earth Guardians worked hard to support greater protection for these lands, and now these thieves race their machines through our waters and soil, destroying our Mother, desecrating her and mocking people who care for her," Chapoose said. "Arrest them! Arrest them!" cried Serawop, and the crowd joined her in chanting for the arrest of the trespassers.

"Who is here to speak for the thieves?" Serawop asked. "And why is the sheriff letting this happen? Because they are white men? Would they look the other way if Indians violated the law? No, no, no, no. This is wrong. Arrest them. Arrest them."

Law enforcement personnel stayed well back from the well-behaved crowd. Carbon County Sheriff Cortland Hackney issued a statement later in the day affirming his commitment to enforcing the law and his desire to end the Recapture protest peacefully.

Speakers from the Northwestern Band of the Shoshone, the Skull Valley Goshute, the Paiute Tribe of Utah, and the Navajo Nation reinforced the frustration their people felt when it appeared that the ATV riders were being left alone and even supported by the government. "If those Recapture people were Indians, the government would have mowed them down the first day," said Chapoose. "They would have had another Wounded Knee."

Representatives of environmental groups and elected officeholders joined the Native Earth Guardians in calling for government action to end the Recapture protest. "The government needs to assert itself," said Rachel Larsen, of the group Great Old Gals for Wilderness. "The government needs to show that it will not abide lawlessness in any form," she said.

* * *

A small group of armed supporters of the Recapture group assembled across the street from the rally but were quickly cordoned off from the marchers by Salt Lake City Police. Several of them carried signs, and one banner read "Recapture Are Roads," which Serawop pointed out from the podium as a perfect example of the kind of people they were up against.

Native Earth Guardians plans to join the environmentalists' protest camp in Buckhead Wash to raise awareness of the issues at stake.

OLD WOMAN SPIRE

I had to think about that for a while. And no, I didn't feel lucky to be about to die here in the desert, even if it is a place of beauty. I'd rather put it off for a while. Like forty or fifty years. I wondered where Speck was. I hoped she was OK.

I took another sip of water and realized that I had maybe one or two small sips left.

"What time do you think it is, Frank?" I asked.

"Almost noon," he said. "Eleven fifty."

"Maybe sitting here until our blood thickens and our brains dry up and we die like Abbey's hiker isn't the best strategy," I said. "Feel like walking?"

"Sure do," Frank said. "It might be our only chance at this point. Let's do it."

I gathered my gear together, rubbed my eyes, shouldered my pack, picked up my cane, turned up the gully, and waited for Frank.

"Want to lead the way?" I asked him.

"Follow me," he replied, and started up the trail.

We started out briskly and were beginning to breathe heavily by the time we were halfway up from the bottom of the gully to the crest of the game trail, following the route Lily had taken yesterday. Frank was probably thinking exactly what I was, but afraid to say out loud. Something's happened to Lily. She would have been back by now if she had just hiked to the water—either to the potholes we had talked about or to the seep at the Old Woman spire. Whatever it was, whether she was hurt, lost, captured, no matter, we had to find water soon, or we would be done for. The horror of thinking something has harmed Lily cloaked me and drained my soul.

We settled into a steady pace as we angled up across the slope toward the crest west of the wash we had been following. Frank stopped at the top, and we rested for a few minutes.

"She came this way and headed down into this next wash," he said. "Pretty straightforward. And Speck came this way too."

The afternoon sun was hot, and my mouth was dry, but I determined that I would save the last of my water as long as I could hold out.

"Should be all downhill from here, right," I said. "And when we hit the bottom of the badlands, we can either head for the potholes or turn for the spring at the Old Woman. I'm thinking the Old Woman is closer."

"I think so, too," said Frank. "I can see the spire from here. Shouldn't take us more than oh, about an hour maybe, to get there. We're making pretty good progress."

"Knees holding out?" I asked. "We're starting some pretty good downhill. That'll take a toll."

"They'll be all right." Frank said. "A nice cool drink will go a long way toward making my knees feel better. I'll be OK."

We took the rest of the hike at a more relaxed pace, measuring our progress by our thirst, looking every once in a while at the Old Woman, to see how much farther we needed to go. My eyes burned and my vision was blurry, but I was able to stay behind Frank and look around occasionally. I thought about putting a pebble in my mouth to help fight my thirst, an old Boy Scout trick I had heard of, but my mouth was so dry I was pretty sure a dry pebble would have just stuck to my tongue and made things worse. Not only was my mouth dry, my eyes were hardly watering, and my sinuses seemed to be bone dry as well. I realized that I was nearing a crisis and that my organs were probably starting to react to dehydration. Keep it up, step by step, I told myself. I started counting steps. I often count things. Steps, stairs, people, houses, anything. I'm a compulsive counter. I know how many steps each set of stairs in my house and office has and how many steps I take between the bedroom and the bathroom, between the house and the garage. Maybe I've been preparing for blindness all my life. What a terrible thought. Blind people must count steps. Surely they do. I imagined myself walking blindly around my house, happily remembering that five steps from the kitchen, I needed to turn right and head down the hall for six steps to the door of our bedroom. I had just reached 670 steps when Frank shouted "Look out!"

I had no time to react before I was hit hard in the chest and nearly knocked over. A slap of wet tongue hit my face. "Speck," I cried, and sank to my knees. "Speck, my goodness, Speck."

I hugged her and kissed her and she jumped all around and I could feel that her coat was wet and she smelled like a swamp.

"I told you she'd be all wet and muddy," Frank said. "We're almost there, almost to the seeps."

I didn't count, but it was probably only 100 steps to the spring. We took our packs off and filled our bottles.

"We want to be careful and not drink too much too fast," I said, knowing that we would be tempted to gulp down a gallon or two.

"Good idea," Frank said. "Spread it out, let it seep in to all the nooks and crannies. We have time. No rush."

"Any sign of Lily," I said, trying to look around.

"Looks like she's been here," Frank said. "Her tracks are here. And, well, shit. There are others too. Hers are fresher, but somebody else has been here pretty recently. Somebody with big boots."

"Damn," I said. "That can't be good."

That'll Be a Good Look

We settled in and made ourselves a little camp in some oak brush 100 yards or so from the seep, up on a small rise that gave us a view of the spring and the surrounding area. We sipped water and chewed on dried meat, and we wondered who had made the footprints and if they had anything to do with Lily's whereabouts, and we worried about our friend and what it might mean for us.

"Sometimes I wish you could talk, Speck," I said. "I really wish you could."

Gradually we became rehydrated, and some of our energy returned. My eyes felt a little better, although I could tell that there was something serious going on with them. Maybe they were badly damaged, maybe the infection was getting worse, it was hard to know. The smaller wound in my forehead was healing, but the larger one, the deep and painful one, was festering. I'll probably have a big scar there. It'll be a good conversation starter. Yes ma'am, that's where I took a bullet in a gun battle with a pirate. Maybe I'll lose one eye, and I'll wear a patch. Yep, that'll be a good look.

"Looks like there were two people down by the spring," Frank said. They didn't spend much time at the seeps, just kind of walked around a little and left. Lily wasn't there too long either. Probably just long enough to drink and fill her bottles. I bet she saw the footprints and took off as soon as she could. I didn't see anything to make me think they ran into each other. Down near the water at least."

"I guess we could head for the cave in the morning," I said, thinking out loud, "If she's OK, she knows where we're headed. Kinda. No. No, we can't do that. We have to find Lily. We'll use this as a base camp and search for her. That's what we'll do. We need to find her. She was trying to help us and got hurt or lost or something. There's no way we're leaving here without her."

"Yeah. She might need us, bad off as we are," Frank said. "And we can try to figure out what's going on with the other people. Maybe they're your friends. Maybe they're rescuers, good guys. Maybe they found Lily and are searching for us, who knows."

"There's a lot we don't know," I said. "I'm with you though, maybe my friend Bill made those tracks. Maybe we'll be rescued and out of here by tomorrow."

But we both knew that there were many possibilities that did not end happily, and for the time being, we chose not to focus on them. At least, we chose not to discuss them. I thought we were both wondering if the prints were made by unsavory characters, people we would not be over-joyed to see. And we were both probably running through scenarios of what we would do, how we would react. People say worry doesn't get you anywhere, but worry leads to planning, it leads to thinking things through, and it helps you prepare. We didn't need to prepare for running into friendly people, but if we weren't prepared for problems, we'd have little chance of dealing well with them.

"Why do you think the government has let this go on like this?" I asked. "Are they afraid of these guys? Afraid of what might happen next?"

"Maybe they recognize the legitimacy of the movement," Frank said. "They know that these people have a valid point and they are backing off."

"I don't know about that," I said. "I really don't. I do think that if the Recapture Brigade had been made up of Natives or Blacks or Hispanic or middle-eastern-looking people the insurrection would have lasted about fifteen minutes."

"I hadn't thought of it that way," Frank said. "But we could think up all kinds of 'what ifs' and none of them would really matter. Not have any real bearing."

"But what is true is that these Recapture people are nearly all white people. White people waving American flags," I said. "They're not Black. It's a lot easier to justify shooting brown and Black people, especially if they're young and male. They're seen as The Other by a lot of people, people in power, including police and military. They're a threat to white people and their grip on everything. If they were to take up arms the country would throw everything it had at them."

"So you're saying that legitimacy has nothing to do with it? That the validity of their complaints doesn't matter?"

"Yes. Yes, that's exactly what I'm saying. And, well, the Recapture Brigade's complaints aren't legitimate anyway, by any means. They're alive and hunting us down right now because they are white and patriotic, and the government is leaving them alone. If the government blew them up, a lot of white people would be upset. And more of them might get out their guns."

"So you're saying that the government might be worried that things would get out of hand?" Frank said.

"Exactly. And it could. For all the wrong reasons," I said.

"That's where we'll disagree," Frank said. "Some of their complaints are at least reasonable. At least they should be discussed."

"Yep, that's where we disagree," I said. We sat quietly for a few minutes. "Shit, Frank, I'm sorry. We're in this together. We don't need to be arguing. Sorry. We can debate this whole thing next week. When we're not hiding in the bushes wondering where Lily is. And hell, where Speck is. Have you seen her? She was just here."

"No, I don't see her. Maybe she went over to the spring to get a drink. I, um, I can't see her over there. We're losing the light, but no, can't see her. I'll keep an eye out."

Breaking News from Channel Nine News
Liz Nuñez reporting

"Channel Nine News *has obtained new information that may be relevant to the case of the persons missing in the vicinity of the land-use protests in the Price, Utah, area. At least three people have been reported missing and may have fallen victim to foul play in the San Rafael Swell just to the south and west of Price. Two truck drivers, Craig and Lily Clark, have been reported missing, along with their semi and the contents of its trailer. Spokespeople for the Recapture Brigade say the couple voluntarily gave their truck and its contents of food and related products to the protest, but their associates and families say they would not do such a thing. Another man, Salt Lake geologist Stan Watson has been missing in the area, and more recently, Frank Saccomano, a reporter for the* Carbon County Drumbeat *newspaper, on assignment to cover the protests, has not been heard from for several days and is feared missing. Saccomano's wife, Velma, reported receiving a garbled voicemail from her husband the evening of June tenth, the day he left town, that seemed to indicate that he was in some kind of trouble. She reported it to Sheriff Cortland Hackney, who told her he would investigate, but she says she has heard nothing from her husband or the sheriff in days."*

"Please tell us, Mrs. Saccomano, what you heard on that voicemail."

"Well, I was out watering the garden and away from the phone, so I wasn't able to answer when he called. He left a message, but his voice was breaking up, and I could tell there was something wrong. He said something like 'they took my truck' or something like that. I couldn't really tell, and it only lasted a minute, maybe less, then it was over. I know the cell coverage is bad out there, but he has a satellite phone with him. I don't know why he hasn't used it to call for help, unless, well, I don't know, unless he really is in some kind of trouble or hurt or something. I wish the sheriff would go out and look for him, but they keep acting like nothing's wrong."

"How do you know he wasn't calling from the satellite phone? Maybe he was using it."

"No, the caller ID showed his cell. I tried to call him right back, but he didn't answer. I even tried to call the satellite number, but he didn't answer it either."

"Mr. Saccomano knows that country pretty well, doesn't he? You don't think he's lost, do you?"

"Oh, heavens no. That whole area is like his backyard. His family ran cattle out there for years. He spent every summer out there when he was a kid. No, he wouldn't be lost. But if something happened to his truck, or if somebody did something to it, like I said, it sounded like he said 'they took my truck,' then, well, that makes me worry. His knees are bad. He's going to have his knees replaced next month up in Salt Lake. He can't walk far, and that worries me. This whole thing worries me. He is friends with Drew Peacock, you know, the guy who started this whole thing, so maybe Drew will help him. I hope someone does because the sheriff doesn't seem to want to do anything."

"Thank you, Mrs. Saccomano. Well, there you have it, yet another family member has reported a loved one missing in the area of the protest, but none of them are receiving much assurance from the sheriff that a search or even serious consideration of the fate of their relatives is underway."

"We will follow this and related stories as they continue to unfold. Reporting from Price, in Carbon County, Utah, Liz Nuñez, Channel Nine News. *"*

Speck must have found her

Soon the night was fully dark, and I worried because Speck had not returned. She might have chased after a rabbit. There are quite a few cottontails around, maybe she went after one and got turned around. No, she wouldn't have gotten lost. I worried about the people who had made the footprints. Had she approached them, did they catch her and keep her? Or worse? I called and whistled for her and finally gave up when my voice got rough. Well, this is not the first disappointing development of the last few days. And just when I thought we were getting close to possible escape, to possible rescue. We could be at Dark Lord Cave in two days. But dammit, where are Lily and Speck. I sat back against an oak trunk and folded my arms across my chest and immersed myself in disappointment.

A sharp cracking of a branch and rustling of leaves had us both reaching for our weapons. I could hear Frank stand, and as the sound got closer, I felt a rapid rush of fear rise in my chest.

"It's Speck," Frank said, and she ran to me and greeted me with a madly wagging tail, a kiss on the face, and then just as suddenly, she spun around and sprinted away.

"Hey," I called, "Speck, Speck, come back!"

We listened for the sound of her running through the undergrowth, but heard only silence. What was going on? Where could she be?

"CaCaw, CaCaw," came a call from over near the spring.

"What the fuck?" Frank said. "What's that?"

"CaCaw, CaCaw," I replied. "CaCaw. Over here."

"Huh?" Frank said. "What are you doing?"

"It's Lily," I said. "That's our call. It's her. Speck must have found her."

And indeed she had. Speck came running up, and steps behind her came Lily. I rose to greet her, and she, Frank, and I stood and hugged and laughed and cried. We hopped and cheered with delight, and joy swirled over and around us as Speck ran in circles and danced along. Lily turned to me, and we embraced. We held each other and swayed back and forth. I cried. Relief ran through me, and I pulled her in tight. I wanted to hold her forever.

"God, I'm so happy to find you guys here," Lily exclaimed, stepping back. "When Speck came running up I wondered if something had happened to you, since she never leaves your side. I started crying, then when she left me and then came back, I hoped it meant that you were here. This last couple of days have been a nightmare. A freaking nightmare."

"When you didn't come back, we thought something had happened to you, so we came here," I said. "We've been OK except for about running out of water."

"Well, there were two guys here yesterday," Lily said. "Or I would have been right back with water. When I got here I saw footprints around the spring, so I filled the bottles and was going to head straight back to you when I saw them. Two men, like army dudes, carrying guns and all covered with gear. They were over there, north of here, walking west. I don't think they saw me, but I just watched them until it was almost dark, and then I headed back to find you guys. That's when I got lost."

"What do you mean?" I asked.

"I went back the way I came down, but somehow I got on the wrong game trail and I wound up all the way back at the top of the badlands, you know, where we were a couple days ago, before we started down. It took me a while to find our trail, and then by the time I found the place where I left you it was late and you were gone and I, well, shit, I thought all kinds of bad things might have happened to you. Man, what a day. Thank God you're OK. I'm glad Speck came back after me. I'd still be hiding out there, worried about walking up on some freaking pirates.

"We saw the footprints," Frank said, "but we didn't see any people. Maybe they've left the area. Could you tell anything about them? I mean, what if they were friendly. Well, how would you find out until it was too late to do anything. If they weren't friendly, I mean."

"For now, we're all back together," I said. "And, Speck has really risen to the occasion. Thanks Speck, you've saved our sorry asses a bunch of times so far."

"I'm so happy to be back with you two, I really am," Lily said. "Last night was awful, and if I hadn't found you just now, I'd be about done for." She came over to me and sat close and put her arm around my knees. I reached out and put my hand on her shoulder. I wanted to tell her how much I had missed her, but was afraid I'd say too much, say the wrong words.

"Well, we've all been worked up and frightened, and now we can rest a little and make some plans," I said. "Let's get a good night's sleep, have a little to eat, and head out early in the morning. I think we can almost make it to Dark Lord Cave. We could be to the cave, and maybe to people who will help us, by the day after that. Let's make that our goal. Something to plan for. Something to set our sights on. Let's rest and do what we can to get out of this hell in the morning."

Like Grammy's Turkey Dinner

Coyotes cried, fought, partied, howled, and generally engaged in vocal mayhem for most of the night, keeping Speck on edge and occasionally disrupting our sleep. When Speck bristled to the edge of camp, growling, and the first songbird calls announced the coming day we rose, readied our gear, hoisted our packs, and headed to the spring, where we drank and filled our containers. Lily led the way and Frank took up the rear, while I stumbled along half-blindly in between. We were like horses returning to our barn after a long day of work, and with eager steps we made our way toward Dark Lord Cave and dreams of release from the clinging oppression that had been smothering us. The earliest light silhouetted the distant sandstone shoulders that marked the head of Muley Canyon, the entrance to our passageway, the familiar and welcoming avenue that led to the Cave of Our Salvation. We strode across long exposures of slickrock, as smooth as a sidewalk, and struggled through drifts of the finest sand, each step sinking in the liquid-like powder that filled our shoes and slowed us down, at times nearly halting our progress.

When we crossed a sloping flat, thick with waist-high sage that forced us to weave and wind our way through the fragrant, flowering, spiny shrubs, Frank remarked on how many rabbits we were flushing out. When I heard the sharp report of a firearm, I jumped but knew immediately that Frank had shot a rabbit. When we stopped in a dense stand of junipers, Frank built a small but hot fire, and when it had died down, laid some piñon and juniper fronds and needles on the coals, then the skinned carcass, and he covered it with more needles and coals and topped it all with a layer of branches, duff, and soil. Small puffs of smoke curled from a few rifts in the oven's domed earth covering, and Frank seemed pleased with himself.

"This'll be the best meal we've had in ages," he said. "We'll remember this rabbit for the rest of our lives, I'd wager."

"I think we're in pretty good shape," Lily said. "Considering that we've not gotten too far. I bet we've only gone maybe two miles, and the day's half over."

"Those dunes sucked," I said. "Glad to be past them."

"Yeah, they killed my knees," Frank said. "I'm sorry for slowing you down, but, well, I'm having a tough time."

"You're all right, Frank," Lily said. "We'll be fine right here if we need to rest your knees. We'll drop into that Muley Canyon in what, only another couple miles, then it's all downhill to the cave, right Stan?"

"Yeah, we could make it in one day from here. Like, oh, four or five hours of walking. And easier hiking than today."

Lily took the binoculars and climbed up on some rocks a short way from our picnic spot. The aroma of the roasting rabbit mixed with the pitchy smell of the needles made my mouth water. I haven't had a decent meal in, what, about two weeks? Last normal thing I ate was a gyro sandwich from the Greek place in Price. It seemed like another lifetime.

"I don't see any sign of those two army dudes," Lily said. "And we haven't crossed any trails or people tracks. I'm hoping they're out of here. Back with their loser buddies." She sat down and leaned against a juniper. "Hey, that's smells great. Like Grammy's turkey dinner. She always put a lot of rosemary in her birds. Smells like that. Kinda."

The rabbit roasted and steamed for what seemed like an eternity of tortuous temptation. At one point Frank poked a small hole in the earth oven with a stick and poured in a little water. He quickly resealed the hole. "That'll steam it up a little, make it nice and moist."

And it did. Frank was right. It was the best thing I had put in my mouth since that gyro sandwich eons ago. The meat was moist and tender and delicious. Lily agreed.

"Man, Frank!" She cried out. "You're doing the cooking from now on. We'll have to start calling you Emeril! This little bunny is deee-licious!"

We gnawed and sucked on the bones and broke the long bones open and slurped the marrow, and we thanked Frank for making this the best meal and the best day ever. Frank's knees were painful, and he said they were swollen, and since we were sure we could make it to Dark Lord Cave in one day, we decided to settle into our camp and enjoy what we were calling our Last Day in the Swell. Or our Last Day in Hell. Lily scouted around some more and shot another rabbit, and we prepared it the same way and feasted well into the evening. We saw no more sign of people, and Lily reported that she had walked to the drop-off into Muley Canyon and that it was a pretty easy walk that we could make in less than an hour, even with one man limping and one man walking around blind. From the drop-off to the cave was only about two miles, so I figured we could be at Dark Lord Cave and possible rescue by tomorrow afternoon.

When I lay back to sleep, the coyotes cried out like they were having a feeding frenzy, and I imagined them eating cottontails and smiling as we had. The sounds of the cavorting carnivores made Speck nervous, and she paced and occasionally growled and eventually settled down between my sprawled legs. I thought of Chris and filled my mind with images of her and my friends Bill and Ron, and I imagined finding them at Dark Lord Cave, and as I drifted to sleep, I dreamed that they had pizza and beer and we made a big fire in the front of the cave and ate and drank and played guitars and partied all night long while the coyotes had their own party just beyond the light of the fire.

You're under arrest

When Speck stood and growled, I thought nothing of it, since she had been on edge all through the night, but when an intensely bright white light shone right in my face, through my crusted-shut eyelids, I awoke with a start, just in time to be thrown into an adrenaline-ignited explosion of fear and confusion, when a loud commanding voice broke the stillness of the night.

"Put your hands where I can see them. Do not touch your weapons. Move slowly and nobody will get hurt. Hands up. Now!"

I couldn't even open my eyes to see what was going on. I could hear Lily and Frank scrambling around under the tarp and trying to figure out what to do. Should we try to get away, or should we do as ordered? Always the first to be compliant, I raised my hands above the tarp and kept them in front of me as I slowly sat up.

"Hey, you, I mean it. Hands up," came the voice again, and I could hear some scuffling. "Stay right there, right there! Hold your hands out in front of you. Do it!"

"OK then, OK," another voice said. "That's better. Everybody just calm down, and nobody will get hurt. We are officers in the Recapture Brigade, and you're under arrest."

"Under arrest?" Frank said. "You can't arrest anybody. You're not law enforcement. You can't arrest us. Jesus Christ. Under arrest!"

"You are under arrest for murder of a member of the Recapture Brigade and suspicion of three additional murders. We are officers of the Recapture Brigade, and this is our official territory. We are authorized by our command to detain you and bring you to headquarters to stand trial. We are also authorized to use deadly force if necessary, so do not make it necessary."

"May I rub my eyes, to clear them?" I asked, not wanting to be shot for moving my hands. "They're infected, and I can't open them."

"Go ahead," the first voice said. "Just keep your hands up in front of you."

When I had gotten the crust from my eyes and rubbed them to clear them a little, I opened them just a tiny slit. Two very bright lights shone on us, one apparently from a headlamp on a person standing a ways back from us, and one from a handheld flashlight from a person squatting just beyond our feet. I couldn't see well, but when my eyes had adjusted to the light, I could tell that Speck was sitting next to the squatting man, and he was petting her.

"I see you've met our guard dog," I said.

"Oh yeah, she's a great dog. We've known each other for a day or two now."

"What?" I asked. "What do you mean?"

"Well, we've been patrolling this area for a couple days. We figured you'd be headed in this direction. And we knew you had a dog. She just ran up to us day before last, down by the springs. I gave her some jerky and thought about keeping her. Willis here wanted to shoot her, but I figured it'd come in handy if we did find you to have her know us and like us, to think we were OK."

I shook my head in disbelief. Well, maybe faux disbelief. My dog, bought off by the enemy for some beef jerky. Good grief. Well, at least they didn't shoot her. And, if she had barked and raised a fuss tonight, they might have shot her just now. Maybe just as well that she was friendly.

"Well, who wouldn't sell out for some beef jerky," I said. "I don't blame you, Speck. I'd probably have done the same."

"Speck, that's her name?" the man laughed. "I was calling her Slick, since she just appeared, then she was gone, just like that. Slick. Not too far from Speck, really, is it, Slick?" He petted her one last time, stood up, and switched off his light. "Willis here is going to keep you covered, so don't try anything tricky. I want you each to stand, one at a time, starting with you, the female, and I'll put some zip ties on your hands. Sorry about that, but I need to make sure you're not going to do something foolish like try to escape or grab a weapon. Come on, ma'am, I won't hurt you."

He tied our hands together in front of us and around our ankles and joined them together with a short length of nylon cord. He attached a longer cord to each of us and connected them to a carabiner.

"Look," he said. "Let's not make this any more difficult than it needs to be. We will take you back to headquarters, and we'll have a trial. Maybe you'll be punished, maybe not, but you're accused of killing some of our people, and we need to investigate and make sure justice is served."

"Well, you are the ones who should be on trial," Lily said, anger welling up in her voice. "You people hijacked our semi and shot my husband and chased us all over, and stole Frank's truck and were about to shoot him. We're the fucking victims here, and you fuckers have the nerve to tell us we're going to go on trial. Bullshit! I call bullshit on your little fucking army game. Fuck you, assholes! Fuck you!"

"Shut up, bitch," the one called Willis shouted out. "You are the minions of the socialist pigs that are ruining this country, and you are the enemies of the Recapture movement. We could execute you right now, and it would be justified. Completely justified."

I could tell that he was affecting a threatening posture, holding what appeared to be a very tricked-out AR-15 rifle pointed straight at Lily's face. Great. She just gave him all the justification he needed, justification he was probably waiting for, hoping for, to blow our brains out.

"That's enough, both of you," the first man said. "Back off, Willis, she's just talking. No need to engage. Stay above it. Sorry, ma'am. I know how you feel. Nothing I can do about it. I have my job to do, and I'll do it as a professional. Please, everyone, just calm down."

DIVINE LEADER

"I apologize, Captain," Willis said. "Now you people, you listen to Captain Shumway, he's in charge of this operation, and he has orders from the general to bring you in. And he follows orders."

"And who is this general?" Frank asked. "Is it Drew Peacock?"

"Yes," replied Shumway. "You know him, correct?"

"Oh, just since first grade," Frank said. "About seventy years, that's all. So he's a general, huh? I think he was a corporal in the army back in the day. Guess he's given himself some promotions." Frank chuckled.

"General Peacock!" Lily said. "Does he have a dress uniform covered with medals and ribbons, like a real general should? Like a South American dictator? Does he have you call him Divine Leader, or is he content to be just General Peacock?"

"I know it may seem amusing to you," Shumway said. "But he did not proclaim himself to be anything. He was elected and put in command by the members of the Brigade. We needed a leader, and he is the most knowledgeable and best suited. He's a good man, and I support him 100 percent."

"He is a good man," Frank agreed. "He's just not what I consider the general type, that's all. In fact, he's the reason I got tangled up in this whole mess. I was headed out here to interview him for the paper."

"He knows you're out here, and he asked me to look out for you," Shumway said.

"What about us," Lily said. "Did he tell you to just hogtie us and bring us back so he can videotape some asshole cutting our heads off and post it on social media? Is that his plan?"

"Calm down, lady," Willis shouted, stepping forward.

I took a deep breath. I hadn't thought of the possibility of being executed this morning, but the way Lily put it, I immediately saw images of us kneeling on a sand dune while some General Peacock strutted around yelling about taking back America from the socialists and Mexicans and then shooting us in the head.

"Again, everyone just back off a little. Now, I'll make some coffee. We have energy bars to eat, and we can head for the road. We can probably make it to the Temple Wash Road this evening, and we'll be picked up and be back to headquarters by tomorrow. There's plenty to eat there, we can all get cleaned up, and I'll assure you that your side of the story will be heard. I'll treat you with respect, and all I ask is that you do the same."

He left the camp area for a few minutes and came back carrying two large packs, which he leaned up against a juniper trunk. Willis stood with his rifle trained on us while Shumway made coffee, and we sat back down and every drop of hope seemed to drift away through the trees with the faint breeze that moved slowly and somberly down through the stunted and twisted junipers and away from our desired destination, Dark Lord Cave.

I FELT LIKE A WHORE

We shared a cup of instant coffee between the three of us captives, and it was incredible how warm and wonderful it was. I could hardly remember ever drinking coffee before that was so warm and fragrant, and that tasted so remarkably rich and bitter and fulfilling. I felt like a whore drinking coffee provided by our captors and enjoying it. Shumway gave us energy bars, and they were delicious beyond belief, and I realized that deprivation had enhanced my appreciation for things I had formerly taken for granted or not even given much thought. I savored every tiny bite of the crunchy, salty, sweet, nutty bar, and I put the wrapper in my pocket, out of habit I guess. Littering is not part of my behavioral repertoire.

"Go take a look at Watson's eyes," Shumway said to Willis. I hadn't heard my last name spoken aloud in quite a while, and it sounded odd, like they were referring to someone else.

"I'm going to shine this light near your eyes so I can see what's going on in there," Willis said. "I'll try not to shine it directly in. Let me know if it bothers you."

The gentle, thoughtful demeanor seemed a stark change from the man who had been so threatening a few minutes ago. I didn't think about it too much, though, as I welcomed someone taking an interest in my eyes. Maybe he could help. Maybe he could help me see. Or keep me from going blind.

"You've got some scratches on your corneas, and a little bit of infection going on," he said. Not good. And you've got an infection going in this puncture wound in your forehead. How did you do this?"

"One of your buddies shot him, that's how," Lily said. "Back at the stock tank."

Willis kept looking at my wounds. "Well, he's fortunate, because I don't think he's going to have any lasting damage if we can get this infection under control. Doesn't look like you have any fragments of bullet in the wound, and it clearly didn't puncture the skull, so it's better than it could have been, I'll just say that."

Willis turned and zipped open a pouch. "Lean back and let me put some of these drops in your eyes," he said. "It might burn a little, but it will help a lot. It's an antibiotic ointment. I'll give you some oral antibiotics too and clean out this head wound. You're in pretty rough shape. You really need to see a doctor."

Willis worked on me for nearly an hour. I felt a great sense of relief to be having someone who seemed to know what he was doing attend to my wounds. But then I remembered that just a short while ago he was pointing an automatic weapon at us and threatening to use deadly force. Maybe he was just making sure I could see him when he put a bullet in my head and completed the job the Viking had started a few days ago.

"That ought to do for now," Willis said. "Anybody else need first aid?" He looked over toward Lily and Frank.

"Frank's knees are bad," Lily said. "He's having a hard time walking."

"What is it, Frank," Willis asked. "Arthritis, or something new?"

"Both," Frank said. "I am scheduled for knee replacements, one after the other, later this summer. Cartilage is gone. But I banged the right one pretty good a couple days ago. It's pretty painful."

"Let me take a look," Willis said. "Can you roll your pant leg up?"

Frank's knee was swollen and badly bruised. I couldn't see that well, but I could tell that it looked awful.

"That's bad," Willis said. "I'm surprised you can even walk."

"Well, we haven't exactly been out for a stroll, Lily said. "We've been running for our lives. From you. And Frank's a badass."

"I can tell," Willis said. "That's got to be painful. Each step. I'm not sure I can do a lot for you. This is a fairly serious injury. Actually, between the two of you, you've got some pretty grave medical issues. I'll give you some ibuprofen and see if we can get the inflammation under control. Maybe you can try walking in a little bit."

Willis went over to where Shumway was standing, and they spoke quietly for a few minutes before Shumway came over to us.

"We need to get walking if we're going to get to the road by this evening," he said. "I know you'll want to get cleaned up and have some decent food, so let's start getting ready to move."

My eyes were burning from the drops Willis had put in them. Frank was rubbing his knee. Lily stood.

"Look, I know you want to take us on your version of a death march so you can show your prissy Peacock your prize captives, but these men are in pretty rough shape," she said. "We can't walk five or more miles. We barely covered two yesterday, and it was mostly easy walking, and Frank hurt himself even more walking that much. No. We aren't ready. We can't hike out of here."

"Get your asses up," Willis said, in a loud voice. "You heard the captain. We need to move. Now!"

"Put your gun down, Gomer," Lily said. "You saw the shape these guys are in. Come on, lighten up."

Shumway and Willis walked a few steps back and talked some more, this time seeming to argue, while trying to keep their voices low. I thought of parents trying to hide their quarrels from their children. After a few minutes, Shumway turned to us.

"OK, here's what we're going to do," Shumway said. "We'll give the medicine a couple hours to start working. Bring the swelling down. Then we'll head out. I'm going to send Willis here back to the spring for more water. The rest of us will just wait here. We'll start walking this afternoon."

To get back to the real world

Shumway and Willis spent a few minutes moving their gear around and consolidating equipment. While Shumway looked on, his hand resting on his holstered sidearm for us to see, Willis undid the cords that bound us together and secured them through a loop of larger rope, presumably so we could all be tied together or separated as need be. They filled a large collapsible container with water, and Willis collected all the empty bottles, strung them together on a length of nylon webbing, and slung it over his shoulder.

"Be back in a couple hours," he said, and started walking.

Shumway watched him go, sat down on a low juniper branch, adjusted his baseball-style camouflage cap with a Cabela's logo on the front, took out a map and studied it.

"We're only about five miles from the stock tank," he said. "Where you had the shootout."

Nobody responded.

"We thought you," he nodded to Lily, "we thought you might be the only one who made it. We didn't know if you were all still alive. When Phil made it back, he told us that he thought you, Saccomano, had been shot, and he thought he had got you, Watson. When we found Marty's body by the stock tank and saw footprints leading away, we weren't sure what had happened."

Nobody responded.

"That's not what you're wanted for, though, shooting Marty. It's for the man by the truck. The man with the black beard. Gus. Gus Rosenberg. He was my friend, and you executed him. You executed him. You fucking executed him."

I looked at Lily. I could see her eyes widen with rage. I looked at her, shook my head, and put a finger to my lips. We waited. Shumway seemed to be upset thinking of what had happened. I tried to think of a way to start. I didn't know how to start, and that's how I started.

"I don't know how to start, but I want you to know that we did not kill your friend. We did not execute anyone. We would have let him live. We let Phil live. We called him the Viking because of the way he looked. We left him tied to the truck. No, we didn't kill your friend. Phil did. Phil shot him. Right in front of Lily. And me. He didn't know I was there. He killed your friend because your friend was protecting Lily. Phil wanted to rape her, and your friend wouldn't let him. So Phil shot him. Right in the chest. And he just dragged him out of the way, dying, like a sack of fertilizer. I could have killed Phil then. Maybe I should have, but we tied him up and left him there. I should have known that he would blame everything on us. And he made Frank his prisoner, and that other guy was about to shoot Frank, and we had no choice but to start firing. If he hadn't been such an asshole we might have avoided a lot of crap. But we didn't kill your friend. He died because he wanted to protect Lily from a psycho rapist. And that's the truth."

Shumway looked at me, and at Lily, and back to me.

"We're telling the truth," Lily said. "I shot that guy, that other guy, Marty, but he was about to blow Frank's head off, in cold blood, for no reason. The Viking—Phil—he knows that. I shot at him too, after I thought he had killed Stan." She put her hands to her face and wiped her eyes. "This has been the worst thing that has ever happened to me. I don't know who any of these people are, who you are, how we got in this mess, but I know some assholes killed my husband, and Stan and Frank and I have been fighting for our lives. All we want is to get away. To get back to the real world. Back to sanity."

"Believe me, I never imagined things getting like this, out of control," Shumway said, looking straight at us. "We were protesting government overreach. That's all. We were planning to get back to our families after a few days. Maybe face some trespassing charges or something, and have a big trial and make our political points. I came out here with my buddy Gus, and the next thing I know, he's got a giant hole in his chest."

This isn't a Girl Scout hike

The sun was getting hotter, and I scooted over a little to move into the shade. Shumway took his cap off, ran his fingers through his short, sandy-colored hair, sat the cap on the log beside him, and held his head in his hands. I worried that he would become upset, and perhaps violent. I looked around to see where I could run if something started. I could see the guns piled behind the tree, on the other side of him. No chance to make a break for them, the way we're tied up. I took a deep breath and tried to remain calm.

"The hijacking that went bad, that's when everything started going out of control," Shumway said. "That survivalist and his kid, the ones, well the ones I guess you shot, they botched it. They were supposed to talk you into letting them take your semi, you know, then you claim they took it at gunpoint, nobody gets hurt except for the insurance company. We had done that once before. Well, it's understandable, kind of. You hit a pickup truck with your semi at the rest area. I guess they were trying to block the

"

road. Well, his wife, the kid's mom, she was in that truck. Got hurt pretty bad. They were pissed. That's why they chased you. That's when they started shooting. That's when it went bad. Really bad. We'll all face felony charges. We're all screwed. I'm just going to do what I promised to do, which is to bring you in. Then, well, then, I don't know. I just don't know."

We sat for a while and hoped he would unwind. Shumway stood and paced around the little camp. He looked for a few minutes in the direction of the Old Woman spire, where Willis had gone for more water.

"And don't be too freaked out by Willis," he said. "He's a little gung-ho. Too enthusiastic sometimes. But he's a good guy and a hell of a medic. He'll take good care of your eyes. And your knee. He'll do his best. He will."

I opened my eyes a bit and looked over at Frank and Lily. They sat in the dirt beside me, tied, as I was, and looking down, staring at the ground without expression, without much sign of hope, or even life. I blinked my eyes, removed bits of sandy crust from the corners with my fingers, and tried to look about.

After the initial burning, the eyedrops seemed to be helping. My eyes felt a little better lubricated, and the scratchiness seemed to have lessened. When I opened my eyes a little, things were not as blurry as they had been. Maybe the medicine Willis had given me was working.

"How's your knee?' I asked.

"'bout the same," Frank said. "It's wrecked. Pretty much wrecked."

Willis appeared in camp shortly after noon. He hung the webbing with the water bottles over a branch, leaned his rifle against a juniper, took off his pack, and came right to me.

"How are these eyes?" he asked, putting his hands on my face and opening one of my lids. I started to tell him that they were feeling better, but he coughed and started speaking. "A mess. They're really a mess." He turned toward Shumway. "It'll take a few days for the antibiotic to have any affect. He's going to be more-or-less blind for a while."

He walked over to Frank and motioned for him to lift his pant leg. He dropped to one knee and looked Frank's leg over.

"How's it feel, any better?"

Frank shook his head.

"Have you tried walking?" Willis asked.

"Frank nodded. "A little. Pretty painful."

Willis drew in a breath, looked me in the eyes, and turned toward Shumway.

"I've done what I can." he said. "These two aren't in great shape, but we can push them. They'll just have to do it. This isn't a Girl Scout hike, fellas. Get up and let's get going."

Shumway readied our tethers, gave us each a water bottle, and rousted us up. "Come on, we're going to walk out of here."

"Can we get a cane or a crutch or something for Frank?" Lily asked. "There's the stick Stan was using, over there with our stuff. Maybe Frank can use that."

Shumway got the cane and gave it to Frank, who stood and gingerly tested his right leg.

"Let's get going," Willis said, raising his voice. "We have some ground to cover." He motioned with his rifle. His message was clear. "Follow the captain."

I motioned with a nod for Lily to lead the way. She started down the trail behind Shumway. Frank started after her. I could tell that his knee was really bothering him. I followed Frank, with Speck at my side, and Willis brought up the rear.

The way was mostly level and winding as we made our way east through the juniper forest that contained an occasional piñon pine and pockets of sagebrush and greasewood. Frank struggled to keep up, even at a slow pace, and when we dropped into a shallow gully, he fell when starting up the other side. I stepped forward and helped him to his feet, and I could see from his face that he was suffering. He was sweating profusely, despite the slow pace and gentle, cooling breeze. His face was red, pinched, tense. His eyes glistened. He tried to ascend the gentle slope of the gully and fell again. I reached to help him up, and Willis pushed me aside. He reached across Frank's back, took him under his arm, nearly lifting him off the ground, and helped him to the top of the rise. There he stood for a moment while Frank gained his balance. Willis looked at Frank, and I could tell that he saw what I saw, a man who would not be able to keep up.

Willis walked past Lily and went to Shumway. I listened, and caught fragments of their conversation but did not like what I heard. Willis seemed to be arguing for leaving Frank behind. Maybe leaving me with him. Or shooting him. Willis was pushing Shumway to decide. At one point Shumway shouted, "You go. You go and I'll stay here with them," and Willis shouted back, "No, you need to be the one. You're the captain. I'll take care of these prisoners. I'll take care of them."

I worried what he meant by offering to "take care" of us. I really didn't like the sound of the conversation, but we were prisoners. Our fate was completely in the hands of these men. And Willis scared me. A lot.

Shumway looked over at us and motioned for us to sit down. "We're going to take a break," he said. Willis tied our tether to a tree trunk, checked that it was secure, and he and Shumway walked to a spot out of earshot and continued their conversation.

"I'm sorry," Frank said. "I'm trying. I'm screwing everything up. My knee is just not working. I'm sorry. I'll volunteer to stay. I'll just stay here, and you all can go ahead."

"Shut up, Frank," Lily said. "We're not leaving you. We'll all go down if we have to. We're all screwed anyway."

"Well, they might just shoot me right here," Frank said. "It wouldn't surprise me. Not a bit."

"That's not going to happen," I said. As if I knew anything. I felt that our fate was completely random, with no real way to know what might happen next. We could all be executed. Or just Frank. Or we could all be left behind. I caught myself thinking maybe if they shot Frank they would spare me and Lily for a while. And then I tried to make that thought go away, but I couldn't, and when I saw Willis walking toward us, rifle in hand, I put my arm around Speck and thought that it would be really weird to die this way. But then, wouldn't it be weird to die any way. My mind raced, and I realized instantly how insanity worked.

"Frank is fucking the whole thing up," Willis said, with a touch of anger in his voice. "And you being blind doesn't make things any better. If it was up to me I'd leave both of you here, maybe pop you both, and only take her back." He nodded at Lily. "At least she can walk and see."

"Who are you—God?" Lily looked at Willis, staring straight at him as she slowly rose. "Your little game makes me sick. These are good men you're talking about. You make me sick. You are sick. Fuck you. Fuck you!"

"Calm down. Nobody is getting left behind. Captain Shumway thinks your lives are worth saving, for some reason, so he is going to hike out and bring back ATVs for the rest of us. I'm your keeper. I have to stay here and babysit you, a cripple and a blind man. And a bitch." He glared at Lily.

Great. As soon as Shumway walks over the hill, we're all getting a bullet in the head. He'll tell his pals we tried to escape. They'll say it was justified. Great. We're done for.

Shumway walked and stood in front of us. "I'm leaving Willis here with you. He's a medic, and he can take care of you until I get back with more help. I'll bring ATVs in to haul you back to Recapture Camp. You'll be OK until then. I'll be back by tomorrow night. You have plenty of water. I don't need to take much, so, well, OK then, I'm heading out. Listen to Willis. He's in charge."

LIKE A TRIO OF HAMSTERS

Shumway turned and headed east. I looked over at Frank and Lily. We shared a sense that things had gone from terrible to horrendous. I felt a dark, heavy weight settling down on me, a cloak of inescapable fate from which there was no escape, only resigned acceptance, as though I were a condemned prisoner being led down a hallway to his doom. Willis sat with his back toward us, facing south. I looked at the zip ties around my wrists and the knotted nylon cord that bound them. If I started biting the cord now, I could probably chew through it eventually. I put the cord in my mouth and started gnawing. Lily saw what I was doing and started chewing on her cord, and in a minute Frank joined us. We were gnawing away like a trio of hamsters, and it was exciting because it was the most positive, hope-generating thing I had done since these maniacs captured us. The cord was wet in my mouth, and I was making progress. I could tell that I was tearing through the outer sheath and starting on the next layer. A few minutes more and I could, what, tackle Willis? Run away? Grab a rock and hit him over the head? If Lily and I both rushed him, maybe we could overpower him and take his rifle. I took the cord from my mouth and dropped my hands when Willis stood. I motioned to Lily and Frank to do the same. We all sat with our hands in our laps as he walked over toward us. I had the feeling that I looked like a kid who had just been caught shoplifting, with guilt painted all over me. I think I was even smiling a little bit. Appeasement, one of my finest qualities, makes me sick.

"You shouldn't be chewing on those cords," Willis said, leaning his rifle against his pack. He stood, took a knife from a sheath on his belt, and walked forward.

This is it. He's going to kill us with a knife. I scooted back but was stopped by the juniper behind us. There was nowhere to go.

Willis went to Lily. She stared straight at him. Goddamn, she is brave. She's not going to cower, she's going to make him look her in the eye. Jesus.

Willis reached down with his left hand, took the cord that bound Lily and cut it.

"Here, let me see yours," he said to me. I held up my hands, and he severed the cord. He then cut Frank's.

"What, are we now supposed to run, so you can say we tried to escape, so you can shoot us," Lily said. "What a chickenshit. Fucking chickenshit."

"I know that's what you think. What you should think, that's what I've been trying to make Shumway think. And all the Recapture people. I'm not one of them. I'm a federal agent. I work for the Department of the Interior. I acted like a maniac so these Recapture people would trust me. And it's worked so far. I think. I know it seems crazy, and that you don't trust me, but I have to take the chance. I'm a spy. If Shumway comes back and finds out who I am, he'll execute me on the spot as a traitor. Any of them will. My job now is to get you three out of here. I promise I will do everything I can to bring you to safety. And I'm sorry I called you a bitch. That was Willis. He's an asshole. I'm Nick. Nick Thomas. Here, let me get rid of those zip ties."

He cut the ties from our wrists and stepped back. We rubbed where the ligatures had bound us and looked at each other. Should we believe him? Can we trust him? It was almost more overwhelming than before. We now had to decide if we could accept Willis. . . Nick as a colleague, an ally, someone who only moments ago was our oppressor, an enemy who threatened to kill us. Were we being tricked? What cruelty was he foisting on us? My knees threatened to give way with the weight of the new responsibility placed on them. I wondered what Frank was thinking, how he would react. I didn't need to wonder about Lily's take.

"Now listen. You can tell us a story about being a good guy now, but you've been a complete turd, twice the turd that Shumway was, and frankly, I don't think I can trust you. I don't think I can believe your story. It seems too, well, shit, I don't know, too good to be true."

"Look, I know how it sounds. It sounds crazy, and it is. I have been a turd. But now I'm going to make it up to you. You are the reason I was sent here. To help people like you. To help you. Here, come over here." He gestured toward our stacked gear. "Your things are over here. Your guns. Come get them. Please don't use them on me. We'll need to look out for each other. But take them, go ahead. I'll lay mine down. I trust you. Maybe you'll be able to trust me eventually. I hope so."

We got our things, and Willis, now Nick, asked Lily to stand guard, mainly to scan the terrain to the east and make sure Shumway didn't return. He opened his medical kit and cleaned and applied more ointment to my eyes. When he looked at Frank's knee, he apologized.

"Frank, I have to let you know that I caused you a lot of pain today. I told you I was giving you ibuprofen for the inflammation in your knee. I really gave you an allergy pill. Nothing that would help your knee. I knew you would have a hard time walking, and I wanted it to slow us down and stop us. I'm sorry. Here are a couple ibuprofens. And when we need to get going, I have some pain pills and a good wrap for your knee. We'll need to get away from this spot either later this afternoon or in the morning, and I'll do what I can to make you comfortable. Carry you if need be."

"Where do you think we should go?" I asked.

"I was hoping you'd have an idea," Nick said. "Shumway is headed for the Temple Wash Road, which is a few miles east of here. I know we don't want to go that way, but I don't know the territory, and, well, he has the maps."

"Um. . . well, we've been talking about where to go," I said, glancing up at Frank, "but we haven't really come to any conclusion."

I was hesitant to tell him of our plan to go to Dark Lord Cave. I wanted to trust him and have him on our side and be our hero and help Frank and me and Lily and take us to safety, but I was still hesitant. Frank seemed to agree with me.

"I know this country pretty well," he said. "We have a few options, but it all depends on where we think the militia people might be. Definitely stay away from the Temple Wash Road if they're patrolling it. What about the Dragerton Trail? Think they might be that far north? Shumway say anything about how far north they were going?"

"I never heard that mentioned—the what—Dragon Trail?"

"Dragerton."

"No. I did hear them talking about how they had to stay away from the, um, Something Mining District. Said the BLM had a guard station and checkpoint set up there. A few of our, um, their men had been stopped and captured there."

"The Van Deusen Mining District? Does that sound right?" Frank asked, looking over at me.

"That's it," Nick said. "Van Deusen Mining District."

"That does it then," Frank said. "We're heading north. Straight north to the Van Deusen Mining District and the Dragerton Trail."

"Have you been there?" Nick asked. "How far is it?"

"Yes, I've been there, and so has Stan here. It's a place we're pretty familiar with. We were heading there when you, well, when you jumped us. We can get pretty close with just a day's walk, even with my gimp leg."

"Tell you what," Nick said. "It's getting kind of late to start out this afternoon. We'll let your knee rest up and get the swelling down and head out in the morning. It'll feel really good to be getting close to civilization. The Dragerton Trail. I like the sound of that."

THE LAST SUPPER

Frank and I looked at each other. Frank nodded. I looked over at Lily, standing near the top of a rocky outcrop a short way from our spot, scanning with binoculars, my AR-15 slung over her shoulder. I think we're going to be all right. The future seemed a little brighter. We were back on track. Heading for the Dragerton Trail, which was the old road just north of Dark Lord Cave, a road that has been closed for years but that still appears on maps and is used by ranchers to drive cattle. Maybe, just maybe, things were going to work out. The thought of seeing Chris and Bill, anyone familiar, seemed to be a most improbable and incredible dream, something of no special note just a short time ago and that now shone brightly as the most desired goal imaginable, and it was becoming more real, coming more into focus. Lack of hope and desperation changes a person, but rekindling a dream restores faith that tomorrow is worth looking forward to and planning for. Tomorrow seems likely, and it may be better than today. I took a deep breath, and it felt like I was starting on a new adventure, pushing off into a river that was flowing fast and smooth toward home.

My eyes were feeling better, and Nick cleaned them and applied ointment as evening fell. He wrapped Frank's knee with an elastic bandage and moistened it, so the evaporative cooling would help keep the swelling down. He brought a pack and placed it under Frank's leg to keep the knee elevated when he was sitting or lying down in camp.

We took turns standing guard through the night. Nick assigned us to two-hour slots, and he kept track of whose turn it was and what we should be paying attention to. It felt good to be working as a team, and I'm sure that was his intention, because I don't think he slept at all. I took that as a sign that he was aware of the level of danger we faced and that he considered the threat to be significant. I worried considerably about whether my growing trust in him was misplaced, something I accepted only because I wanted him to be trustworthy, and because it was the easiest thing to do. I decided that the only reasonable course of action was to trust him but with an asterisk, trust that was constantly under scrutiny, trust that was conditional on continuous affirmation.

I jerked awake to the beeping of Nick's wristwatch alarm. He turned the alarm off, rummaged in his pack for the small stove he carried, put on water to heat, roused Lily, and called to Frank, who was on duty.

"How's that knee doing, Frank?" Nick asked when Frank arrived at the camp.

"Better," Frank said. "A lot better. Not fantastic, but the swelling is down."

"Here, take these," Nick said, reaching a cupped hand toward Frank. "A little more ibuprofen and some OxyContin. You can use the cane, and one of us will stay by you to prop you up if you need it. We're going to try to cover some ground today, and, well, we want you to be comfortable."

"Thanks," Frank said. "I don't want to hold you up. If I do, just let me trail on behind. I'll be fine."

"No way, Frank," Lily said. "You know what happens to the slowest buffalo or wildebeest—lions get it. We won't let any lions get you. Or Recapture-ers. Take your medicine. You'll be skipping along in front of us once those OxyContins kick in."

The aroma of the coffee and the first little taste seemed to invigorate me. I sensed that the end could be near. The end of the ordeal that had overwhelmed us. "This is the end, beautiful friend, the end." I hummed the tune as we readied our gear and hoisted our packs, and Lily led the way north, toward Dark Lord Cave, the Dragerton Trail, and rescue, friends, family, safety, showers, and a change of underwear. I could hear the organ playing and Jim Morrison singing along with me as I made my way down the trail, happy to be able to see just enough to find my way through the faint light of the pre-dawn woodland. This is the end.

Our limping, bandaged crew made steady progress over mostly level and relatively easy terrain. We maintained a moderate pace, and Frank was able to keep up, although it was clear that he was working hard to keep us from knowing how difficult it was for him. When we reached the bottom of the canyon that we would follow to Dark Lord Cave and the Dragerton Trail, sandstone cliffs rose on both sides of us, sometimes several hundred feet of sheer vertical walls separated by only twenty feet of sandy canyon bottom. At times the canyon widened to several hundred feet, with sage-covered dunes migrating along the canyon sides and out from the mouths of side drainages, and in many places we saw the fantastic paintings of the ancient inhabitants of the canyon, sometimes isolated figures, sometimes in groups of a dozen or more. Looming life-sized and larger human or ghost-like figures, with animals, birds, insects, unknown and unusual creatures from visions and tales and nightmares, and they seemed to be watching over us. Speck found a part of a dead and dried rabbit, and her happiness at such a find overflowed and enveloped all of us. We took a break in the cool shade at the foot of a sheer cliff face that rose and overhung us slightly. Nick produced energy bars, and we ate in silence, somewhat mesmerized by an intricate panel of painted figures on the wall opposite us that seemed to be lined up for a portrait of the graduating class of an ancient acid trip.

"They call that one The Last Supper," I said. "Kind of reminds some people of the da Vinci painting."

"If you say so," Lily said. "I'd call it something like Judgment Day. Looks to me like a bunch of scary judges and ghosts looking right at you. Getting ready to seal your fate."

"I like to think about what it might have looked like when it was painted, like 2,000 years ago," I said. "It looks pretty intimidating now, but can you imagine coming around the corner here and seeing that when the paint was fresh and bright? Must have been pretty impressive. Still is, and the paints have been fading for 100 generations."

"You know, we're only about a mile from Dark Lord Cave," Frank said.

"What's that?" Nick asked.

"Oh, it's an archaeological site," I said. I worked there a few years back. Big cave, great place. Has a nice spring in the back. We were kind of heading there, thinking it would be a good place to hide out, and maybe, just maybe, I've been thinking, well. . ." I looked at Lily and Frank. They both nodded.

"I've been thinking that maybe my friends would meet us there. Or leave us some supplies or a phone, or, well, I don't know what, but I have a friend who knows about the site, and we always talked about what a great place it would be to go in case of something like this happening, so, um, we're heading there. You never know."

Frank rose and steadied himself with the staff. "You got me excited. Let's get our asses on down the canyon. See what's going on at Dark Lord Cave."

LIKE YOU DO

As soon as I saw them, even through tear-blurred eyes, I stopped dead in my tracks and threw my left arm out to signal the others. I slid my hands to a ready position on my holstered pistol, dropped to one knee, squinted, and scanned the entire width of the canyon as far as I could see. Nick was right beside me, and after a few moments of seeing nothing more, he stood.

"Just the ATV tracks?" he asked. "Did you see anything else?"

"No," I said. "Just the tracks. Sorry if I overreacted. I was in kind of a zone, and when I saw the tracks, I about shit."

"You didn't overdo it. We need to be extra careful from here on out. Who knows who could be just around the next bend? Could be your friends. Or the BLM. Or Shumway and his crew. You never know."

"The cave is only, well, just about a quarter mile maybe, just around the bend." I stood and pointed. "Just past that talus on the left, in the Navajo Sandstone about fifty feet above the canyon floor. You can almost see it from here."

"Tell you what," Nick said. "You three stay here—Lily up in those rocks. You, Stan, over by that tree. And Frank, you get down in these bushes. I'll go ahead and see if it's all clear down to the cave. Seem OK? Here, Lily, I'll show you where you should be."

Nick and Lily took off. He stationed her in some rocks that had a view both down and up the canyon. When Lily was in place, Nick waved to me and Frank, ducked into a crouch, and hurried down the canyon.

I sat comfortably in the shady canyon bottom, leaning up against the trunk of a large cottonwood tree that had fallen nearly down some time in the distant past, somehow recovered, and regrew a vertical trunk at an almost ninety-degree angle from the original tree that fell. The melodic descending call of a canyon wren provided a soothing and beautiful ambience. I hoped Nick wouldn't encounter bad guys at the cave. Then I worried that he might run into Bill and some of my friends, and they would not know each other and might start shooting. Shit. I stood and started hurrying down-canyon. A gun battle between Nick and Bill was worse than my worst nightmare. I ran, not knowing what I would do or what I would encounter, but I ran, following the sandy gravel bed of the dry canyon, my feet sinking in the soft substrate, sending small stones skittering about with each step.

"Stan, Stan, stop, Stan, stop!"

I heard Lily calling to me. I lurched to a stop and turned to look up at her. She was pointing down-canyon. "Nick's coming back. He's waving for us to come on down. You don't need to run."

I stood and caught my breath. I didn't know what I would have done if there had been shooting, other than run into the middle of it and get myself filled with lead. I could see Nick heading back toward us, and Lily was coming down from the rocks. Frank walked up behind me.

"Where were you going in such a hurry?" he asked. "Did you see something?"

"No, I just let my imagination run wild," I said. "Like I do sometimes."

"Like you do," Frank said. I looked at him. "Like everyone does. Like you do."

"Cave seems all clear," Nick reported. "Looks to me like these ATV tracks were made a few days ago, and whoever made them didn't even go up to the cave. And, um, no friends camped out in it either, sorry to say."

I shrugged. A wash of disappointment swept over me. I knew it was incredibly unrealistic of me to think we would find a cave full of friendly people waiting to escort us away from the danger of the Recapture Brigade's San Rafael Swell Jamboree, but I guess I had been letting the image float around in the movie theatre in my head for long enough that it seemed likely, even inevitable, that the cave would somehow be our portal to safety and everlasting happiness.

"Let's go see," I said, and started walking.

Breaking News from Channel Nine News
Liz Nuñez reporting

"Channel Nine News' Liz Nuñez has breaking news from the Recapture protests near Price. Liz?"

"Thank you, Dick. We have some news that turns the entire protest and the story of missing travelers on its head. We have been talking with a Colorado man who claims to have been part of the protest movement, but because of the way things have been handled and gotten out of control, has left the protest and come to Price. He is willing to speak out about what is going on."

"Thank you, sir, for agreeing to appear on camera. Can you tell us your name, and a little about how you came to be part of the protest?"

"Yeah, my name is Al, Al Shumway. I'm from over in Colorado, Dove Creek. I heard about the protest, and since I oppose heavy-handed government, I came to join in, me and my buddy Gus, Gus Rosenberg."

"Can you tell our viewers a little about why you left the protest? What prompted you to want to tell your story?"

"Well, um, yeah. The protest has gone bad, I guess you could say. There's some people who have, well, ruined it for all of us. They've turned the whole thing into a civil war or something. There've been some murders, including my friend Gus, and those truckers, one of the truckers was killed, hell, a bunch of people have been killed."

"Murders? Those are some serious allegations. The official word has been that the truckers are safe, and the protest has been peaceful. Now you are saying that is not the case?"

"Not at all. I believed it, well, mostly believed it until a day or two ago. I knew there had been some trouble, with the second camp and all, but I didn't realize what has really been going on. And maybe the people in the main camp like General Peacock don't really know what's going on either."

"How could they not know, if what you say is true? One of the truckers has been killed? And your friend, and others? How could they not know?"

"Well, they knew about some of it probably, but not all of it. One guy and some of his pals, they've been acting like their own militia, and they've done some things that are, well, just awful. They've ruined the whole thing. Ruined everything."

* * *

"It is clear that you've taken this pretty hard, Mr. Shumway. Do you want to tell us, well, what might be done? What can the sheriff or anyone do to bring this to an end?"

"I don't know. Maybe go in and try to get control of the place before some more really bad stuff goes down. And it could get really bad in a hurry."

You said that one of the truckers was killed. Is the other one safe? How about the geologist, and the journalist? Do you know anything about them?"

"Well, the husband, the trucker, he was killed, and the others, the woman, and the two other men, they're in the custody of one of the protesters—the real protesters, you know, not the crazy ones. But the crazy ones are hunting them. That's why I came out, to try to get some help. Otherwise, well, it could be a bloodbath. A real bloodbath."

"It looks like the sheriff's deputies are here and want to talk with Mr. Shumway. Can you let us know how this changes the situation? Sir, will you tell our viewers what is going on? Are you planning to intervene in the protest? Sir, when can we find out what is going on?"

"As you can see, the sheriff's office does not want to talk at this point. They have taken Mr. Shumway away in a police car, I assume to question him about what he knows and to find out if they need to act to stop what Mr. Shumway says will be a bloodbath. He is clearly very emotional about what has happened and said that his friend, a Mr., um, Rosenberg, Mr. Rosenberg, was killed, clearly a traumatic event."

"The statements made by Mr. Shumway shine a whole new light on these very confusing, and often shadowy events."

"We will do what we can to bring you every detail of what is going on as this bizarre situation unfolds. Reporting from Price, in Carbon County, Utah, Liz Nuñez, Channel Nine News.*"*

Open the Damn Thing

Dark Lord Cave, or Muley Cave, as it is known in the guidebooks and archaeological publications, is a grand cathedral-like space carved in the smooth, unblemished sandstone by millennia after millennia of patient grain-by-grain removal of stone by the wind and water of this majestic canyon. High-ceilinged, twice as deep as it is wide, it was of perfect, classic proportions and had been home, school, hospital, dance hall, church, playground, morgue, wedding chapel, art gallery, kitchen, refuge, concert hall, burial ground, and bedroom to thousands of people over many thousands of years. I could almost hear the voices of its past inhabitants as I entered it, a feeling I sometimes had when I entered an archaeological site. I often thought I could hear children laughing and playing, and I heard them now, and I smiled. The towering hollow-eyed red-caped figure that dominated the wall near the entrance was familiar and welcoming, not menacing, as so many found it to be. There appeared to be no fresh human tracks in the soft sand of the cave floor. I walked to the back and dipped my water bottle in the stone-rimmed catch basin that held the coldest, freshest-tasting, most delicious water for miles around, brought it to my lips, and sipped the magical water of this most magical place. My friends were not here, and I was disappointed, but the incredible power of the cave, one of the most significant places in my life, the place where I had proposed marriage to my wife, Chris, comforted me and lifted me up.

"See anything?" Lily asked, walking up behind me.

I shook my head. "Well, I can't see very well, but no. No sign of anybody. Nothing. We'll just have to head for the trail, Dragerton Trail, and hope we'll run into the BLM. It's only a mile or so away. We can head there now if we want."

I wandered around in the cave while the others filled their water bottles and rested. Over by the far corner, I found a small mason's nail in the wall that I had placed there several years back as a mapping datum when Bill and I had worked in the cave. We had removed old backdirt from one of Professor Manson's excavation units to expose one of his stratigraphic profiles to take tiny samples of the sediment for analysis. We had taken about ten samples, each only about the size of a golf ball, and had refined the dating and environmental reconstruction for the entire 11,000-year human occupation of the cave. It was research Bill and I were most proud of.

I smiled when I looked at the edge of the area we had excavated. It was so well backfilled that there was no indication that a hole had ever been dug in this spot. Good work, boys, I said to myself, congratulating us on the quality of our restoration. Right in the middle of where our excavation had been, I noticed a tiny piece of yellow string lying limply on the sand. We must have forgotten a piece of mason's line, I thought, and bent to pick it up. When I pulled on it, it snaked out of the ground for a few inches, and then stopped. It seemed to be stuck, or attached to something. I pulled a little harder and it slipped from my hands. I knelt down, wrapped the string around my hand, and tugged. I could see the sand starting to give way around where the string emerged from the earth. I pulled a little more, and the string started to move. It's tied to something, something kind of big. I brushed the sand away with my hand while tugging on the string. Before the sand filled back in, I caught a glimpse of something smooth and bright yellow. It seemed to be pretty big. I continued brushing and hit a hard, angular piece of plastic that protruded from the smooth yellow surface. A handle. I grasped it and pulled. Suddenly it came loose and the sand caved in around it. It was a large plastic suitcase. A Pelican case, the kind of water- and sand-proof cases river runners and scientists used in harsh environments like this. And it was heavy. Somebody had buried this here.

I pulled the case free and started walking toward the others, who were now sitting near the mouth of the cave.

"Look what I found," I said.

I sat down in the sand and laid the case out in front of me.

"I know who put this here!" I said, my voice rising in excitement "See this." I pointed to a stylized pronghorn antelope design stenciled on the flat side of the case. See this WA symbol? It's my friend Bill's company. Wanzi Archaeology. He left this here, right where I would find it."

"Well," Lily said. "Open the damn thing!"

Rock Henge for Dinner and Drinks

I flipped the two heavy latches that secured the lid against the rubber watertight seal. A slight vacuum held the lid tight, and I turned the knurled knob of the threaded relief valve. A sudden hiss of air rushed in, and the lid popped free. Lily hovered over my shoulder as I lifted the top. A piece of ivory-colored paper, clipped to the cover of a paper-bound book, lay on top of a gray cloth that covered the rest of the contents. I picked up the book and unfolded the paper. Neatly printed, in ink, it read:

Summertime, and the livin' is easy
Fish are jumpin', and the cottonwood's high.

"Huh, I said. The lyrics to *Summertime*. A Gershwin tune."

"What's the book?" Lily asked, reaching to pick it up.

"Aww, jeez." I said. "This tells me that Chris put this together. Or at least helped. It's *The Dalai Lama's Book of Wisdom*. It's my book. It's one I turn to whenever I need a little inspiration or, well, just a reminder to be tolerant. Kind. It's, it's. . ." I took a deep breath. "It's perfect. Just perfect."

I thumbed through the book for a moment and stopped at a dog-eared page. Page 70, a passage I have turned to on many occasions. I read it to my companions:

"The supreme source of my happiness is my calmness of mind. Our country can be invaded, our possessions can be destroyed, our friends can be killed, but these are secondary for our mental happiness. The ultimate source of my mental happiness is my peace of mind. Nothing can destroy this except my own anger."

And from page 73:

"However, according to our experience with anger, if you do not make an attempt to reduce it, it will remain with you and even increase. Then even with small incidents you will immediately get angry. Once you try to control or discipline your anger, then eventually even big events will not cause anger."

"You know," Lily said, "what kind of pisses me off is how you're sitting there reading from some book when there's a whole treasure chest sitting in front of you, and you are not digging into it."

"You'll never destroy my peace of mind, ma'am," I said, laughing at her joke. "I'm sure I can find a passage about patience in here to read to you. And tolerance too."

I made an exaggerated scowl, then dived into the case. The gray cloth was a drawstring bag, which I lifted out of the case and pulled open.

"Let's see, I said. Freeze dried food. Beef stroganoff, turkey something, chili mac—all kinds of yummy stuff."

The crew cheered.

"A first aid kit. Probably no OxyContin, though."

The crew booed.

Here's a little stove, some fuel canisters, um, and what's this?"

I held up a silver implement with a black handle.

"Espresso maker," Lily squealed.

"And here's the coffee to go with it." I said. "And some little cups!"

"Now we're getting serious," I said, keeping my hand in the bag. "I mean, really serious."

I slowly removed my hand.

"A fifth of George Dickel!" I shouted. "And a box of See's Candy—dark chocolates!"

The crew cheered.

"Let's see, not much else. A Swiss Army knife. A flashlight. Some Vitamin C packets. Tea bags—Guayakí yerba mate, my favorite. And, um, huh, some doggie treats. Hey Speck, want a dog biscuit?"

Speck wagged her tail and danced around and sniffed the case and its contents and I am sure could have told me exactly who had packed the goodies and what they had eaten for breakfast.

"We're eating well tonight," Nick announced. "And this shows that you were right. Your friends thought you might come here and left supplies. Maybe they'll be checking back. You never know."

"Think we should hang around here, or should we head down for the trail—the Dragon Trail?" Lily asked.

"Dragerton Trail," Nick said. "Isn't that right? Well, that's where we're going, but I'd like to scout things out before we head right down there. Also, I'm a little bit concerned by those ATV tracks. I'm thinking we ought to find a place to spend the night that's more protected. Like not easy for an ATV or truck to drive to. Back in the trees somewhere, maybe."

"I know just the place," Frank said. "And it's only about a half mile from here at the most. You know what I'm talking about, don't you Stan? The observatory. Rock Henge."

"Oh shit, yeah, great idea, Frank," I said. "It's on top of Cottonwood Ridge, just over there. We call it the Cottonwood Plaza. Lots of people call it the Medicine Wheel, or, like Frank said, Rock Henge."

"Well, I'm intrigued," said Lily. "Let's go."

"Everyone fill up your water bottles, and let's help Stan carry all this loot. We're going to Rock Henge for dinner and drinks. Whoopee!"

MOLLIE'S NIPPLES

Cottonwood Plaza is a flat, open, level clearing at the top of Cottonwood Ridge, a rocky promontory between the Cottonwood Creek drainage and Muley Canyon. Stacks of stones, or cairns, are arranged in strategic points around the plaza, and at least some of them appear to be of astronomical significance.

When we reached the spot, we dropped our gear in the center of the plaza, and Frank walked around the perimeter.

"You can see why we call it Rock Henge," he said. "Each of these piles of stones marks a spot where the sun and stars line up at different seasons. The Fremont people probably used this as a calendar. Helped them know when to have certain ceremonies or to plant crops. It's pretty mystical if you ask me."

"Yeah, Frank's right," I said. "Although it's probably Ute, not Fremont, nobody's really researched it. There's nothing else like it around here. A lot of archaeologists discount it as modern, but, hey, it works. I've seen it. On the summer solstice, the sun rises directly between the twin peaks of that mountain over there—I think they're called Mollie's Nipples, right, Frank?"

"Yeah, except we always called it Gunsight Peak. Mollie's Nipples is kind of, well, you know, racy."

"Who's this Mollie?" Lily asked. "She's got some pretty perky boobies. Or had, I guess."

"Anyway," I said, "on the solstice, the sun comes up right in the center, between the, um, nipples, and lines up directly with this cairn over there, and if you stand in the center, it's a pretty incredible sight. And it only happens on one day each year."

As we stood there contemplating the significance of the spot we were standing in, and the fact that it had been constructed years ago, a thought screamed into my brain, as if a piercing ray of sunlight came directly through my crusty and watery eyelids.

"Nick, what's the date? What's the date today?" I asked.

"Um, the um, twentieth," he said, pushing up his sleeve to look at his watch. "June twentieth."

"Well, holy shit," I said. "Holy fucking shit. It's the solstice. Tomorrow morning is the solstice. We can see it. It's the perfect day to be here. I can't beleive it!"

"Let's party," Lily said. "Solstice in Rock Henge. Freeze-dried beef stroganoff and Tennessee whiskey. A real freakin' party." She started dancing and twirling around the plaza, and for a moment I thought I could hear drums and singing and children laughing, and I felt a little of that happiness and calmness of mind the book Chris had sent me reminded me was so important.

"You know what," I said. "I think that note in the treasure chest was meant to bring us here. It's some of the words to the song 'Summertime.' Well, tomorrow's the first day of summer. And the line 'and the cottonwood's high,' that's not what Gershwin wrote, but we're up high, at the Cottonwood Plaza. We might have visitors tomorrow! Where's that whiskey?"

We broke out the Dickel, and I took a swig and passed the bottle to Lily.

"Oh, my," I said. "That's a feeling I haven't had in a long time. Goddamn, that's strong!"

"A taste of back home!" Lily exclaimed, taking a first-class pull on the bottle. She made clucking noises and put her right hand under her armpit and flapped her arm like a wing.

Frank took a gentlemanly sip and passed it to Nick, who put the bottle to his lips for a taste but no more.

"Don't get me wrong, I love the stuff, but, well, I'm still on duty. Maybe tomorrow."

We started arranging our camp, and I set up the stove to heat water for our selection of freeze-dried entrees. The stove roared, and the water was nearly boiling when Nick came over, held his hand out and signaled me to turn the stove off. He put his finger to his lips, looked at us for a minute, and walked to the edge of the plaza where it overlooked Muley Canyon and Dark Lord Cave.

"Everybody stay down," he said, and he ran to his gear, took out his binoculars, picked up his rifle, and hurried back to the edge. "ATVs," he said. "Three of them."

"Maybe it's Bill," I said. But we knew we had best be prepared for disappointment. And worse.

Lily and I exchanged a quick glance. It seemed to carry a lot of information, as much as a long conversation or a series of letters. Excitement, disappointment, fear, anger, anticipation, commitment, tenderness, strength, resolve, love. I opened my pack, took out my binoculars and handed them to her. I put a full magazine in the rifle and held it out to her. We nodded to each other and to Frank, and we readied ourselves. Lily crawled to the edge of the plaza and crouched down behind one of the cairns. Carefully, she eased up alongside the stacked stone monument and peered into the canyon below. She brought up the binoculars and scanned for a few moments, then ducked back down, looked over at Nick, and shook her head. She turned back toward me and said the one word I hoped she would not say.

"Viking," she said. "The fucking Viking is coming up the hill after us. And he has two other guys with him."

An act of learning
and ritual

Nick signaled to us to all come over to him. Frank and I joined Nick and Lily a few feet back from the edge.

"There are three of them. That guy Phil, the one you call the Viking, seems to be in charge. I don't recognize the other two, but they've got hats on, so it's hard to see faces. Can't miss the Viking. They're coming up, following our trail. They're not in range yet, but when they are, we should hit them with everything we have. They're following our tracks, so they know about where we are, and we won't be revealing anything to them. Lily and I will coordinate when to start. Stan, you and Frank just stay back for now. Your sidearms won't be of much use until they get closer. I'll take the Viking, and Lily, you try to get whichever of the others gives you the best shot. And stay down if he finds cover and starts shooting at us. He's carrying a big sniper rifle."

I couldn't see a thing from where I sat, and waiting, not knowing what was happening, was torture. Every once in a while, Nick or Lily would say something to each other, but I couldn't really hear their words. What seemed like hours later, but which was really probably less than fifteen minutes, during which time I saw a nighthawk swooping back and forth above our plaza, and the light turned from yellow to gold as sunset approached, I heard Nick say to Lily, "Ready? Get a bead and fire when you have a good shot. I'll fire when I hear you."

A slow twenty seconds ticked by, and I heard Lily count "three, two, one," and the firing began. At first, all I heard was the sound of Nick and Lily firing, but within seconds, return fire answered. I sat between Lily and Nick and handed them fresh magazines when they needed them, and Frank and I reloaded magazines when they handed us spent ones.

A lull in the firing brought silence to the canyon and plaza. Frank and I looked to Lily and Nick for insight. What was going on? Had the enemy run away? Had they finished the enemy off? I was formulating a happy scenario in my head when the cairn just above Lily's head exploded, rocks tumbled and crashed down around us, and Frank grasped his leg and gasped. Nick let loose a barrage of fire while Lily ducked down and turned toward me and Frank.

"You guys OK?" she asked.

"I'm bleeding," Frank said. "Not bad. What the hell was that?"

Lily shook her head, as if to say "I don't know." She leaned over and looked at Frank's leg. "It's just a little piece of one of the rocks. Must have shattered. Just a little cut." She held her hand on the wound to keep pressure on it.

Nick ceased his firing and spoke quietly as he put down his rifle and looked through his binoculars.

"Lily hit the first guy. He's down, maybe for good. The other one ran off. I thought I hit the Viking, but he must have ducked down in a little wash or something. He's down in those trees on the first ledge above the canyon. That," he pointed to the cairn, "was his 'fuck you' to us. His .50 caliber sniper rifle. Tore the hell out of those rocks. Just think what it'd do to one of us."

That cairn has stood for many years, and one bullet sent stones flying. A person long ago had carefully placed them there, an act of learning and ritual, and they were violently thrown about in a fraction of a second by a maniac who was trying to kill Lily.

"What can we do?" I asked. "Should we be doing something?"

"He can't hit us from where he is," Nick said, "Unless we try to move. We're pinned down. If we had rope, we might be able to go over the other side, but it's a sheer drop off. Maybe we can find a way. We'll look. We really need to keep watching the area where he's hiding. You all keep your heads down. I'll try to see if I can safely watch. Go ahead and make some dinner. And some coffee. We may be sitting and waiting for a while."

AND THERE ARE STILL NO RULES

I started the stove and reheated the water. When it was boiling, I poured water into two opened pouches of freeze-dried food—beef stroganoff and chicken and rice, stirred to mix them, and set them aside. I heated water for coffee, and when it was ready, signaled Lily and Frank to come eat. I took a cup and bowl to Nick, who had found a protected crack at the foot of a cairn that was partly shielded by a juniper tree so he could watch for movement.

"See anything?" I asked, handing him a spork. He shook his head. "I can see where he was, but I can't be sure that he is still there. Hope he hasn't moved to a new spot. I think I hit him earlier. Maybe he left to get help. Not knowing is the hardest."

I nodded in agreement. "I still can't see worth crap, but I'm sure Lily or Frank would be happy to give your eyes a rest."

"Thanks for the food. And the coffee. We'll just have to stay hunkered down. I guess the next move is up to him. Them. Until we get desperate."

"When'll that be?" I asked.

"Dunno. Depends. If we don't see anything else, we'll make a move to get out in the morning. If they show up and the shooting starts, well, who knows. You never know."

I crawled back over to where Lily and Frank were sitting and ate some dinner. The coffee hit the spot, and I was thinking about starting some more water when I heard a very faint, low sound that sent chills through me. I cocked my head and cupped my hand behind my ear.

"Hear that?" I said. "More ATVs?"

We all listened for a few seconds, and then it was clear that the sound was not ATVs.

"Helicopters," Nick said. "More than one. Military. You can see them now, off to the west." He pointed.

I couldn't see anything, but the harsh *whap whap whap* of the rotors rose in intensity and then dropped as the helicopters passed from north to south, some distance to the west of us. We all sat quietly for a few moments, contemplating the situation.

"Might be heading for the Recapture camp," Frank said. "They're going in that direction."

That was what we were all thinking. Maybe the military had been called in. I felt a rush of optimism sweep through me and thought about cheering when I sensed a very subtle faint hissing or whistling noise, followed instantly by an overwhelmingly loud screaming, rushing, roaring sound that flattened me to the ground and made my heart race and adrenaline rush through me as it never had before, and I closed my eyes and prepared to die. And then it came again. And again. And again. As I lay glued to the ground I dimly realized what we had heard. Felt. What had nearly crushed us with its power. A blast of wind hit us a few seconds later. Planes. Barely over our heads.

"What the fuck," I said, trying to look in the direction they had gone.

"Fighters," Nick said. "Holy shit. Fighters. A10s, I think. Right over us. Not a couple hundred feet, I'd guess. Something's going on. Some shit's goin' down. I'd hate to be over at the Recapture camp right about now."

I was breathing rapidly and my hands were shaking. I don't think I ever experienced something as instantly, overwhelmingly frightening in my life. My God, the power that just passed over us was greater than anything I could imagine. And they were just flying by, ready to bring instant death to people. If they had been targeting us, they would have fired missiles from miles away before we even knew they were coming. We would have been blown to bits without even knowing we were in trouble. I was trembling as though I had hypothermia. I looked at Lily and Frank, and they were trying to shake the stunned looks from their faces.

"Holy shit is right. Holy fucking shit," Lily exclaimed. "Holy fucking shit!"

"That was close, too close," Frank said. "I could feel the shock wave from them. And the wind. I might have wet myself. Man, my heart is racing. Christ, that was something. Really something."

Nick was right. Some serious business was going down. The planes were headed south, in the direction of the Recapture camp. No messing around, the big guns were here. Something like that is nothing to the military. An easy job. No surface-to-air missiles to contend with. No advance warning. No bunkers. Well, who knows, they may have bunkers. Who knows anything? I don't know a thing about what's down there or what's happening, but I'm glad something is happening, and I hope it helps end our ordeal. I found myself wondering what would happen if they dropped bombs or shot missiles at the camp. Would it start a forest fire? Did they consider what damage such an attack might cause? Would it harm Dancing Water Creek? Would it pollute it? Jesus, Stan, do you think they should have done an environmental impact statement or an environmental assessment? Gone through NEPA? I guess those things are suspended in case of emergency. Or war. Is this an act of war? Is our military waging war on its own citizens? Maybe they are classified as traitors, so the rules change. Since I took off for Moab another lifetime ago there have been no rules. And there are still no rules. I wondered what the Viking thought of the planes and helicopters. Maybe he was heading for his ATV to get out of here or go help his buddies. Forget about us. I hope he forgets about us. I looked around. The sun was getting ready to set, but there was still plenty of light. I tried to look in the direction of the Recapture camp to see if I could see smoke or anything but saw nothing. What if there is a mushroom cloud? What if they nuke them? Would we survive? Now you're really drifting, Stan. Falling apart. Hell. But you never know.

Lily took the other binoculars and wiggled up behind a hole in the low parapet to help Nick keep watch. "I can see the spot he was firing from before, but I don't see anything. Maybe he's taken off."

"We can hope," said Nick. "We can hope."

A GOOD DAY TO DIE

My hands were still shaking and my heart was racing from the star-tling rush of the planes flying so close overhead. I made some more coffee and took some to Nick and Lily. Nick put down his binoculars and took a sip of the coffee. "Thanks," he said. He rubbed his eyes. "We're gonna have to figure out where to put our gear and where to dig in for the night before it gets dark. I think we ought to kind of spread ourselves out a little around the edges of the plaza, up against the parapet or the cairns for protection. We don't know what might happen, or where it might come from."

I nodded and looked around at the plaza. Roughly circular and about fifty feet or so in diameter, it was ringed by a low, one- to two-foot-high stone parapet wall, fallen and slumping in some places, punctuated by eight stacked rock cairns, some fallen, several nearly three feet high. On the east and south sides, the cliff fell straight down from the parapet, and on the north and west sides, the ground sloped away more gently. "I'll start organizing the gear and finding good spots for us," I said, and crawled back to the camp area.

"Uh, oh," Lily said, her voice low but full of alarm. She raised up on one knee and peered through her binoculars over the parapet. "He's moving. He's heading up on the far ridge." She pointed so Nick could look in the right direction.

"Goddamn it. He's heading for those rocks at the top of that hill. He's setting up to knock us all off."

"Should we run?" I asked. "Could we get out of here while he's moving?"

"That would be suicide," Nick said. "He's watching us. And his partner might be waiting to ambush us when we run. Like when he starts shooting at us from up there. In about five minutes."

I could see a rocky promontory farther down the ridge, higher than we were, that would clearly give him a nearly unobstructed view of our compound. We would be easy targets, even though it was a long way. "Our rifles won't reach that spot, will they?" I asked.

"No, but his will," Nick said. He appeared to be thinking,

"You guys keep watching," I said. "Frank and I can start piling our gear and more rocks along the north wall and the cairns to give us more shelter. Better walls to hide behind. Come on, Frank."

Frank and I rushed to pile all our gear against the north parapet, and we started dismantling a couple of the cairns and bringing the stones to heighten the north wall. We had only been at it about five minutes when Nick told us all to take cover. "He's up in those rocks, and he's getting his rifle ready. He could start shooting at any time."

I ducked down behind the north parapet, called Speck, and made sure that there were places for the others. I placed water bottles nearby and laid our packs atop the stone wall to provide a little more cover. Nick got down directly behind the northern cairn, and made a place to watch the sniper through one lens of the binocular.

"I'm sorry I put us in this position," he said. "I should have thought this through. I've let you all down. I'm really sorry."

"It's not your fault, Nick," I said. "Frank and I wanted to come up here. It's a great place. It's protected us so far. Who could have imagined a sniper on a ridge a half mile away picking us off? Nobody. Nobody."

Hiding helplessly behind the crumbling stone wall was an exercise in facing my deepest horror. The future has always frightened me. I worry about what is around the next bend, whether a car is going to come into my lane, if a gas line will explode, if lightning will hit, if I will have a stroke or a heart attack. I have always worried about something striking me from out of the blue, something I could not prepare for, something that would end my world, my life, in an instant. I greatly feared the notion that I could be here one instant, gone the next. And here I was in the most vulnerable spot I had ever been in, waiting, completely at the mercy of random events unleashed by a maniac. The stone wall I hid behind was riddled with gaps and crevices. A bullet at the right spot could penetrate the wall, break into pieces, and fill us full of holes. Should I try to meditate? Should I pray? Should I think of Chris? I hugged Speck close to me and felt her snuggle tighter. I felt a good feeling rush through me. I've had a good life. I've had a great life, a privileged life. I'm in a beautiful place, a sacred place, a place of great power. I felt that power enter me. I felt strength. This is a good place to die. A good day to die. I did not think of the Viking or his sniper rifle or of the Recapture Brigade or of the horrors they'd wrought. I closed my eyes and saw beautiful, white light, and I felt warmth and beauty and love, and I was nearly lost in the meditation when a blast shook me from behind, and I felt as if something had shoved me and I lurched toward Speck, and I heard her yelp and jump up and run away, and I called her name and heard a gun report and then another and I cried out for Speck, and I heard Lily shout to me to get down, and I could feel a sharp pain in my left arm and I reached toward it and my entire arm was wet and I realized it was blood, and I heard Nick shout "Goddamn it!" and start shooting.

Instantly Lily was kneeling over me and tearing at my shirt, looking at my arm.

"Lily, get down," Nick screamed, "Get down!"

Lily ignored him while she worked on my arm. I could hear rapid firing from Nick's position, and then more. Frank was shooting too. Lily lay on me, pinning me down, trying to stay low. She took a bandanna from her pocket and pressed it hard against my arm and took a deep breath and let it out.

Rifle fire rang out both near and distant, and Lily shoved and dragged me toward the parapet. She again lay on top of me, covering me. I put my right arm around her and held her close. I wondered if I would die here. I wondered if at any second a bullet would tear through both Lily and me and end everything. I tried to pull her down as much as I could, and neither of us moved, and the firing was intense and rapid and then, without warning, it stopped.

Be like a rabbit

We hunkered down and lay still in the silence. My arm throbbed with burning pain. I could still barely see, but I could tell that Speck had been hit too—a corner of her left ear was torn away. I felt it and pinched it between my fingers to stop the bleeding.

After a long moment of silence, the most complete and unnerving silence, during which neither Lily nor I took a breath or even moved a muscle, and during which I thought every thought I had ever had a hundred times, Nick finally spoke.

"OK, OK then, this will never do. If we sit here he'll pick us all off. It's almost dark, but he probably has night vision glasses and can sit up there and take us out one by one," he wriggled over to get closer to where the three of us huddled behind the tallest and most substantial cairn.

"We'll wait until it's a little darker, then I'll make my way over to the spot over there, closest to those trees," he motioned with his chin and a pucker of his lips. "I'll give you a heads up, and then go over the wall and race for that little bunch of trees and rocks just above the drop off. If I'm quick enough, he might not be ready, might miss it completely. Or at least not get off a good shot. Then I can work my way toward him and hopefully get close enough for an effective shot."

"And what if he spots you and, well, what if you don't even make it to the trees," Lily said. "What'll we do then? What if, I mean, shit." She leaned into me a bit more. "Damn."

"Well, it's a risk. But we're all vulnerable here. If I don't try something, he'll take his time, and none of us will make it. None of us. I think I have to give it a try. I really do."

We knew that he was right. He was the only one with even the slightest chance of changing the equation, altering the situation from one of complete hopelessness to something slightly better. And if the Viking saw him and shot him, well, that would pretty much do us all in.

I reached out my good hand and grabbed Nick by the shoulder. "Thank you, Nick. We know how much you've done for us. Be safe. Thank you. Be safe."

"Should we start firing or something, you know, to give you some cover?" Frank asked. "Say, if we started firing from here, and you bolted from over there, by that third cairn?"

"I don't know," Nick said. "If he isn't watching, any firing will give it away. And if he is, I don't think it will do much good. I wish I could think of something, but I can't. Just lay low, and I'll do my best Usain Bolt sprint to the trees. It's only what, about twenty yards or so. Shouldn't take too long."

"Be like a rabbit, Nick," Lily said. "Be fast, but don't run straight. Go a few steps one way, zig, then zag. Don't be predictable. God, Nick, be safe. And fast. Like a rabbit. Just like a rabbit."

"It's getting pretty dark, Nick said. "I'm going to start making my way over there, to the cairn by the edge. Once everything's been quiet for a while, maybe in an hour or so, I'll give a little whistle, and head for the trees. Like a rabbit. Usain Rabbit. This'll work. It will. I'll see you later. In the morning. And I love you, too, all of you."

Staying close to the parapet, Nick wriggled his way to the spot on the circle closest to the trees below. The slightest breeze moved the air down-canyon but made no real sound, and the first stars gently pierced the darkening sky. The silence was profound, especially so after the violent and chaotic eruptions of gunfire, helicopters, and the explosive intensity of the jets as they passed overhead. A little sound might be nice. What was going on over at the protest camps? Were there battles going on? Were people dying? Would we die tonight, huddled here together, three people and a dog, crouched behind an ancient wall made not to deflect gunfire but to delineate a special place, a sacred place, a place of refuge. It's our refuge now. Maybe it'll protect us. Please let it protect us.

A low whistle made Speck lift her head quickly, and it sent a sharp pain through my injured arm. A shuffling sound was all we heard.

"He's over," Lily whispered.

Several seconds of silence passed. The longer the silence, the better the possible outcome, and I found myself almost subconsciously counting, the way I automatically do when lightning flashes. One, two, three, four.

And then the thunder clapped, and clapped again.

"Oh God," Lily cried. "Oh God."

The silence that followed and the darkness that enveloped it and us seemed infinite, as though we were hurtling through deep space. Our very existence seemed suspended, as we pondered the moment. Was Nick dead? Would we be dead soon? In an instant? Were we next in line for the firing squad? None of us moved, and the silence of the night was drowned out by my racing, random, wretched thoughts.

THAT GODDAMN DOG

For about an hour, the longest hour of my life, despite the ache in my injured arm and my crusty, itching eyes, I willed myself to remain motionless. Frank and Lily were likewise, without any movement or sign of life, like statues stacked together where they had fallen from an ancient wall. Even Speck seemed to understand the need for quiet and stillness, until without signaling or forewarning of any kind, she pulled back, out from my embracing arm, and leapt over the parapet.

"Speck," I called out, in a sort of shouted whisper. "Stop."

"Be still," Lily said. "Let her go. Let her go. She'll be back"

There was nothing to do but let her go. But where and why had she run? Had she heard something?

But she did not come back, and we heard not a sound through the long, cool, dark night. We took turns keeping watch and trying to sleep, but none of us could. Where are the soldiers? Where are the helicopters? Is it just the three of us and a crazed maniac on the top of a hill in the remote desert canyons of central Utah? We knew that we could do nothing. That if we moved, even to pee or peek over the parapet, we would likely be blown apart. So we waited and wondered about our friends and protectors Nick and Speck.

As the deep darkness of the heart of the night descended, a slight rustling in the brush along the southern edge of the plaza caught our attention. Nick? Speck? We held our breath, anxiously listening.

"Nobody move. Nobody move. Hands up. Nobody move," a voice boomed.

"Oh fuck," Lily said. "It's him."

And it was. The Viking. I could not see him, but could tell that he was on the outer edge of the parapet, and I assumed he had his weapon trained on us. Shit.

"Everyone stand. Stand!" He shouted. "I can see you, so drop all your weapons or you will all die right now. Stand!"

We struggled to rise. My legs were nearly asleep, and I swayed when I finally stood upright. Frank and Lily rose and faced south, so I turned with them, still unable to see anything.

"Spread out a little," he ordered, and we did.

"Over here, come into the middle over here, away from those rocks and packs," he commanded, and we stepped forward, away from the spot where we had crouched for most of the night.

"Well, finally, finally I have you. I've been waiting for this. Especially for you, sweetheart. You fuckers killed my buddy Marty. You all piss me off, you worthless pieces of shit. You made a mess out of everything, and now you're going to pay. One by one. Who wants to go first? Old man? How about you? Why don't you step forward. Come on, step up old man. I should have shot you that first day, then we wouldn't have had all this trouble. Come on, old man, so your buddies can see you die.

"Hey, fuck you, you asshole," Lily shouted and stepped forward. "Shoot me, you limp dick turd. Fucking asshole!"

Lily strode forward. I could now see just a little, and the Viking held a pistol in his outstretched hand. I could also see my 9mm pistol tucked into the back of Lily's pants.

"Come on sweetheart, come on over to me. This way I can plug your buddies and save you for last. Come on, come on over here."

Lily did step forward, and as she did I saw a rapid movement near the parapet that sped toward us. Speck!

"That goddamn dog," exclaimed the Viking, and he swung his weapon toward the movement. A shot rang out, then another.

"No! No!" I ran forward and dived toward Speck. "No!"

I tried to tackle Speck, but she was too fast. I landed on my belly and skidded across the ground, my hands brushing her legs, my arm protesting in searing pain. She ran on past me, and more firing rang out, *bam, bam, bam.* I rolled to look up at the Viking, and he lurched in my direction, nearly launching himself forward and landing hard on the packed earth of the plaza. His face smashed flat against the ground. I edged backwards, away from him.

I was only a few feet away and could barely make out his features, but I could hear his breath erupt out in a sort of grunt, followed by a gurgling sound.

Not a Growl, Not a Bark

"Stay down," everybody stay down," came a voice from the perimeter. "He might still be dangerous."

"Nick," Lily cried out. "Nick, is that you."

"Yeah, it's me. I'll cover you. Go to him and make sure he's dead. Get his guns away from him. Here, I'll give you a little light." The light from his flashlight was almost blinding to my sensitive eyes, and I looked away, toward Lily.

Lily cautiously approached the supine hulk, pistol drawn and pointed at his head. She kicked the weapons away from his outstretched hands, bent forward to look closely at him, then stepped back.

"He's dead. His neck is half gone."

"OK, then," Nick said. "Come help me. Now I need a little help. And be cautious. There might be others. Even Shumway. He could be back, looking for us."

Lily went to where Nick was draped over the low wall of the parapet. Frank joined her and they helped him over the edge.

"Oh God, Nick, your leg," Lily exclaimed.

"Yeah, he hit me. It's bad. I put a tourniquet on it. May lose it. Doesn't hurt though. That's good."

"How did you, I mean, shit, how did you get up here?" Frank asked.

"I really thought he'd come look for me, but he didn't. I didn't move after I went down, and I guess he thought I was dead. When I heard him heading for the plaza, then heard the shouting, I knew I had to at least try to get up here, so I crawled. Wasn't that far."

"My God, Lily," Nick continued. "I didn't even get off a shot. You moved so fast, you were amazing. You saved us all from that horrible man."

We all went to work helping Nick find a comfortable spot next to the parapet and helped him attend as best we could to his wound. In the confusion I had forgotten about Speck, and clucked my cheeks.

"Has anybody seen Speck?" I asked. "Do you think he shot her? He was going to, and now I haven't seen her." I clucked my cheeks and whistled.

"No, no, here she comes" Frank said, "I don't think he shot her. Again. She was really racing. She distracted him long enough for Lily to draw her weapon and start firing. Speck helped Lily save us. She really did."

"Yeah, she did," Nick said. "And she came to check on me after I got hit. That dog deserves a medal. I hope she's OK. Now let's all settle in and wait for morning. Keep our eyes and ears open. We may be in the clear, but, well, you never know."

I crawled up against the parapet and held my hand over the wound on my arm. The pressure eased the pain and helped slow the bleeding. Again, we tried to be inconspicuous and still, with only our minds moving, pondering, churning. Speck snuggled in with me, and again we waited.

The idea that Shumway could be coming was unnerving to us all. He would have others with him, and as Nick had said, he would be coming for us, and gunning for Nick. Or Willis, as the Recapture people knew him. Lily and Frank took positions by the cairns on the west and north sides of the plaza. We all checked our weapons, and I tried to clear my eyes with some eyedrops from the first aid kit. I gazed up at the multitude of stars in the dark night sky, but rather than sharp points of light, I saw only a scattering of diffuse, blurry spots.

I was exhausted, and I'm sure we all felt the same, but I was sure I couldn't sleep. My mind raced with images of Shumway and dozens of Recapture Brigade goons storming over the parapet and shooting us or taking us prisoner. The wound on my left arm gave me a constant, sharp pain, and I could not lift that arm very high, nor could I lay on that side. Speck's ear had swollen up and gotten hard, but it was no longer bleeding.

She kept wanting to shake her head but I tried to keep her still because shaking made the wound open again and sent blood flying.

We'll have some nice scars to show Chris when we get back. I hope these are all of them. I hope we get back. We seemed to be almost out of trouble a couple of times, only to have something bigger and more frightening happen. God, I hope Shumway is far away, down at the Recapture camp. Maybe it's gone. Leveled. Maybe Shumway is gone. Blown all to hell. I kind of liked him and feel bad wishing him harm. But if he is here, hunting for Nick, and for all of us, then to hell with him. Thoughts and fears rocketed through my mind, and I was jolted back to the present when Speck abruptly stood.

"What is it, girl?" I mumbled, not fully aware yet of anything. "What is it?"

She took off as though launched. Not a growl, not a bark, just took off. My arm jerked painfully away as she leapt to a full speed sprint toward the north end of the plaza.

"Speck," I called in a loud whisper. "Speck's run off."

"She bolted right past me," Lily said. "She must have heard something."

I got up and crawled over to Lily. "Any sign of her?"

"No, but I can hear something in the brush. Over there."

I heard branches rustling, and then a dry stick cracked close in front of us and something ran by, followed closely by something else.

"What was that?' I asked Nick. "Could you see anything?"

"No," he said, "nothing. It was like another dog was chasing her. Or she was chasing it."

"Maybe a coyote," I said.

We sat and listened, and heard no more movement in the brush. Several minutes passed, and my worry for Speck, and for what it might mean for us, mounted. Had she chased a coyote? Would it lead her to its pack, where they would kill her and eat her? Was Shumway here with an attack dog? God, I hope Speck is OK. She's saved me and been my friend through this awful time, God, I hope nothing bad has happened to her.

Nick and I sat and listened, but there was only silence. The air was so still, not even leaves were rustling. I could hear a ringing in my ears, but nothing, nothing from Speck.

Then, suddenly, we heard,

"CaCaw, CaCaw," coming from down in the trees below us.

"What the fuck," said Nick, rising up and readying his rifle.

"Hold on, Nick. Hold on," I said. "Let me answer."

"CaCaw, CaCaw," I called.

Immediately we heard back,

"CaCaw, CaCaw. Stan? CaCaw."

"Bill," I shouted. "Bill! CaCaw, CaCaw!

Dancers and shamans
celebrating

Speck cleared the parapet between my face and Lily's with a velocity and suddenness that seemed to rival that of the fighter planes earlier in the evening, and right on her tail was a similarly swift flying missile of brown and white fur. Speck skidded to a stop, whirled around, and greeted me with kisses and a happy tail that wagged her entire body with it. Her brown and white pursuer did the same. I rolled onto my back, my wounded arm screeching in pain, my eyes squeezed shut, my face contorted in an uncontrollably exuberant grin.

"Knuckles! Knuckles is here," I squealed. Speck and her best friend left me and raced in joyous circles, trying to turn each other into butter.

I stayed on my back, my entire body tingling as though I had been electrocuted. Bill, Bill was here. We were going to be OK. It was over. It was really over.

Bill, our friend Ron, and two special agents from the Department of the Interior were here to save us. They hoped we would be here and had worried that Phil, the Viking, might have found us, which he had. They knew that one other Recapture soldier had fled when the shooting started and had been captured by other federal law enforcement personnel near the Dragerton Road. They told us that the area was now clear.

"What about Shumway?" Nick asked. "We thought he could be hunting us."

"No, said the agent who was attending to Nick's wound. "Shumway probably saved you all. He went to the sheriff and blew the whistle on everything that had been going on. He told us that three of the missing people were still alive in the custody of a protester named Willis and that Phil was hunting them. Well, we know that Willis was Nick here, and that we had better end this whole thing before it got much worse. These friends of Stan's, Ron and Bill, they've been a huge help all along, and they were pretty sure of where you'd head if you were OK. Oh, and agents raided both of the protest camps last evening. No casualties on either side, from what we've heard."

They reported that protesters had all been asleep—or had been put to sleep, I guessed—and the agents had had a relatively easy time subduing them. They called in a helicopter to take Nick, me, Frank, and Lily to a hospital, and when it arrived and we departed Cottonwood Plaza, I hugged and thanked Bill and Ron. "It was Chris," Bill said. "She organized everything. Once I told her where I thought you'd go, she took over. You're a lucky man, Stan."

I am. I'm a very fortunate man. I thought of how Chris had organized friends to help us. I looked over at Lily, who had saved me over and over again, and who, I knew now, I loved deeply. As the helicopter rose straight up from the plaza, I reached over and held Lily's hand,

Lights illuminated the medicine wheel, and for a moment I saw dancers and shamans celebrating the arrival of the solstice, and I knew that a balance had been restored. The issues that had led to the protests had not gone away, and I knew that the tensions that had erupted and caught us in a deadly nightmare would linger and fester. I vowed to work with Frank and Lily and Nick to tell the story of our ordeal, of how Lily and Speck had been called upon and had risen to the posts of heroes, of how Frank and I had taught each other a few things and how I thought we could work out new ways to look at this place, this so-called wilderness, which was not a wilderness at all but which was a part of us, a place where we must live and make a living, a place that must be treated like a friend—listened to, cared for, nurtured, and loved.

For this place is not just a playground or a goodie bag to be taken from and never replenished. It is us, and we must be responsible for its upkeep and its nourishment, we must find ways to not destroy ourselves because we thought of ourselves as apart from place. I promised myself that I would make this trip to Moab the best thing that has ever happened to me and transform it from a nightmare into a vision, to become a man, like the man on the wall of that first little shelter that protected Lily and me when we were most vulnerable. The man who had two little helpers, one on each shoulder, who showed him things he could not see, told him things he could not hear, let him feel things he had learned to ignore.

I want to be that man, and Lily and Speck and Chris and Bill and Frank and Nick, and even Shumway have made that possible. My desert night-mare is over, but my journey has just begun.

Epilog

Everything after we lifted off from the plaza is a blur. When we landed at the hospital a small crowd descended on us, including television crews, law enforcement personnel, and hospital staff. The sheriff shooed everyone but the medical crew away. "They're not talking with anyone until after they have been seen by the doctors." The staff wheeled Nick on a gurney straight into the hospital. Others helped the three of us into wheelchairs, one nurse walked Speck on her leash, and they hurried us in through the doors of the hospital and into a fairly small room with bright lights that made my eyes water. I heard toenails clattering on the linoleum floor, and through teary eyes I saw Speck dancing and leaping to greet Chris, who was hurrying toward us. We hugged and cried, I could hear wails and tears as Frank's wife Velma knelt by his wheelchair and wept, clutching his legs as he leaned forward and embraced her.

Oh God, Lily, I thought. She has no one to greet her. I looked over and saw a tall man walk up to her. "Uncle Pen," she cried, and burst into uncontrollable tears. "Oh Lily," the man said, dropping to one knee. "Dear Lily, praise the Lord you are now safe. Praise the Lord."

We all embraced our loved ones for several minutes, as weeks of fear and worry worked their way to the surface and erupted in outpourings of emotion. "Chris, I want you to meet Lily," I said, taking her hand and reaching toward Lily. "Lily saved my life, Chris, I owe her everything."

"Oh Chris, I am so happy to meet you. Stan has told me all about you. And he saved me. We both saved each other. You have an incredible husband, Chris, take good care of him." I could hardly catch my breath as I watched these two women, two women I loved, wrap their arms around each other in a tight embrace.

"I'm Pendleton Shuffler," the man who had greeted Lily said, as he extended his hand. "I'm Craig's uncle, and his partner in the trucking business."

"I'm so sorry," I said. I couldn't think of anything else to say as we shook hands and nodded, acknowledging the horror we both had endured, and knowing that, for now, it was over.

Acknowledgments

Thank you to everyone who read the manuscript, offered suggestions, helped with editing, was nice to me, or had anything to do with getting this story into print, including Barbara Evert, Nick Jones, Shley Kinser, Steve Trimble, Brenda Cowley, Melissa Bond, Kurt Proctor, Amie Tullius, Dorothee Kocks, Jim Sayers, Diane LesBecquets, Kyler Willett, Jim Jones, Jeannine Jones Willett, Jonathan Thompson, W. Michael Gear, Kathleen O'Neil Gear, Bill Davis, the late Speck Evert-Jones, Dan R. Miller, Cody Rex Chamberlain, Andy Nettell, and Lowell Norris. Special thanks to my editor, Diane Bush.

www.ingramcontent.com/pod-product-compliance
Lightning Source LLC
Chambersburg PA
CBHW061205210726
48294CB00006B/1764